Sea Change

Sea Change

S. M. Wheeler

TOR®

A Tom Doherty Associates Book
New York

This is a work of fiction. All of the characters, organizations, and events portrayed in this novel are either products of the author's imagination or are used fictitiously.

SEA CHANGE

Copyright © 2013 by Shannon M. Wheeler

A Tor Book
Published by Tom Doherty Associates, LLC
175 Fifth Avenue
New York, NY 10010

www.tor-forge.com

Tor® is a registered trademark of Tom Doherty Associates, LLC.

Library of Congress Cataloging-in-Publication Data

Wheeler, S. M.
    Sea Change / S.M. Wheeler.—First edition.
        p. cm.
    "A Tom Doherty Associates book."
    ISBN 978-0-7653-3314-8 (hardcover)
    ISBN 978-1-4299-6733-4 (e-book)
  1. Kraken—Fiction.   2. Friendship—Fiction.   3. Quests
(Expeditions)—Fiction.   4. Fantasy fiction.   I. Title.
    PS3623.H447S43 2013
    813'.6—dc23

                                        2012043818

Tor books may be purchased for educational, business, or promotional use. For information on bulk purchases, please contact Macmillan Corporate and Premium Sales Department at 1-800-221-7945 extension 5442 or write special markets@macmillan.com.

First Edition: June 2013

Printed in the United States of America

0 9 8 7 6 5 4 3 2 1

Sea Change

Acid flowed at the table more often than wine and had long since ceased to cause Lilly alarm; her attention remained on the soup even as Father asked, "Does the thought of me still pain your head, love?"

Cool, Mother replied, "I fear I am coming down with some strange illness, for I suffer still. I should go to the baths and—"

His habit was to swallow such lies with a drought of the liquor at hand, but tonight the bottle had been emptied already. "And by what means will you have a child of mine while resting there?" He laughed, a deep, drink-rough noise. "Mourning the parting, will you lie with me the night before—then abort whatever is thus got and have a bastard by another man, to return to this house and claim—"

"Lilly." Mother looked to her, fire on her tongue such that all her husband's anger seemed but sparks. Here was not the woman who called Lilly *sweetheart* and cradled her face between her hands; in such a temper, she looked taller than

Father, her presence heavy with the soot of past fury. "Dinner is over. Go to your room."

Lilly filched a glazed bun from the table because she refused to go without something sweet; wrapping it in a napkin as she went out, she shut the door behind her then put her ear to the keyhole. She dismissed the thought of capture, for the servants were all stiff-faced and silent at the edges of the room, or gone away to the kitchen if they could, ashamed to serve a family that would descend into this crudity—unless all households of old blood were thus, and all servants must foster the ability to overlook lapses in decorum.

Though not given to eavesdropping, this argument concerned her; younger siblings would mean a sea-change, a reshuffling of priorities, danger along with freedom. The thick door muffled their voices but it didn't matter; when their war came to open battle they fought lustily, snide murmurs giving way to shouts.

"If you won't have my child—"

"I promised you one, and that one is enough." She spoke now in her country burr, the honest voice; and softer, almost inaudible: "I will not die with the second."

"I know. I know. But you're better than your forebears. And what is she, this girl?"

Giving a short laugh, Mother said, "Your child."

"But no sweet girl for me, not soft-eyed: no, sharp and sea-loving—"

Miss Scholastika caught Lilly by the ear, and dragging her by it as she only did outside of Father's sight—though happy to do so when Mother watched—took her from the door. Both of them stayed quiet; Lilly bit her lip with eyes brimming, and Miss Scholastika kept herself to the pinch-mouthed look that the toothless excelled at. Only when they reached Lilly's room did the servant release her and ask, "How shameless are you to be eavesdropping?" Her voice quavered—not angry, but fearful. "There are things a child shouldn't hear."

"They voiced those before I left," Lilly said, reasonable, and flinched as the woman's hand came up; but Miss Scholastika only rested it against Lilly's cheek, the side of her face where the skin looked darkly bruised, brown and black, swollen.

Whispering, now, "Both of them love you."

"Yes. Father wants a daughter he can parade or a son to become a merchant-marquis in his place, though." Lilly moved away, smiled—and meant it. "Ma'am, I am happy."

"You don't know what that means," the old woman said, bitter, and before leaving added, "Turn your mind to your books, child. I will want to hear what you know about our neighbor kingdoms tomorrow."

Lilly did no such thing, knowing that the servants' ability to turn a blind eye extended to her behavior. Slipping off her satin shoes and stockings and full skirts, she donned instead last year's skirt—it fell just above her ankles and still fitted her waist—and on her feet put the soft leather shoes Mother gifted her with a conspiratorial wink and a finger held over her lips.

The sash window, oiled, slipped noiselessly open. Beneath it was springy lawn which straightened after she passed, showing no footprints to betray her. When her legs were shorter, the path through garden to the slender broken shell path down to the sea had seemed long; now she ran to meet the sea, the salt air scouring off her gentlewoman's skin.

The water churned active today, the low sun golden on its whitecaps and the spray hands that reached for her; it was playful in the manner of creatures that ate humans with a smile. Once a water-woman had beckoned her with a scaled hand and a sharp-toothed grin, just like that.

The path she took she sometimes walked in the late evening when the night slithered in hollows; she had never fallen on it. These steps she knew: over skittering shale with impressions of strange animals and through a tangle of ocher stones, on a sedge-thick strip of land from which one could hear the gulls but nothing more, and down again to a slope of dark stone that plunged into the ocean. She patted the still-hot bun in her pocket, eyes scanning the water for a wake or the break of a smooth burgundy curve, and saw far-off a patch of ocean that did not gleam with the sun. Grinning, she waved her arms to him: *I'm here, I'm here, come fast.* It seemed he dawdled; for some time nothing broke the surface again.

Until eight slick, suckered limbs weaved from the water, with their immense strength rolling aside the boulders that lay at the bottom of the slope. Behind them came a sleek and rounded shape, ridged in a brow over golden discs of eyes which were bright as the gold crucifix in Father's study—and held more love than any dead man's gilded face. She demanded of the kraken, "When did you get so sneaky?"

"I've been hunting seals." His voice rumbled and sang high at once, wind moaning in cliffs, nipped short in the narrow passages and shaking the larger. "You are troubled."

"No, no . . . a little. Come close, I have a present for you."

To her side the sea creature came in a roil of tentacles. Two of those settled around her feet, the delicate tips curled around her ankles. He loomed well over her, eighteen hands high at his tallest, though at the moment he compressed himself lower to the ground so that he might look her in the eye. "I *will* return to your troubles." Then: "A present?"

With panache she plucked the bun from her pocket and unfurled the napkin around it. She felt quite proud at this newest offering—steaming still, citrus-scented, and only lightly squashed.

"The things you humans eat!" He took it with such gentleness that the sugared sides bent only a little. The top of it he stroked. "Sticky. And so soft." One last pass, and then he tucked it under his bulk. "Stings a little on the inner mouth—and crumbles at the beak. Interesting! What do you call it?"

"A bun with icing and orange zest." She rested her hand above his eye. "Should I bring you other desserts?"

"Oh, yes." He ruminated a moment, singing faint whalesong under his breath. "Should I bring you a seal?"

Again she laughed. She did often with him and rarely at home. "I don't think my teeth are up to it."

"Squid?"

"Cannibal," she replied without the least rancor. He kept a sort of sea monster kosher for her: no men at all nor capsizing of fishing ships for their freight of fishes.

"Since you're not interested in a gift from me to match yours, tell me your worries." He shifted, blocking the wind.

She flicked a dismissive gesture. "Oh, they come at my age."

"They have not for me."

His brow-ridges made convenient places to set her hands when she wanted contact. "You're younger than me. Another year and you will be full of woe with your coming of age." She shook her head. "Marriage—society—they should be a part of my life now, but are not. My company consists of yourself, my father's merchants, my mother's maids." Now it was her turn to ruminate; lightly, he pressured her ankle. "The house is restive. They want a more elegant daughter to parade about."

"I would parade you in the hall of the monarchs of the ocean, if you could breathe water."

"I know." She tapped her cheek, indicated her wetted feet. "I would suit it, wouldn't I? But until such a time as I develop magical abilities, I must be canny and fear what they might in rashness do. Marry me to some brave young man willing to take an ugly wife for the sake of my father's gold, perhaps."

"Why would they be foolish? You never spoke of them that way," said he.

"They were born country folk," she said quietly, "and the fear of failing their nobility is in them. Young ladies are married to young gentlemen, you see, or else become maiden aunts. Or— my father fears that. My mother does not fear or does not show fear, ever."

"You don't speak of these things to me." Remonstration, there; they could tolerate much from each other, but never lies, neither explicit or of omission. Misunderstandings were too potentially dangerous.

"I could only explain them clearly now, I think." She breathed out, glanced towards the sun riding the horizon. "I'm not used to fearing the future."

"Then don't. You tell me that the future is choice and the present a starting point." Those words came first from Father but sounded so different in the kraken's mouth that it might as well have been a different maxim. "Why assume that the present will not give you better choices?" He touched her cheek.

"Think of sugared buns and stories and sundials for now. Brave young men can be met when they come. I could relocate them for you. Does that make you feel better?"

"However impractical and short-sighted—yes. Now tell me about seal-hunting, Octavius."

On her eighth birthday, her parents held the first and last party in her honor. In a new cream frock and with her black hair tamed into a complicated braid, Lilly felt quite delighted—numb even then to familial conflict. Father yelled about putting in the open what ought to be hid; Mother stayed silent until he paused a moment, then asked, "Are you ashamed?" He said no more. Lilly suffered a moment of shyness when Father crouched down to tell her, "Don't confirm in their minds that you are hell-spawn, all right?" He patted her cheek, then went to greet the guests in his strange, terse manner.

Lilly walked beside her mother a while, crunching through the new-fallen leaves and nibbling at deviled eggs, waiting to be talked to. No one did, though they glanced at her a little; they were local gentry mostly, a few wealthy shopkeepers from town who had met her before when Mother took her into town. The whole place smelled of cologne and perfume and sounded like a chicken coop, of which she rather disapproved— she liked this garden for thinking, not playing.

Mother talked to a delicate-walking, rounded woman about the production of linen—how it was made, traded, stitched into gowns—with the lady exclaiming in surprise, eyes round, at the complexity of it all. In the middle of a sentence, Mother gently tapped Lilly's shoulder and pointed towards a knot of children. No words; none needed. Lilly obeyed.

They bunched like sheep before the dog as she came close; one of them made the gesture against the evil eye, which she accepted with a shrug. "Does the party please you?"

A boy emerged from the herd—well-fed, well-clothed, her cousin by Father's sister, a relative mocked often over dinner because she had come running to beg for money when her noble husband ran out. Young von Graf, Father called her cousin, and she couldn't quite remember his first name. "We're too afraid of the spells that must be all over this place."

"Well, let me assure you that I haven't encountered a single one in all my years living here." His name was not so important; he had an ugly sneer. Perhaps he knew about Father's mockery.

He said, "Does it count as encountering if you lay it down yourself?"

"Yes, I imagine it does."

He spat; she flinched, but he did it so weakly that it splashed onto the ground a good foot in front of her. Flushing, he said, "They say the ocean washes off witchery. I'll go down there to protect myself." And away he stomped.

Lilly looked to the others, spreading her hands a little, asking: *Are you that foolish?*

A girl piped up, "There is a good lawn for playing on."

The child must know that Lilly would not participate when she wore a new, light-colored frock; the dozen of them went scampering away. Biting down on her hurt like a dog chewing a wound, she retreated back into the crowd of adults, nodding to those she knew, looking for Father. He would be sympathetic to her plight, being sensitive as she to the negative reactions she garnered. More sensitive, perhaps; he drank over it, while she only paced the house sometimes.

Searching, she didn't know herself searched for until a heavy hand on her shoulder spun her around. Old von Graf scowled down at her, recognizable on account of being swarthy with a quite aristocratic beak of a nose. "Where is my son?"

Lilly stood on her toes and tilted her head to the side, looking towards the lawn. "He isn't with the others? I suppose he really went down to the beach, milord."

He shoved a little when he let go of her, but hesitant; perhaps the count believed his wife when she said that her brother would give them money. "I'll check the house." Away he bulled through the crowd, the gentry parting before him with nervous titters.

Counterproductive, that. Being responsible insofar as being the source of fear that drove her cousin from the grounds, Lilly circumvented the guests and took the little broken shell path that led to the tame beach which lay a terrace below the garden. Kicking imported sand from her shoes, she stared out into the waves, lost for a moment. *Deadly, wild, fickle,* her mother called it, *a place for sirens and not little girls,* after which words she would turn Lilly's head gently away. She must have known that once the salt-thick spray touched her daughter's face and the waves crashed a welcoming song, Lilly would be enchanted.

A witch couldn't be enchanted, could she? That proved she was human if nothing else would.

Young von Graf, she reminded herself, and finding a set of footprints leading away to the brown rock and tide pools which made up most of the coast, she padded into unknown territory. However smitten her heart might be, prudence was ingrained; there were mysteries enough to prod in the tide pool daughters of the sea, scuttling crabs that pinched to make her squeal and silver fishes that panicked at her shadow. She went

around a dead fish and the gulls feasting on it much as she had
the guests and their champagne and escargot, though with far
more fascination for the birds' laughter and the fish's strewed
entrails.

Another glance around revealed no cousin; she would have
to confess to the priest that she felt no guilt over this, as she
doubtless should have. A foolish boy could suffer real hurt in
this place.

Just then there came a tea-kettle, jester-laugh noise, over
which one of the birds flopped its wings and jabbed its beak.
Something still alive hadn't nearly the charm in being eaten as
a dead thing; not thinking much, she rushed the bird with waving arms as she sometimes startled the starling flocks when the
servants weren't watching. Crying insults at her, the gull took
flight. One couldn't save a thing and not take a glance to see
what it might be; Lilly crouched and stared down into the shallow pool over which the bird had taken such interest.

The thing in it was bright red, craggy-skinned, and the size
of Father's fist, which was to say not very large but with a great
deal of presence; around it limbs coiled like petals circling a
flower's heart. The water came halfway to the top of its bulbous body. It made kettle noises at her. Good sense rolled right
out of her head with the silly thought that adventures started
with such things; plunging her hands into the water, she drew
it out on her palms.

Its limbs whipped out and made erratic lightning shapes and
a hard little beak pressed against her skin. It had the most beautiful eyes, beaten gold with a human's pupils, and she thought:
like the sea monsters on the best illuminated manuscripts. After it
got over its startlement, or perhaps decided she would neither eat

it nor be frightened, it promptly squeezed her fingers in an eight-fold hug. Curious, she touched the top of its head and found the skin not slick like the rest of it, but papery. It needed a better tide pool; one where it could hide and be fully submersed. So she stood and went to find one, venturing closer to the water.

A few steps and its skin smoothed, darkened to a pleasant sienna, like the rocks. "What are you?"

She wavered, startled and perhaps a little wide-eyed. "I— well, I'm eight today. Eight and a bit lonesome at the moment, and I suspect overprotected."

It had a fluting voice, lispy. "I will trade you company for some of your protection. I know many good conversationalists I could introduce you to: kelp, sharks, rivulets flowing into the sea . . ."

"The protection is on loan from my parents. I don't think I can give it away. Thank you, though." She inspected the pools that hemmed her, squinted down at the waves rattling the shore a bit too far beneath her feet to be comfortable. "Do you wish to be *in* the ocean?"

"Oh, no. It is wicked today. Look how far away it left me!" He whistled what might have been a sigh. "You turn your back one moment and the waves pull away, sniggering."

She crouched to let him inspect the options. "Does the ocean talk?"

"If you listen. Most hear only *hush, hush*, but that's her telling them to be quiet so that she may speak." Then, without so much as a countryman's "bye," he dripped off her hand into the pool, the movement startlingly liquid.

She pouted after him until rocks rattled behind her. Scrambling to her feet, she turned expecting something demi-human with bright eyes and a sly smile and unspeakable desires; instead she looked into the frightened, scuffed face of Young von Graf. "I must have been wrong—this is your element, not the garden." He spread his palms, all bloodied and gravel-studded. "I fell! I'm the best athlete at my father's country estate—I would never be so clumsy without a spell."

"Maybe the others let you win." She deserved the glare that won her. "I mean—can you get back? I could lead you."

"Right over a cliff, maybe." He jerked forward, caught up her chin to tilt it to the side, looking at her birthmark. "This is the Devil's mark, then. It's not so scary. Just ugly. Is your beauty what you sold to get your witchy powers?"

Dry, thinking of what her father would say in this situation, she asked, "Does that mean you think the other side of my face is pretty?"

His hands dropped to roughly clench her shoulders, smearing the good cloth with his blood and dirtiness, which she wasted a shocked second being offended over before she realized he meant to shove her.

Catching at his wrists, she said, "I'm not on speaking terms with Satan."

His lips pulled back off his teeth in a grimace, but before he could carry through, he fell with a squealing, childish scream of pain. He slicked blood across his hand and calf as he fumbled at the wound, whimpering. His trousers caught on the rocks, tore, as he scrambled back; gaining his feet, he bolted. Lilly went back on her heels, an offer of help dying in her hands. He must have been fine after all.

A weight on the bottom of her skirt made her tense, but it was only the little sea creature climbing up her side to perch on her shoulder. It was flushed to scarlet again and sang what seemed to be a victory song, two of its tentacles waving after Young von Graf's retreating form like a pit fighter inviting an opponent to come back at him. It was a cool, dampening presence, its cheek against hers, one of its limbs curled against her nape. She realized that the warm liquid soaking into the shoulder of her blouse was her cousin's blood.

"Can we talk more now?" It calmed. "I would like to talk until sundown, until tomorrow morning, until the evening after that—"

"Wait," she said, "my parents will worry, and I really must eat and bathe and study and do other necessary things."

It touched her cheek. "I made you sad. Sirens weep, too."

She had cried, a little, but not at him. "No, *he* did. You just frightened me a bit."

"That isn't better!" As if afraid to hurt her, his tentacles all curled up close to his body—which meant she need reach up and steady him with her hand.

She breathed out, considered. "I have one question. Can you refrain from being a sea *monster*? Eating people, sinking ships—that sort of thing. I could pretend I didn't know but that's not the right thing to do."

"People?" he said, dubious. "There are so many people. I can't eat stones."

Lilly blushed—she held a talking sea creature on her shoulder and she did not stop to think that his prey, thinking beings, would be considered people, too. "Humans. I'm sorry to be so biased, but the thought bothers me."

"Lots of creatures have that sort of loyalty." He patted her cheek as if testing her reaction, then uncoiled to hold himself up again. "All right. I won't eat humans if it means you will speak with me."

"Yes, thank you. I am pleased—no, I'll say as I thought. I am very, very glad to talk with you. But I can't spend all my time here, I'm afraid." She tilted her head back, eyes catching on the clouds boiling white on the horizon. "Things like that," she gestured at them, "aren't good for young people. Would you hear me if I called your name from this beach?" She blushed, wondering if he might slither contemptuously away at her presumption. Dogs came when called, not people.

"Yes!" He knotted around himself, hiding. "But I haven't a name."

"Oh." She looked to him, thinking: eight limbs, gold eyes, both intelligent and merry. It called for something with an ancient but teasing feel. "Octavius! Or Octavia. Which would you be?"

"The first one. I like the noises." Again those arms wriggled with excitement. "Octavius, Octavius—I'll have a name to tell the sirens when they say I will never grow big, I will say, *I must match my long name by growing long.* And the selkies cannot eat something with such a strong word-weapon." He giggled, touched her cheek again. Fascinated with the texture of her skin, she realized. "Thank you."

"I didn't know it meant so much. I'm glad I could give it to you." She sighed, checked the sun. "But I have been gone far too long and someone will worry. I must go."

"But you will be back tomorrow?"

She looked to the ocean. "Yes. And the day after."

———

Perhaps it should have shamed her when her parents met her with closed faces. Mother asked, "Have you hurt yourself, then?" and Father snapped, "I can see she's not. Did you shove that boy? Your cousin. Did you go down to the beach?"

"I apologize," she began, and meant to clarify, but before she could Mother caught her up by the elbow and led her towards the chateau. When she glanced back, Father had pasted on his merchant face and was turning towards the crowd.

"He can only gloss this over so much," Mother said in an undertone. "Do you like painting, Lilly? Needlework? Maths and reading?"

"Watching Father at the books—is that maths?" As they came onto the front stoop she brushed self-consciously at the shoulder of her frock, but that only smeared the stains. "Are you angry?"

Mother did not answer until she had closed the door behind them. "No. How could I be? I expected this." She reached down, took the ribbon from the end of Lilly's hair, and finger-combed it straight.

A heavy coat made it possible to go down to the water, where she would tuck Octavius against her belly and listen to him tell stories of the distant places he traveled to. The open water was dangerous for him, he said, but some things could only be seen when one was small enough to slip into little spaces. Today he had talked her through the process of weaving sea-grass baskets, and though the first try had been messy, the second was a perfect little bowl that held water as tightly as any china dish. Though they could have stayed forever on the beach, they parted; he had to begin his next journey, and she needed to study her French.

The maids responded poorly to the basket when she showed it to them and questioned her at length as to its provenance; thankfully none of them brought up sea creatures so she could truthfully answer *no* to all conjectures. Figuring that she'd best broach this subject with her parents before the servants did, she ventured up the floating staircase—an architectural and not magical feat, much to the disappointment of her younger self—to her father's study. There a screen and portentous-eyed statue provided a hiding place from which to assess the situation.

"Shall I find another serpent for us to kill? Would it make you yourself again?" Mother's sharp voice. Lilly thought: *I should retreat now.*

Father, then, sounding lost: "No. I worry."

"Where is the man I married? Look at your shame." When she felt affectionate, she called her husband brave. Having asked about it, Lilly knew this was because her father had decided to be both a merchant and a noble, though the latter should have prevented the former. Perhaps he had been a soldier once, too; they were never clear about that fact.

"He spawned and like a trout died of it."

Lilly preferred not to be called spawn. Padding back down to the top few stairs, she stepped on the creaking one, then came up and around the screen. Curtsied. "Mother, Father. Might I interrupt?"

Father stood before the desk and Mother behind it, sitting in his vast leather chair with ankles and wrists delicately crossed. She should have looked dwarfed by it and did not. He said, "Come in, Lilly."

She did, holding up her treasure. "I learned how to do this. I'm proud to be so crafty."

"Yes, yes, we are too." Father wandered over to lift it from her hands, turning it this way and that. "Who taught you?"

She shrugged.

"A man?" Mother inquired.

His voice harsh enough that Lilly could imagine him as a soldier, he snapped, "By God, woman, she's eight!"

"All the more likely, then." Mother rose. "Listen, Nikolaus— Lilly. Why must you never be alone with a man?"

"Because many of them would like to marry me for our money," Lilly said, bored with the reiteration of this lesson. How could her father not be aware of it? At least it distracted them from the basket, which Father dropped back into her hands. "Some men will force the issue." Lilly looked into his eyes, thought she detected disappointment. "Mother has left out the details."

"I—" Father stood tense. "You don't *need* to know. That's why—"

"No parent can watch their child close enough to protect them better than they can guard their own self. I came to you pure, did I not? You may thank what my mother taught me for it. Besides, so long as you treat her as a dog that needs to be trained—not as a girl that is raised—I will undertake her instruction." She rose to her feet. "We can talk later. Are you not meeting that spice merchant today? Put on your impressive face, dear. The one you wear at present doesn't suit you."

Still groping after sense, he said, "You were a tailor's daughter, and she is—"

"And she is the daughter of a tailor's daughter." With which she swept out of the door. Lilly always thought her mother's stride more elegant than the mincing of most ladies, but—a tailor's daughter? Truly?

Father laid his hand on her head. "I didn't think you so . . . aware."

"Aware? Sensible, Mother says." She tucked the basket behind her back so that it didn't come up again. "Spice trade is important. I won't bother you anymore."

"And you understand *that*, too?" He squeezed her shoulders. "I should speak with you more often, child."

A man who looked so wounded needed salve, but she remembered far too many rebuffed hugs to make the offer. "I would like that, Father," she said, and ducked out the door.

At the bottom of the stair she met the spice merchant. Tall, dark, and swathed in fine red cloth stitched with grey and gold, he had the sway of a sailor in his walk and the active eyes of a bird. Looking unimpressed but mild, he followed a manservant—Mother must have summoned him for Father's sake. Since she stood on the fourth step up, Lilly could look levelly into his eyes.

He smiled in what seemed to be genuine affability, but he was, after all, a seller of goods. "Lady Lilly, I presume?"

She curtsied and attempted to come down the stairs at once, which proved to look quite a bit like tripping. She dodged his helping hand, smiling fixedly. "Yes, sir. I'll be on my way."

He bowed to her and solemnly said, "I am sure you are much relied on. I would not detain you."

"Sir, might I know the name of he who is gracious enough to say so?" Maybe that came across as her mother did when faced with rudeness; the manservant, who had fallen back in despair upon seeing Lilly on the stair, waved his hands as if to push the words back into her mouth.

The merchant reminded her bizarrely of Octavius when his expression of surprise gave way to amusement. The other smile *had* been false; the true one showed more around his eyes than mouth. "The Sheik Efreet, milady." He inclined his head.

"I apologize, Sheik, for my daughter. She is willful." Father stood at the top of the stairs, his voice far more grave than contrite.

The spice merchant *tsk*ed and flipped his hand as if brushing away a pestering fly. "It is no problem, Marquis. I have three children at home and the youngest manages to be wayward, though she is still in the cradle. But we must be to business, if you will excuse us, lady."

Lilly floundered, then tried, "Of course. It was my pleasure to meet you."

"The pleasure is entirely mine." Yet he was distracted already, the smile falling from him as he looked up at Father; he went up the stairs without being invited. To him, the sheik said, "I'm most interested in this prospect of autonomy, milord." He spoke the term of respect as some spoke *brother*: kinship, equality, but not fondness.

She showed Octavius a sundial, but he never understood why humans would construct such things. The position of the moon and the sway of sun's path across the sky, yes, but not such little units as hours, minutes, seconds. He found them silly. The years, though— those he counted with her, by season, by his own growth from palm-sized to hip-high to shoulder-height.

She had a good life to lead, she thought: tutors, her father prying better deals from merchants with wine and the implicit threat of his witch daughter at the table, trips with Mother into town to buy necessities and "observe real life," introduction to the fine horses that Father kept but never rode. Above all else: her wandering with Octavius. They traded stories, and he showed her what mysteries the ocean washed up on their little shore.

When he was still small, they would meet on the tame beach, and she would carry him up to the chateau to sneak with him through the gardens and even the halls, showing him human life. In return he brought her to places where the ocean let a part of herself be seen by the dry world; once she met a ribbon fish who spoke an elegant greeting and inquired after the state of the sun. Upon hearing it still burned bright, it twisted away to seek deeper waters once more. The sharks were kind, also, though they spoke less and watched more.

She took up another language, Arabic, and Father would drag her into his study with a faint whiff of alcohol on his breath and show her what the accounts meant. Mother continued to give her practical, frightening knowledge, just as when she was young; but now, in reversal of the usual parental pattern, she added fairy stories to the mix. This increased attention meant she could not meet the kraken as often, yet life remained at an equilibrium of calm happiness, even when Octavius' growth meant they could no longer sneak onto the chateau grounds together.

The ocean wore a pungent cologne on summer days as hot as this, but Lilly would have tolerated a rotted sardine hung around her throat for the sake of the sunlight on her skin and a breeze to brush away sweat. On a scraggy-limbed bush she hung her shoes and broad-brimmed hat and hiked her skirt to knee-height with the use of a belt.

At their beach, Octavius greeted her by thrusting a much-rusted device towards her, something alike to the inner gears of a watch, though so sorely degraded that she found it difficult to discern one piece from another. "I found it on a ship," he said, "and I cannot understand what it is."

"It seems . . ." She turned it over in her hand, careful of a sharp-edged barnacle that clung to the back. "Something like a clock, perhaps?"

"*You* do not know?" He curled a tentacle around her wrist, delicately retrieving the thing. "Why, I will have to return it. A human thing at the bottom of the sea is free to whoever takes it up, but it must be the product of a different animal—one who, perhaps, meant to return to it."

"You are not a very discerning thief to have chosen this of all sunken treasures," she teased, touching the ridge of his brow; she no longer had to bend to do so. "I fear I am losing my function as your guide through the human world. Where you bring to me sights, I can only tell stories."

"But what stories they are. You approached with an expression that said you have found another worth telling." He swept a rock free of sea wrack and gestured grandly for her to sit.

"Here." She handed him a small bag in which she had put a handful of nuts and seated herself. "For some time I have heard hints and whispers about midsummer and all its properties. You look perplexed—but then the weather doesn't mean much to you. Well, it is a day of some mystical note, and I hear that some commemorate it more fantastically than others. There is a place—" she waved down the coast "—not so far from here

where there is an ancient abandoned church and a cluster of
hovels in which live pagans." There came times when no
amount of explanation could communicate an idea; despite
considerable conversation on the topic of religion, they had
settled on his understanding the terms to be a manner in which
humankind categorized itself. "They have been described as
having the antlers of deer by day and the bodies of wolves at
night—which seems rather odd, but not altogether unlikely."

Octavius turned an almond in his tentacle, positioning it by
some precise measure that she could not discern, and with a
flex of muscle cracked it neatly down the center. He offered her
the nut thus shelled. "After the griffon and the horse—"

"Yes, precisely." She watched him manipulate a hazelnut,
which by the relative delicacy of its shell presented something
of a problem for him—the first she had given him ended as
crumbles and splinters. "However, I imagine that being wolf-
bodied might interfere with their midnight festival, which it is
said involves much dancing about in scandalous clothing and
sacrifices to devils."

He hummed, thoughtful, applied pressure light enough to
fracture the shell then pulled it apart with two suckers, pre-
senting the meat with a triumphant whistle. "When is midsummer?"

"Oh, not long off. That is why there is so much talk about
it." She tilted her head, recognizing Octavius' smile, inasmuch
as his posture of happiness could be compared to a man's expression. "What do you plan?"

"There cannot be too many ancient abandoned churches
along this coast." He stretched, one tentacle touching the approaching front of the tide; it would drive them higher, soon

enough, or else apart. They often used the ocean's timing to prevent her staying too long and arousing suspicion. "The night is not so good as the depths for sneaking, but we might slither close enough to look down on these rituals. Then you might show me something of humankind again."

She hesitated in the act of taking a cracked nut from him. It was certainly not her habit to venture out at such a time. Yet— she would be accompanied by a sea monster. Besides, when would she next have a chance to see pagans go about their dark rites? "Yes, I believe I can find my way here after sunset, but I must be back before morning."

"Or your dress will become rags and your mother a dove?"

She seemed to recall that particular fairy story went another way, but then, his version could doubtless be found, too. "Nothing so interesting." Lilly pulled her toes back from the encroachment of stinging sea-spray, nose wrinkled. "But who knows what strange stories would be told after the townsfolk heard the uproar of my being missed?"

Later, when he found them, he told her first, "There are antlers set like wreaths on their doors, and their dogs are very much like dogs, and there is a ruined church at the center of their town—are they the correct ones, do you think?"

They determined that yes, they would likely be; if not, the trip would be no hardship, for Octavius indicated that the path was an easy one to tread. Though he had found the place by ocean, on a new moon night he had also gone by land, and Lilly trusted him on his assessment, for he was well accustomed to her abilities after so many years playing among the stones of the coast.

He could not have told her how difficult it would be to go over the sill of her bedroom and into the fragrant night. Pulling her jacket tight around her though the night was not cold, she stepped hesitantly away from the chateau and thought: *Octavius will worry if I linger here.*

She knew that she should have brought a lantern before she even left the garden; the gravel seemed to move more loosely underfoot in the dark, and the moon was not so much help with clouds tracing fingers across its face. The path to their beach proved easier, for she was accustomed to finding a path of particular safety, here. She could see Octavius by the coiling of his limbs, the moonlight catching in the ripples of the ocean. She grinned, put her foot down wrong, skidded the last few feet to his side. With a huff of embarrassment she got back to her feet, waving aside Octavius' offer of help.

"Should you have brought a lantern?" Octavius piped a noise of repentance, guilt. "I did not think, though you said that your eyes are not for the night—"

She rested her hand on his side, asked, "Will you guide me?"

This proved to be better as a dramatic gesture of friendship than as a practical plan of action, for even with his best effort Octavius could not warn her of every knot and hollow, and she was not patient enough to toe forward in fear. Once, he caught her arm with his tentacles when she would have gone face-first to the forest floor, startling them both. She laughed at that, and said, "I should hope I never go blind, for even with the best of all creatures to lead my way, I am most terrible at being sightless."

When the light of the town showed through the trunks, it served only to confuse her more, and after she caught up against three trees—alarming Octavius most terribly—she closed her eyes and let him lead her through the last of it.

He touched her cheek, said in his wave-shushes whisper, "From where shall we watch?"

Peering through the undergrowth which tangled at the forest edge, Lilly saw that the place was ramshackle, its houses built of sea-warped boards, the livelihood of the people made clear by the boats laid belly up beside their homes and the lines and fire pits set out for fish smoking. A bonfire cracked the air on the packed dirt of the town's center, but even its inconstant light could not make the three dozen townsfolk gathered around it seem sinister. They were clearly poor and also clearly in high spirits: the women wore bits of ribbon pinned to their blouses and the men stepped about in buckled shoes.

Here the branches obscured her vision, but if they were to creep far from the woods, they would risk discovery. Certainly it would not suit to put their backs to the ocean, for though Octavius would then escape with ease, she had not yet tested how far her strength extended in the water.

The townsfolk moved with purpose around a table laden with a cheese wheel here and a great deal of fish there. The viands were interspersed with a great deal of woven wreaths and flower circlets, which made them seem a little less scanty. Over it all hunched the husk of the church—or what was not, perhaps, a holy place at all, for it made no sense for a place of community to be situated outside the bounds of ordered society. It could be a madman's lonely blasphemy; this dark impression was furthered by the fact that the bonfire's light did not reach it.

"This way." She tapped his temple, pointed to indicate that they would skirt along the edge of the forest. "If someone sees

me, wait a moment. They will be confused, I think, and I
won't be in danger."

Octavius asked, "Why would you be?"

She was already some strides away; she whispered, "Let's
talk about it later." In the dark, skulking around a strange
community—it was not the time to speak of the violence in
human nature.

She made more noise than Octavius, who moved so
smoothly that he brushed aside the foliage rather than breaking through it as she did; the fear when her foot came down on
a stick with a snap of particular loudness was delicious-terrible,
a sensation that ebbed as she realized that the townsfolk
were too occupied in their laughter and preparation to note
little noises in the forest margin. With some disappointment
she noted that they spoke the same language as she, and further did not have an accent any different from those in the
town which lay a short ride from the chateau.

They reached the foot of the building just as the music began: an accordion and bock and she knew not what else. This
masked her stuttered laugh, partways between amusement and
disappointment, to find that this grand church or madman's
steeple was in fact half illusion, for it was placed on a tumble
of stones that formed quite a regular shape. The building itself
was a wooden lighthouse listing somewhat to the side, its sides
spattered by gull dung.

"Well." Octavius arched his tentacle that she might use it as
a step to reach the ladder that hung down from the elevated
door. "Was it better as a shadow at a distance?"

"I find that it is best as a perch." She glanced over her shoulder, checking that the townsfolk did not show awareness of

them. They were entirely too occupied dancing in a manner that she found impressive in terms of vigor, though no more devilish—if not less—than the foot-tangling complications of a waltz. Well, perhaps they were getting warmed up. Testing the slats, for she was not overly certain of this building's integrity, she scrambled up to the top. It smelled of birds and faintly of old fires, though the pit at its center seemed unused. "There must be something worth hearing about this," she said, "for once it was needful and now it is not, and change makes for interest."

Octavius did not respond because he had not followed her up.

Horrified, caught by the thought of her friend shot down by silent and terrible weapons such as fairy darts, she rushed to the edge of the lighthouse, throwing her weight precariously against its slender hand rail, and looked down into the dark with the expectation that she would see the remains of her friend leaking sea-blood and ichor.

Octavius had knotted himself most thoroughly around the rungs of the ladder, each limb curled around this part or that, his malleable body flattened against the building. Voice small, he said, "I have never been this high up."

Thinking of the first time she had gone into deep enough water that her feet could no longer touch the bottom, she made a noise of sympathy and reached her hand down, though it was more reflex and sentiment than help. "I could come back down. We could watch from—"

A cacophony of shouts and bellows and various half-human noises went up from the crowd, but it was for the purpose of welcoming a barrel of ale being rolled out from a cellar.

Octavius lay the tip of one of his limbs across her palm; placing just pressure enough that she could feel the tension of it in her muscles, he slid his way up to the tower top, where he promptly spread himself across the uneven boards, clutching what solidity there was to be had. "Look," he said, "they are most thoroughly roused. Perhaps the scantiness begins now?"

No, it became clear; but the barrel was tapped. By the motion of the moon, not much time passed before the dancing grew uncoordinated and the music considerably more dissonant. Unless the tribute was to joyful inelegance, Lilly did not think any particular propitiations were occurring down below. She clutched her knees and leaned against Octavius, trying to read his mood; she could not recall him ever being so motionless. Considering this, she whispered, "Are you bored?"

"This behavior—it is further drunkenness?" He tilted himself as if to gain a different perspective on the events.

"Yes. There isn't even a spot of debauchery." Lilly did not know for certain what this would look like, but its use in conversation as a most severe and hysterical word indicated that its appearance would not be missed. "Your hearing is better than mine. Are there goats bleating somewhere near? Perhaps the sacrifices come later."

"I'm afraid not." In a brighter tone, he said, "Sacrifices or no, it is a fair night that is spent in your company. What of the future? Since you have never before ventured out into the dark, then you have never seen the ghost ship. She comes close to the shore when the wind blows a certain way."

"If it is a dingy it will be worth having seen in your company. And if she is truly a ship, I will read her name and tell you her history." She took to her feet without care, for surely when the carousers looked up to their lighthouse, they would dismiss any movement as an effect on the eyes of too much dancing and drink. "Perhaps it is best to leave these people to their celebration. Octavius, will it take swimming to see your ghosts?"

"Well, if you wish to see the light of the captain's red eyes—"

Lilly grinned and, going ahead of him to the ladder, asked, "How soon?"

It took some months, but there came a time when Octavius brought her to a jetty where the water licked as high as her knees, most thoroughly destroying her skirt. She did not care, for the ship that moved through the water without creating a wake was the Hellbent, *a name she thought a fancy of her father's. She clutched at her friend with excitement and told him about the princess and the pirate's dog and the book that would not be drowned—the one that had been placed in the hands of the figurehead so that the ship remained afloat despite the cannonball holes in her belly.*

When she returned in the predawn to the chateau, she buried her salt-stiff clothes like a murderer disposing of his victim. When the dark circles beneath her eyes were exclaimed over in the morning, she attributed them to nightmares. At this her mother raised a brow, but her father declared his desire to check her knowledge of geography, and for the day he kept her in his study. While he went about the various paperwork of his business, he questioned her on trading routes, profitable goods, the customs of different folk.

She did not wish to make rote answers to an examination; the experience that began as a joke about drunk fishermen and a misidentified lighthouse and ended with *his* tale come alive—it trembled on her tongue with a desire to be told. Not making a habit of foolishness, she kept silent, and knew that the impulse would fade when she returned to Octavius and planned for future nights.

Octavius grew quite *large, and there came a day when he told her in a voice grown ever deeper, "I cannot stay here."*

Tears were shed before they straightened matters out; she realized he meant he must hunt farther afield and thus be gone for a week or more at a time, and he understood that this irregularity meant only that he must make some sign to show his return. He took to tearing a stone from a pinnacle visible from the chateau the night before he wished to meet her.

Once, there were jellyfish thick on the beach, suicides, Octavius claimed; listing the reasons for despair among soft-bodied philosophers, he showed her the way down to them, careful her feet did not step on their stingers.

He asked: "Do you not hear?"

She replied, "They tell me to hush. I am too loud."

Dinner having brought the family together, Mother shouted "Fine!" at her husband, flinging her fork down. "If you will refuse to speak with me—if you will despise me and accept me no longer as your mate—I will give into this sordid, stupid wish of yours."

He stood and went around the table to her, drew her to her feet; Lilly looked away as they kissed, uncomfortable. In it there seemed not the devotion of doves preening but the sensuality in the snap of wolf teeth. That was soon after her sixteenth birthday, a time when she had begun to see Father as old, grey of temple, and wrinkle-eyed.

As for herself, she buried her thoughts of husbands when Father said, ironical, "I built this house strong for a long line. I suppose the best intentions are those most detested by God."

Without reason to believe that she would be found by a husband, she found a different sort of satisfaction in herself; she understood sexual congress from the mating of animals, listening to the lewd songs of townspeople, her mother's blunt explanations, and incidental self-discovery. Incidental became deliberate. She appreciated somewhat more those similes that compared women to the sea.

Of all the merchants, the most persistent presence was of the Sheik Efreet: gently pleased, understatedly more wealthy with each visit, and greeted with an uncommon respect by her father, he continued to take a fond interest in Lilly. He said that his youngest daughter had developed into precisely the spitfire he predicted, and though Lilly mellowed with age he saw something familiar in her. Lonesome—he admitted once—and thinking constantly of his family, he found comfort in speaking with her. She allowed it, much as she allowed Octavius' friendship: aware of the implicit danger and choosing to take it on.

Her mother grew more pale and distant, a sharp-tongued presence that took pieces from her husband with each snide remark, and in Lilly's mind became not *Mother* but *Anna Rosa, who stays in her rooms*—such things happened. It was better than a true death.

Lilly laughed with the gulls, learned in her home, and for escape from the coast came to rely on a certain horse in the stable—named *Prudence*, but which Lilly called simply the Mare—to bring her safely to the town, no matter what evil eyes were directed at her. Yes—a good life, however circumscribed.

It was spring and everything lived.

Miss Hannah was Lilly's latest tutor, a young woman with a most remarkable store of knowledge who had performed like a dancing bear for Father and been found worthy. The Sheik Efreet teased about coveting her wisdom when she answered a greeting in his own tongue; when she displayed the ability to follow him through three others, he was quite in earnest in his offer to pay her twice over if only she left the marquis' service. Lilly respected the woman—and found her entirely too clever. Like none of her predecessors, she tracked Lilly's walks to the ocean and discerned in them a pattern.

Miss Hannah caught her by the wrist one day and said, "Whatever the details, I will be sympathetic. But you must make plans, milady."

"There are no details," Lilly replied, more startled than distressed. "You were mid-sentence, Miss Hannah."

The next day she found the woman staring in perplexity at the pillar of stone that Octavius had nearly demolished over the years. Though she loathed to do it, Lilly went to Father that evening and said, "Father, I do not think my tutor the best."

"Shall you release her to go work with the sheik? No." He looked up at her, raised an eyebrow. "And why should you find her unsatisfactory?"

"Will you forgive pride? For she tries mine." That earned her a dismissal, and she left more worried than when she came.

"I do not like seals any longer," Octavius told her on their meeting two weeks after; she leaned against him with her hands fisted against her belly as if that might silence the protestations of her sloughing womb. He poorly tolerated this pain of hers, and spent such times being as distracting as possible. The topic of hunting in the far north had been a favorite of theirs for nigh on a year, yet now he said: "There are men who hunt those waters for whales—and oh! the pitiful wailing of that proud people when the harpoons strike their sides. It is entirely unlike their war-bellows when *I* hunt them. One of those men thought to snare me. Do you see the scar? No, don't narrow your eyes so, it is healed."

"Stay until tomorrow," Lilly said, "please. I hurt too much for wandering now, but I would go walking with you." He consented, of course.

Pale-faced and quaking, she returned to Miss Hannah, who said not, "Leave be that boy," as Lilly expected, but: "What monster are you?"

"None, except that I am human." She pulled back, wary. "Have you been drinking, Miss Hannah?"

"I followed you—just far enough to see how you leaned against the bulk of it. . . ." She passed a hand over her mouth, then held it out. "Please. I will tell Lord Rosa, and against such charges there must be some presence of the wrongdoer."

Lilly gave a short laugh that reminded her all too much of her mother. "So that he might see the guilt in my eye? No, Father is with the sheik—and would you disturb that meeting?"

Miss Hannah hesitated, then grabbing Lilly's wrist dragged her towards Anna Rosa's rooms. "The lady will do just as the lord, surely."

Lilly knew she could easily break the weak, clammy-palmed grip, but she went along. Numbness gave way before the dawning realization of discovery. She had laid down plans for just this event and intended to be honest, to take what she would be given. *He is my oldest and dearest friend,* she would say. *A balm to my hurts and a brightness in my day.* Her mother would take the easiness of it from her, of course, but they were always understanding of each other. Her window would remain unlocked, and some night she would sneak down to the kitchens with a knapsack, then go out to the Mare—

Miss Hannah shoved Miss Scholastika from in front of the lady's suite and shouldered open the door, mouth open to voice some warning—froze. Anna Rosa sat at her breakfast table, a steaming bowl before her and a strew of herbs under her hands.

"Witchery," Miss Hannah said, then something in the ancient tongue of her own people, but she cut off the words as she saw which plants lay there. "Abortion?"

"Most foul sins both." The voice like a serpent bite, the woman a snake lashing out when afraid. "And what will you do, servant of my husband?"

"The daughter is like the mother," the tutor whispered, backing out of the room. "No wonder this house is barren." Then she turned and ran.

"There is no likeness," Anna Rosa snapped after the fleeing servant, then pressed her face into her hands, looking too thin, too pale, too hard-faced. "What will happen to you, love? What did *you* do?"

"Nothing that will make Father as upset as this, I imagine." Lilly shook herself, glanced back at Miss Scholastika, who looked a woman apt to die. Ever had she been a faithful servant to her mistress. "I—I didn't mean that. I think I know why. And I appreciate being enough for you."

"*What* did you do?" Anna Rosa asked, rising to her feet.

Though they were the same words, they did not have the same meaning.

"Nothing I have not—" Lilly got out of the doorway, having heard footsteps down the hall. "Nothing that has not been a part of me always."

"Your father called you feral, once." She turned to the man as he came through the door, a bizarre and horrifying rictus grin on his face. Anna Rosa asked, "Are you here to kill me, soldier?"

"I'm here to speak with my lover," he replied, harsh-voiced, and strode past her to the table. "Scholastika! Are these such herbs as cause the miscarriage of a child?"

At Anna Rosa's gesture, the old woman said, "They are such as cleanses the womb, yes, milord."

He struck the bowl from the table, stepping back as the steaming water wetted his pant leg, and turning on his wife, seized her shoulders. Anna Rosa did not flinch; Lilly did. He demanded of her, "Why did you lie to me?"

"Because you would not let me be free of your demands until I did lie with you." She broke his hold with a swift, practiced gesture, forearms knocking his from her shoulder. "And do you call me wrong for that?"

"You are my wife." His eyes strayed to Lilly, and he said, as if distracted: "You look so frightened—do not."

"And what of her? *Why* should she not?"

He returned his eyes to her, and a certain perplexity came over him. "Would you have had me stay a soldier, and you a country maid? Would you never have led a serpent to his death? Would you have not this place, but some cottage to grow old in, losing your teeth and your reason while eighteen grandchildren scurry at your feet? We are as we are made, and she is not my heir. I tried to make her thus—but it takes more than an education to make a gentlewoman. I cannot keep her pent. So give me another child, one who can be—"

"There's something you are hiding from me." Anna Rosa narrowed her eyes at him. "What is it, Lilly?"

Father knew. It was plain in his face, a resignation to loss, a revulsion.

"Will you have me say it?" Lilly asked him.

He looked away from them both. "Confess it yourself, child."

"For many years the ocean has been my companion—the ocean and its creature, Octavius." It seemed for a moment that Anna Rosa did not understand, or wanted to make a different meaning to those words. It was always the sexual hunger of men that she feared to let near her daughter, and never knew what friendship could do. "A kraken, Mother, though he is—"

Anna Rosa bent graceful as a willow for one of the pottery shards, and driving up from the stance aimed to take out the stomach of her mate. But she was withered, even from what Lilly remembered from her childhood, and Father easily caught her wrist, turned it to send the weapon shattering on the floor. They stood together, Anna Rosa panting, Father mean-eyed. She said, "You would let our child become—that?"

"That what?" he demanded. "It must run in the blood, this fascination for monsters—and when I can offer nothing more than monstrousness, why should I deny her?"

"Because she is your blood as much as mine." She wrenched free of him, stepping back though those shards might well pierce the thin slippers she wore. "What life is that? It is cousin to the one that has put these lines in my face, this agony in my womb. How soon would you have her die?"

"I am here," Lilly said, stiff, "and my fate is my own."

"See what you have done?" Anna Rosa looked across his shoulder to her servant. "We travel. Lilly, I would give you something."

"Travel? Travel where?" But Father got no reply; kicking off her slippers to walk barefoot across the room, the woman took riding boots and dress from her armoire and then a jacket, grey and finely worked.

"I meant to give this to you on some significant date—a birthday, given there's little more significant in your life. Remember me by it." Lilly glanced at Father, but he was in whatever frozen place he went at the end of a sour deal, a drinking mood if ever she saw it. Going forward, she accepted the jacket, turning it over in her hand. Quietly, her mother said, "I have made it myself." She shucked her gown, the lines of her body visible through her light shift—a shock, and Father made a hurt noise. Over this she slid the dress, none of it meant as anything but a pragmatic action. As she stomped on the boots, she said, "The grey mare is yours, isn't she, Lilly? I won't take her. Nor you. But you would not come, anyway."

As she passed Father, he caught her arm, but gently this time. "You said forever."

"So long as we lived. Have those young people not died?" She shrugged him off.

"We are yet the same to each other." He was not begging, but bargaining. "I understand now. And a girl needs her mother, a man his—"

"No." That denial rang like bells in winter. "No, our tongues are sharp as ever but our hearts no longer rejoice at the pain." She glanced over her shoulder. "Good-bye, Lilly. I hope your memories of me are fond."

There should have been some fanfare to her leaving, but she did not so much as slam the door, and her maid followed quietly behind her. Lilly watched her disappear around the bend of the hall and struggled to grasp that she would not reemerge, perhaps to say, "Will you slight me ever again? I will truly leave if you do."

The sound of boot heels faded, ceased.

Shocked at this departure, Lilly looked to her father for some cue, but he stared back without the least intelligence in his eyes. She asked, "You knew?"

"A poor father I would be if I did not." He took a deep, painful-sounding breath. "I left the sheik in the midst of deal-making. But I don't think he will take his business elsewhere. That's good, at least. Leave a while, Lilly. Stay out of my sight."

Though Octavius had many stellar traits, being a surface to cry against was not one of them; Lilly muffled the urge and told him, simply, "I would favor a distraction."

"And what you favor, for when that look is in your eye I surely must deliver. Can you wait with me until the moon is high?"

She settled cross-legged on a rock, though that reminded her of tailors, and she blurted, "My mother has gone. She didn't approve of you at all and she approved of my father less." Octavius settled beside her, the beat of his double hearts a more familiar comfort than her mother's lullabies had ever been.

They watched the evening wane, and when the moon had

lifted her face over the water, they set out deeper into the wild. Lilly ventured here—on her own as well as with him. She liked the places where she had to remove her shoes and wade through the cold water of stream mouths and lapping stretches of ocean in which the shore was a cliff and no good for going atop. Salt water healed wounds. Octavius slithered on her right hand, buffering her from the wind.

At last they came to a long jut of piled stones, some old construction long since sunk, a jetty perhaps. She hiked her skirts up to her thighs, pale skin shining in the light with no shame. Out they went; her feet churned silt and her knees parted the water. An urge to dive into the immeasurable dark of deep waters took her; passed. To do so would panic Octavius.

"We got here before them," he murmured, a sound bent by the intervening water. "Good. I asked them this as a favor and they would resent our being late. They do not usually venture so close to the surface, nor to shallow water."

They? She kept silent, for a head broke the surface then, red-haired, skin the color of a blushing rose. This body bobbed higher—lean, low-breasted, a spear in her webbed hands. Her eyes were the antithesis of lamps, glowing black. Four others broke the surface, one of them male, a narrower, smaller creature. All of them raised their spears, and Octavius answered with upwards-curled tentacles.

"I promised them that I would drive their prey back towards them if it slipped over the jetty."

The figures submerged, flipping up fused, paddle-footed legs; moments later, a lean shark flung its head high out of the water, twisting, mouth gaping. Blood was dark on its tail as it curved back into the water, and broke again, rows upon rows of teeth protruding from its extended gums. When next it plunged a darkness plumed across the silvered waves and a scream, wavering and high, shivered through the water. One of the women broke the surface, legs kicking a spasmodic rhythm, her expression distorted. Blood spurted in hideous arcs from the wound of a severed arm.

"Too much?" Octavius asked.

"No."

The woman gripped her spear with her remaining hand and arched, striking the water hard and fast. More blood plumed, unaccompanied by a scream—though she surely would die of her wound, she had struck a final blow.

As with all predators and prey—the wolves on a doe, a falcon on the pigeon—the hunt did not last so long as the slow death after. The people—four, now—lofted the shark's body to the surface and there tore into it, sucking down entrails, gnawing the fatty flesh of its fins, rending chops from its sides. At last the sound of their jaws ceased; together they seized the carcass and dragged it out of sight.

The process was, if anything, cleaner than the slaughter of a farm animal. More honest. Terrifying. She said: "I think they call this catharsis."

"That is a good thing?" He turned an eye to her, flecked with luminescence even when turned from the light.

"Yes."

"One moment—there is one thing better than the killing itself. The reason I brought you here, though I knew from the shine in your eyes whenever I tell of hunts that there is something inside you that sings for such things. Wait here, please." Noiseless, he slipped off the jetty into deeper water.

She had taught him the most polite manners for a kraken; that seemed worth laughing at, just now.

He crested, the working of his siphons stirring the sea around her feet. "They are gone. I can carry you out."

"And I can swim." She pulled her dress over her head and stood in her shift. "Can you carry this to shore?"

He lofted up a tentacle over which she draped the garment, and with care he undulated over the jetty to spread it on a dry rock. He returned swiftly, seeing her push out into the waves. She knew how to swim—her long-ago nurses would be horrified, but she couldn't wade to all the places which her friend wished to show her, and there were days when only the shock of the water could take the stomach cramps from her mind.

The shadow of him swam beneath her now, subtle as a shoal of fish.

Her hands swept through a mass of thumb-sized, putty-soft objects, some of which sank at her touch, others of which bobbed again to the surface. She reoriented, snorting water and wincing a little, and stared around at the lights of—not blood, quite. Stones made of blood and moonlight, their parentage writ on them in a red more striking than a ruby's and a light-glow. They were hardening, going to the bottom; she reached out her hand to catch two before they fell beyond her reach. Octavius rose in the water beneath her, making a platform of his arms so that she could stand in the water, balancing with one arm and swaying with the current.

The stones, drawn close, were one brown-gold and the other brighter, colder. The hunter's and the hunted's. "Such," she murmured, meaning to say, *treasures, beauty,* but there were no words that encompassed them. Anyway some of the ocean got in her mouth and she was distracted by a coughing fit. Then practicality intruded: how did one swim two small things to shore when one wore a shift without pockets? Hold them in her mouth, clenched between her teeth, and risk inhaling them? She thought not.

Octavius ascended higher, and being accustomed to that movement she sat on the curve of his head when she could, one hand braced on his brow ridge. He asked, "Will you let me carry you?"

"Yes," then: "Thank—"

Gently, he replied, "They are meant for you."

There did not exist the story or song or wandering conversation that could outdo those moments, and neither of them tried; the silence of their trip back towards the chateau was both unique and comfortable. She slung her dress over her shoulder, hung her shoes from her fingers, and clenched the stones in her free hand.

Their farewells were quiet, fond. He said, "I am sorry about your mother."

"I'm sorry *for* her," Lilly replied. "I don't think I would hurt at all if Father had gone with her. But they are a broken unit, now—though that has been true for years, today it became final. The pieces shattered and have been swept aside."

When she had gone deep enough in the gardens to be out of sight from the shore, she hid behind a shrub and shucked her shift, pulled on the dress and shoes. It was silly modesty to thus hide herself from Octavius, she supposed, when little enough had been hidden through the soaked undergarment, but it was the gesture, what such modesty meant in friendship, that mattered.

And she was glad of her clothed state when rough hands seized her as she drew herself up to the windowsill of her room, wrenching her inside to fall gracelessly to the floor. She kicked; the stones skittered from her hand. That left her free to claw the arms that held her.

"Lilly," Father said, and the command in that voice stopped her. It sounded reasonable, but the alcohol smell that drafted from his mouth was not.

Calm, she said, "You knew about this."

He released her hands, but as she moved to massage her bruised wrists, he touched her throat, gentle even as his thumbs settled over her trachea. "Yes. I knew you were a little mad. But I didn't know you would lose me my wife."

Lilly could see the twisted logic and perhaps a way to talk him out of it—were he not drunk. She dug at his eyes with her fingers—*her mother* had taught her to do that—then, released, scrambled towards her armoire, where the hairbrush was heavy, metal. She could flee from him to the stable, to the Mare, who would take her elsewhere until full day, the protection of the servants, and the shame of dark deeds brought to light, so that she might gather her things—

He caught her from behind, dragging her to her feet, setting his forearm over her throat, pulling his arm taut with his other hand. She kicked his shins, but there was the strength of the insane in him, and her struggles were weakening meanwhile. Blackness swum over her vision, almost like the sea after dark. In her ear he whispered, "You are innocent, in your way—but you cut bonds, skin, hearts. I cannot fix that. I want another wife, a true firstborn, a new start." His arm slacked a little. "You deserve a last word."

She rasped, "I will leave." By death if not by choice; she preferred the latter, that she might go with Octavius or astride the Mare. She hoped for the second and suspected the third to be sensible. "But I will always be your daughter."

His arm loosened further with consideration or shock or sadness, she didn't give a damn which. She drove her elbow back into his gut and tore herself free while he gasped; staggering to her armoire she took up the brush, turning with it raised in front of her. Steadily. He coughed, began to laugh, wheezing. "Yes. Yes. Mine more than hers."

"Mother could take your breath as well as I just did."

"Reckless girl. Would you have me kill you?" He pressed a hand to his stomach, waiting until his breath evened. The way he held himself did not say *moneyed nobleman,* as it always did: no, there stood a soldier wearing her father's skin. "The King left me too—in the way of kings, by turning the earth so that I stood elsewhere and he remained in one place."

"My death would be a leaving." She edged towards the door. "My presence isn't the one you desire. But will Anna come back to replace me? No."

"Don't talk of your mother like that. She promised me one child—if the first is gone. . . . No. Stop, sweetheart. I'm thinking." He rubbed at his mouth—did his lips numb? Was he *that* drunk? "Will you really leave? Would you wait until I get another wife, another child?"

"I would leave now," she said, and found the scissors on the other side of her dresser. She palmed those, the handle biting into her palm.

"The sheik would wonder. The town would wonder. They would think, *Where have all his women gone?* No. Stay a while.

I won't—I didn't really mean that." He shook his head, shoulders slumping. "She died in a boating accident."

A chill crawled down her neck. "What?"

"When they ask about my wife, I will cry and say, *The ocean took her.*" He looked up, and the light caught in his eyes, the blown-wide pupils, the sweat on his brow. She had seen those under the influence of opium before, in town, lolling on the streets and panting after some distant vision. "It's true somewhat. The ocean did take one of mine. You."

She lowered her arms, uneasy but seeing safety in how he swayed on his feet. "Your absent daughter asks to be left alone, Father." *Nikolaus.* Why did she lose her parents thus?

He made a horrible, coughing noise. "Be it as it may. God help us. Where can I find another woman like her?"

Lilly did not think it the wisest course to find an equal to Anna for his mate, but she did not care at the moment to prevent him from harm. She pressed herself back as he passed, and locked the door behind him. To the armoire's top she let the makeshift weapons tumble, and then dropping to her knees she felt with careful fingertips for the lost blood-stones. They were warm, still, and made pleasant indents in her palm.

Hunching over them, she let herself weep, but quietly, and more for pain and loss—for she had loved her parents, loved them still. This must be how it felt to be betrayed by one's god or one's country, for with this long day heavy in her throat, she could not believe they loved her in return.

The first time Nikolaus summoned her to his study after that encounter, she carried a sheathed knife in her pocket lent to her by the stable hand. At his door she stood some while, meeting him stare for stare; she'd heard before that they were alike in features, the color of their eyes. Always it seemed his were darker, but now that she caught sight of her reflection in the mirror over her shoulder, she saw that it was not so.

"Yesterday, the Captain Marauder asked me who the little servant with the marked face was. He thought you had sad eyes and a boy's hips." He was drunk again, but the study was free of the smell of burnt rope that came with heavier drugs.

She crossed the room and settled in the chair across from him, pride stung. "Such rough men cannot be expected to know how to interpret a household such as ours."

"You stepped aside for him like a servant would. It's no mistake of his." He took up the glass on his desk, and turned it so that the little bit of golden liquor in its depth gathered—*like Octavius' eyes,* she thought, a most disturbing comparison. He was avoiding her gaze. "I want to tell you of people, their relations, and how to appear as you wish."

She sat stiff.

Careful, as if the words were the stones to be set in an unmortared field wall, he said, "I am sorry that we have not seen each other for some time. I expect you here in my study each night that you don't go down to see your monster."

"Do you wish to track my movements so closely?" Those were bitter words and not entirely sensible; it would take little to spy on her. She would have run if she did not know he would catch her.

"You're a smart girl." He waved her closer, a gesture she did not answer. "You can learn what I have to teach."

———

Humans are weak, *he taught her first.* They break very easily.

For the next six months Miss Hannah would not look Lilly in the eye and made no more mention of her trips to the seaside. Doubtless the handprint bruises on Lilly's throat the morning after the debacle convinced her that nobles' troubles were best left to their makers. Spring and summer passed with many hours on the beach— even when Octavius was nowhere near. She sat with the jacket Anna had made around her shoulders and a book or practice ledger on hand. She took the Mare to town and listened to the people there, buying hot bread from the bakery each day until the mistress of the great oven would speak to her.

As Jutta kneaded the morning dough—Lilly had come early, before the dawn, hearing her father stirred and doubtless vicious with the sickness of the night's liquor—Lilly sat on a crate, legs crossed, the Mare dozing where she was tied in the small yard out back. "Ma'am," Lilly said, which always made the baker chuckle. "Can you keep a secret?"

"No," Jutta said, cheerful, and swung her heavy greying braid. "But I'll listen to one."

"I don't know my own history." At the woman's glance, she corrected herself to, "The history of my parents, I should say. How does a couple one half a soldier and the other a tailor's daughter come to be marquis and marquise?"

"They never told you, child?" The *milady* had dropped the first time Lilly challenged it with *ma'am.* "How sad. They must be ashamed. We celebrate them for it." She clapped a hand to her face, leaving a beard of flour. "Oh, I'm sorry, child. I forget that the lady has gone to God."

"You understand why I ask, then." Lilly shrugged off her jacket, laying it aside. "Might I help today, ma'am?"

Jutta glanced out her door; she was friendly, but not a fool, and knew that her customers would spit on her loaves if they knew Lilly had touched them. "Close the door, then—yes. There are never enough hands. Start with the rolls there. They don't sell quite so well as the others in the morning, so it's all right if you are a little clumsy at first."

Lilly did as she was asked then set to the work, thankful for her time swimming, for the baker's muscled arms made sense when one had to fight the dough.

"Be less aggressive with the rolls. They aren't to be squashed like grapes for wine." Watching Lilly until the technique suited her, she asked, "Is this how you mean to pay for the tale?"

"No. This is how I excuse not being at the chateau. It's a useful skill to learn."

Jutta chuckled. "You wish to venture out from the home of your childhood, don't you? You're no different from any bright country lass—it must be in the blood. Well, if you are sensible the story of your parents will cool that wanderlust some. This is how it really went. I heard it from a minstrel.

"Your father started as a soldier for the King's and became honored with his particular favor when, separated from the rest of the army, they battled together back to safety. When the border settled again—the borders are always getting unsettled, you know. It's because people get confused what liege they belong to. Anyway, when things were cleaned up, the King brought Nikolaus—oh, I didn't mean to disrespect—"

"He was Nikolaus then. Do I make these into roll shapes now?" Lilly held up a piece of dough.

"Let me see. No. They're not windowing, see? That's when it will stretch thin—look here at this piece. Then you make it into a snake, and coil *that*. See? Good." She tossed the unready dough back to Lilly, who caught it neatly. "So, Nikolaus went to court. Within the month, they say, he became a sort of terror—like a hunting dog kept alone inside for a family pet. Ravaged one side to the other and scared all the poor courtiers. The King went grey then, they say, and finally he called Nikolaus to his private chambers—not the throne room, because he still liked his soldier too much to make this whole mess public—and he asks, 'Nik, what can I do with you?'

" 'Well,' Nikolaus says back, 'I need to soldier.'

" 'I won't have you dead,' the King replies, and they go back and forth like that until the King offers: 'I'll give you land. I'll give you a title. Do you fancy knight? Not tempting enough for you? A count—or is that too high? A marquis. I'll give you part of the border, a place you can love, and I'll make you a lord marquis.' "

"The minstrel must have been in the King's private chambers," Lilly said, amused, "or got the story whole from my father."

"Oh, he said he was a jester at the time and *was* in the chamber. Clever, child, to realize that. Your father, by the way, would have none of this talk. He said, flat-out, 'I need a wife.'

"This put the King back a bit, and then he pointed out towards the rest of the palace and said, 'Really, Nik? *Really?*' Disbelieving just like that. And Nikolaus said: 'I'll have as a wife the girl I loved, once, in the village of my parents. I left to be a soldier and to die because a serpent owns her heart.'

"The King asked—oh, what did he ask—something like, 'Really a serpent, or a man like a serpent?' "

"Did he ask 'metaphorically or literally?' " Lilly checked herself if the dough windowed, and showing it to the baker was given a nod of approval.

"Yes, yes, fancy book learning you have there." It was said with a teasing smile; the baker slid a rack of loaves from the oven with a rush of warm yeast smell and heat, and put in its place a rack of sweet rolls that had finished rising. "And Nikolaus replied: 'Literally.'

" 'When you come back it will be to a different kind of march,' said our King, but he figured his man would die and so wore black after that—right until Nikolaus came back with Anna beside him, they say. Anyway, the King sent the jester along to bring back the bad news and not leave him wondering. I think the King must wear black now that he heard the lady died, but I don't know that for a fact.

"Away Nikolaus marched with the few coins he would accept from the King—he was, is, a proud man—and his provisions over his shoulder and his gun in his hand. Up the mountains— I don't know which mountains, I'm sorry, but not *ours*—up he went through all the winding roads he'd gone down, once, and he did not have much hope. None more than when he went down. But he was a brave man, too. The minstrel always told us that: 'He's a brave, brave man, and proud, or he would be in this tavern beside me.'

"Around the peak of the mountain you could see the serpent coiled, massive and flesh-colored and with grey eyes like a man's, but so huge that you could mistake them for boulders on the slope. Against his cheek your mother leaned, saying whatever one says to the serpent that has stolen your heart. He would worm his tail down the mountain to catch bears and wolves for his dinner, and go into town with it to wriggle among people's feet until they handed down sweetmeats for Anna. Coming into town like a ghost, not even going to his parents or brothers or anybody else he knew, Nikolaus pulled a jug of rough soldier brew out of his bag."

Lilly sniffed, asked, "Are the sweet rolls done?"

"I was just about to get them. Take up that heavy glove and pull them from the oven, would you? Thank you, child. Don't burn yourself as you turn them out on that rack. Very good. Come back to the rolls. Where was I?

"Yes, here. Then he wrote a little note in the letters the King had taught him and he hoped Anna had learned. She was always a bright girl and he trusted in her. On the note he put: 'My love, you know my name. Tell the serpent to drink of this jug and I will take you away with me to be a marquise, for the King loves me.' Those are exactly the words—the minstrel would talk them in a deep, humming voice when they came up in the songs, his fingers deadening the strings. Nikolaus tied this note with twine to the neck of the jug.

"When the serpent's tail came wriggling into town, Nikolaus gave it the jug.

"That night, the snoring shook the mountains from their crowns to their feet, and Nikolaus jumped astride his horse and felt free to gallop full-tilt to where his sweetheart waited, for he missed her sorely and would die for her even if the serpent had found him out and the snoring was a ruse. But the creature was well and truly stinking of moonshine and sleep when he came around its head, and riding for half the night he at last came around to the other cheek where Anna waited. 'Love!' he shouted.

"And she said, 'Hello, Nik. Help me get this bag over his head. I've been telling the serpent I was making him a sweater all these years, for he gets cold in the winter, but the end I said was for his tail is actually for his head. He is no good with mazes and will knot himself up trying to escape the one he makes of himself in trying to twist free.'

"Nikolaus kissed her, then went to the other side of the serpent, where he held one side of the bag she had made and she held the other. Together they dragged it around and around his vast body. It took them two days and two nights, but that didn't matter, because the serpent still slept off his drink and did not know the sun had risen because of the thick burlap over his eyes.

"When they had him all covered, Anna called out, 'My love, your sweater is ready. How does it fit?'

"First the serpent asked, 'Are the moon and stars hidden by storm clouds? For the night is very dark.'

"Anna called back, 'My love, my love, it is just as you say. You should be glad of the sweater, or you would feel the nip of the cold.'

"The serpent wiggled a bit, then asked rather anxiously, 'I smell a man on our mountain and the sweat of his horse.'

"'In your sleep your tail brought you one of the villagers and you swallowed him down.' She laughed when the serpent made disgusted noises. 'It's all right, love, I checked to make sure he had no nits nor fleas. Now, my love, how does the sweater fit?'

"'The sweater fits tight,' the serpent said, then: 'Have you put it on backwards? It chafes my nose when I try to wriggle free.'

"Anna put her arm around Nikolaus' waist and said, 'My

love, you do so like puzzles. Can't you get free of this one? I made it just for you.'

"Maybe the serpent would have put his foot—which is to say, his tail—down had she not said that last, and demanded she set him free. But he really did love her, though he detested puzzles, so for her sake he tried to wriggle free of the so-called sweater. He wriggled and writhed and twisted and loops of him fell from one side of the mountain to the other. At last he lay in a great big knot, and gasping he said, 'Dearest, could you cut me free? I seem to have failed your puzzle. I am smothering on my own coils.'

" 'I am getting the knife, my love.' Anna took Nikolaus by the hand and drew him towards the serpent's head, and meanwhile he drew out his hunting knife.

" 'I smell man again,' said the creature, but in trying to move only tightened his noose.

" 'You must still have some of the man's flesh on your tongue, my love.' Anna stepped behind the man who would be her husband and whispered in his ear, 'My heart is in his right eye, which is like a cave, and over it a scale.'

"Then Nikolaus stabbed the serpent where the wet gusts of air showed its vulnerable nostril to be. It couldn't have hurt more than a gnat bite, but we all know how bad those can be. When the serpent lunged forward to crush this threat, he tightened himself up all the way, and you can imagine what happened next. Are you all right?"

Lilly cleared her throat, thinking, *How might Octavius be tricked to death?* She turned away to place her kneaded dough on a baking tray. "Yes, ma'am. What happened then?"

"Why, together they opened up the sack and stepped over the

serpent's lolling tongue, pried off the scale over his eye, and went into the cave of his pupil to get her heart. Then they rode down the mountain, she with her arms around Nikolaus' waist, and they were married with all their folks around them in the town church. The minstrel ran ahead to tell the King, and the King met the pair with a pageant and a writ for them to have this very land we stand on.

"The marquis couldn't sit still any more than the soldier ever could, so now he does some shipping on the side. But we're glad to pay our little tithes to a lord who is really one of us."

Lilly groped for some neutral thing to say. "What do my parents think of that story?" She did not want to call the baker a liar and saw little cause besides. The story made sense. Yet she hungered to know the precise truth.

"That is how their minstrel told it. Didn't they tell you about him? There's more than him running back to court—he didn't want to be a jester again, you see. So that doe-eyed soul came with them and stayed until you were born. He was a very pretty creature." She pulled another tray from the oven, then wrapped one of the sweet rolls in cloth and put it in Lilly's hands. "We never decided what might be under his clothes, though he called himself *he*—always with a little smile, though. He looked to the Lord Rosa as if he expected something, and he came down to the tavern to drink like any honest person. If you bought him enough drink he would take to singing and strum on the guitar, and what beautiful songs! Though sometimes he slurred the words, we could always tell when he sang of your parents, because he loved them.

"In those songs you could near see the King, and the Lord Rosa as a young man, and the Lady Rosa in her glory. Hers was a beauty like ours, you know—like an honest girl's, not one powdered and primped since babyhood. I shouldn't say that to you, I suppose—but you don't wear cosmetics, do you?"

"It seems little worth it," Lilly replied.

Jutta did not flinch from the truth of that. "Yet you take such care with your appearance." She reached out, gently stroking Lilly's hair back over her shoulders. "I'm sure it must tangle if you don't tend to it with brush and oil. Would you like to know how to braid it?" She glanced at her own hands, jerked them back with a self-conscious laugh. "Oh, I've got flour on me. And flour on you, now." It made her sound—young, yes.

Young, as she was. "That's all right. I would like to know how to keep it out of my face sometimes."

"It's not for pity," the baker blurted of a sudden.

Lilly laughed, this time, a rusty giggle that she almost didn't recognize as her own. It had been a while. "Of course not. How could I mistake compassion for pity?"

Jutta seemed pleased even as she beat some of the flour from her hands. "No girl should be without a mother at your age. It will be another ten years until mine match you, but I know that already. Sit, child. Let me show you how to put up your hair as the Gallic girls do. I have a sister-in-law from there who showed me."

As the household knew would happen, there came another woman, and it was not clear whether she courted or was courted; perhaps both. Mary Baumhauer was shorter than Lilly, blonde, delicate; the visual antithesis of Anna, but possessed of the same forwardness. "I'm not a noblewoman," she said. "I'm a trader's widow." She had not tried to avoid Lilly but instead talked directly to her, after offering condolences for the grief Lilly still wore in black, as custom dictated. "He was my second husband, but unlike the first he left me a great deal of money. A woman can't manage that much without the King getting to it somehow."

Sometimes she forgot herself and stared at Lilly's birthmark, but that was expected.

When with Nikolaus she laughed often—mostly when he insinuated that he wanted to see her ledgers before they did more than take dinner together—and once skipped out the door like a girl.

Really, she could not be too much older than Lilly. Her first husband had died a year after they were married, she said— when she was sixteen.

Hannah called Mary "your stepmother" long before the wedding was announced, and Lilly didn't contradict her on account of agreeing entirely with that assessment.

Not many months after the woman's first appearance, Nikolaus interrupted himself in the middle of a lecture on how to sell high and buy low with the art of a true haggler to say, "And I'm marrying Mary." He chuckled faintly. "But she's not pregnant yet. You should practice your riding, sweetheart." Not waiting for her response, he continued with his lesson, saying, "I had no money. None! I *had* to learn this and you do, too. I can't send you away with much in the way of funds. It wouldn't be right."

The wedding was held inside the church of the much larger town that lay up the coast from them, the place where most of the merchants touched down to trek to Nikolaus' chateau. He had explained to her that it made him feel powerful that they endured travel by land for the sake of an audience with him.

Only the sheik came by sea, tying his trim, short-distance craft at the chateau's dock beside Nikolaus' unused pleasure boat.

This meant that the sheik, among Nikolaus' merchants, did not attend; as Lilly did not either, she was the one available to greet the man, who had made an appointment that Nikolaus had no intention of following through on. More posturing. The spice merchant clearly knew this, but he was content to take tea with Lilly. He told her about the coffee he normally drank, its cinnamon and cardamom, and of the home he had gotten for his wife so that her and his daughters—no sons, no, just daughters—would not be so sad while he was away. He said, "They can always pretend I'm in another room, out of earshot, out of sight. So your father is getting married, is he, milady? That seems—is it insensitive to say?—rather soon."

"Some men mourn thus, don't they, Sheik?" She hid behind her teacup. "They cannot live with an empty house." She brushed out her skirts, rising. "He made a room ready, Sheik. Shall I show you to it?"

"Ah, he knew he wouldn't be here, did he? Such a complex man is Lord Nikolaus." He moved out of the maid's way so that she could gather up the tea things; he always seemed slightly puzzled by servants. "Well, show the way, milady, and wish me luck if it doesn't strike you as too disloyal. He will doubtless be guarded and unwilling to make good deals for fear that his happiness clouds his judgment."

She raised an eyebrow at him but could not, quite, deny that thought. "I can wish you both fair dealings without filial guilt."

The sheik bowed in answer to Mary's curtsey when he met her the next day, and their brief conversation was all camels and her eyes gone bright as if reflecting the hot desert sun. The sheik never did look at Lilly with quite that sort of interest—or was it merely the preening of one receiving such attention? He certainly looked embarrassed when he caught Lilly's carefully blank expression and excused himself on account of the long way to the home he had spoken of.

Mary cleared her throat. "I didn't mean—"

Lilly crossed the room to her, gently clasped her hand. "You're the best stepmother I could have imagined."

"That's very sweet." She blinked a few times, dropped her eyes. "I thought you might think me . . . Something like . . . Well, Lilly, I hope you aren't offended if I say you are some-what distant."

"Oh, no. Not to you—not in a meaningful way. Ask the ser-vants, if you like. I'm afraid that my demeanor is—" She cocked her head at Mary's laughter.

"Oh, I'm sorry, honey, but you were so *earnest*." She patted Lilly on the shoulder and went—Lilly would later learn—to put some order and verve into the household.

There were gatherings of society people again, dinners for the captains that were not meant merely to convince them of Nikolaus' power. The household became lighter, more practi-cal, its dust swept out and sunlight brought in by hands that knew work and joy and money all, and yearned to make what she must quickly have found to be a cold house into a home. When she spoke with Lilly, it was more warmly each month, though Lilly knew that her own demeanor never changed.

Octavius said, "She would laugh with me, wouldn't she?"

"If I knew how to introduce you," Lilly agreed. "I'm sorry I don't laugh more." She looked to the stars; she liked coming here by night. It made familiar sights into half-seen suggestions, a landscape that might have been anyplace. "I have been thinking: coastal roads are not so hard."

"And I could find you on them, for you are worth looking for."

There had come a fracturing in her life: each moment a lurch forward, every day the expectation not of renewal—and that had always been the anticipation of winter—but of abandonment. She hoarded her heart for Octavius, and shared what warmth was left over with Mary, who did not deserve her ire. Her stepmother seemed to decide that Lilly had been forced into an emotional retreat by Anna's death, particularly when she learned by whose hands the jacket had been stitched. Lilly didn't have the words to tell her that it was merely the warmest she owned.

"I love her for her womb," Nikolaus said. "I will love her more when it's fruitful."

"You're vulgar," Lilly replied, meaning something else. Tiring, perhaps.

"I love Anna for her ability to stab a serpent in the nose." He paused. "Loved. I never did tell you that story."

"I've gotten it from elsewhere. I don't need to know more." She pushed her chair away. "It's late and I must meet Octavius when the moon is over the horizon."

"Octavius? That's a damned stupid name for a kraken." The sloppy look on his face was almost jealousy. So long as he controlled her, he did not really want to share her, she thought, and only his vague paternal sense of her safety—her need to learn how to *be* safe—made him allow her such freedoms as he did.

"I was eight, milord." She turned away and pretended not to hear his words when she had passed beyond the door.

"Well, I suppose it's clever for a child."

Spring came, faded. The pregnancy was a quiet announcement in the midsummer. Lilly came to Nikolaus' door with provisions over her shoulder, prepared to beg what money she could from him, and to her shock and disdain, he started up from behind his desk and said, "No. No, you will wait a while. It will be hard for you to leave your friend, won't it? I'll give you until you are eighteen. You could wait until the babe is born, but I know you won't."

"So you will have me travel in winter," she said, drily.

"Find someplace to settle before it gets truly cold. If you stay close by—well. Just once you may return, and I will pretend I don't know you, and the servants will patch whatever is wrong with you and send you out again."

She bowed to his will only because he would not give her money otherwise, and she was not such a fool to try the roads without a weighted purse. For the first time she did not return to the chateau but spent the night singing shanties and ball-room music with Octavius. She could only sing one part at a time, but he would reunite them into songs, for he could multiply his voice into a choir's worth. At dawn she came in by her window—she didn't often do that anymore, but her current state would rather worry the servants—and, still stiff with sea-salt and perhaps a little wrong-headed with exhaustion, got the idea that it would be sensible to collect those old toys of her childhood that her stepsibling might enjoy.

There were the animals carved from wood with semiprecious jewels for eyes, the porcelain figures of a knight and lady who— on inspection now—she realized must be her parents, though very much younger. The third figure, never her favorite after she had broken off his hands, looked sly and gentle at once. The minstrel, she supposed, whom she never got to meet. She took only the statuette of Nikolaus for the use of Mary's child and tucked the others back into their casket. There were other things: baubles, children's books. She put them all in a box and went to Mary's rooms with them, thinking she might not be in.

Her stepmother answered the door, looked her up from her bare feet to the top of her tangle-haired head, and said, "Lilly! Good morning. Will you share breakfast with me, dear? And what do you have?"

"I appreciate—" Lilly fell silent, startled by her stepmother standing on her toes to kiss her cheek. "They're—they're children's toys. I thought . . ."

"Oh, yes! He told me, once, that he likes to get the best for his children. It's so sweet of you to pass them—and the memories— on." She indicated a table for Lilly to lay the box on and meanwhile closed the door. Coming close, she whispered, "Can I tell you something?"

Lilly tried to finger-comb her hair out of her face. Gave up. "Yes, Mary, if you like."

"This isn't my first child. I had a boy by my first husband— oh, he was beautiful. He caught a fever when he was nine months old, and my husband followed him soon after. For love, I always thought." Mary giggled, a nervous painful sound. "I always want to laugh when Nikolaus goes on about firstborns. I don't know why it's so important to him, but I don't—"

"No," Lilly agreed, "it's not necessary for him to know." She shivered, tried to hide it by drawing away.

"Tea," Mary said brightly. "I promised you tea, didn't I?"

In the corridor that ran between the water closet and the staircase to the second floor she met the spice merchant. Normally she would have made some light greeting and moved on, but she was startled; normally she was alerted to his visits on account of Nikolaus' certainty that the sheik sold at better prices because of his paternal fondness for her. "Sir . . . ?"

The look on his face shocked her, also. He *could* put on the sly mask of a haggler, but never with her, and that he held to now. There worked behind his eyes sorrow, confusion, and in his pause before answering, something far more significant than any of those. "Please, Lilly, call me Saleem."

"After all these years?" The humor—did it count as humor, coming from her mouth?—was sour on her tongue. "Yes, if you like. If we are to be frank, what has happened?"

"Nothing." He smiled, faint. "Have I told you how much you remind me of my youngest? Each day she gets into more trouble, and each day we love her more. Well, perhaps her older sisters don't, but older sisters rarely do." He cleared his throat. "On which topic, when I told her of *you*, the girl across the sea that I met and thought must share some essential spark with her, she got terribly excited and gave me something of hers to pass on to you. She quite loves it, she says, and that she always kept a little piece of her heart in it. She might have meant something else, though. She likes wordplay." During this speech he had drawn a small parcel from his pocket and teased the twine from it.

Lilly accepted it when he held it out. It was light, the wrapping delicate, and inside—her breath caught. It was a box, not much larger than its own lock, the top inlaid with an ocean scene. A hippocampus rearing, nose pointed towards a golden shore. The stones were semiprecious at best, and much of it was stone or wood inlay. Subtle. "You have been wrong all these years, Saleem. We are not alike: I don't have as generous a heart as her, for she has given me this."

"Do you know, she predicted you would say something of the like?" At last a genuine smile came into his eyes. "And in response she declared: '*What is given to one so alike is like having it yourself.*' She trusts my word quite a lot, you see. Here, have the key. We lost the original, so I had to have it wrought anew."

This was gold, with a chip of sapphire, too. Holding these treasures between her cupped hands, she considered how best to pose a delicate question to a man who gave her such things. "Sir," she began, then seeing his arched eyebrow said, "Saleem— has the marquis posed some offer that upsets you?"

His face closed. "I'm not sure—I can't say I know exactly what you mean." He seemed quite desperate that she not know whatever he did.

Delicate, she asked, "Does he expect you to make a different sort of gift to me? He has mentioned before that your people often have multiple—"

"*No.*" Saleem went back on his heels as if dealt a physical blow. "Not for all the good trade in the world would I so betray my wife, nor you." He hissed a breath between his teeth.

"You know your father would make such an offer? Yes, I see it in your eyes. I hoped that he had mentioned it only to me, those years ago. I apologize."

She shook her head. "What for? Consider it a difference in understanding and forget it. It has nothing to do with me."

"No, I suppose. Are you happy?"

"That's a strange question, Saleem. And at this hour I know you have excused yourself but briefly from the study." He kept a steady eye on her; she couldn't help but smile. "We are all significant looks, are we? Each day brings its own happiness and the future promises the same. Is that enough?"

"You're lying," he said quietly. "I know because of what I am told elsewhere. In this you differ from my girl, from Basima. Where did you learn to lie, Lilly? And why do I see you looking so often towards the water?"

She tensed. "There is a line past which even friends—"

"Yes, one sometimes crossed for their good if not their happiness." Briefly, he settled his hand on her shoulder, fatherly. Or like a priest blessing the unlucky. "I'll be leaving soon and must wish you farewell now."

Unwilling to end a conversation on such a poor note, she echoed his farewell and did not pursue the topic. Everyone had their sore points; perhaps Nikolaus had thrown him somehow, and the mention of that long-gone marriage scheme—always doomed to failure—had upset him further.

Given the stress of this encounter, she did not feel entirely surprised that Nikolaus had preceded her to her room after dinner. Though she wanted to make the gesture of stepping past the threshold, she could not make her feet agree to it. "Have you come to send me on my way?"

"The Sheik Efreet is not a good man, you know." He leaned against her armoire, turning the brush she had once threatened him with over and over in his hands. "He is all illusion, lies— an artist of deceit."

"I knew he must be something of the sort. He works with you." There was no madness in him. No drink, even. She strode into her own space, though not quite so bravely as to come within arms' reach. "I don't believe that a measure of a man."

"Is the latter a point against him, though? No, I see it didn't occur to you. There is something sweet in you yet." He set aside the brush with a clatter. "He undercuts the laws meant to protect our homeland. He makes a traitor of me."

"Father," Lilly said, "there are some loyalties that we do not share in the same intensity."

"I would have taken you to meet our King if he had ever in-vited me to." Nikolaus shook his head. "And what matter that? Have you no love of the place that birthed and raised you?"

"What do I know of raising?"

"Your tongue *can* be barbed. Listen. I will only say this once. There is a law against merchants from other countries trans-porting goods from their territories to ours on their own ships."

"You never told me that." Lilly was taken aback. "You can't turn a profit with an empty ship."

"No, you can't. They must use our ships—here and back— and pay for the transportation." Nikolaus bared his teeth. "I don't object on principle, but it does make them hungry, and how could I fail to exploit that?" He strode suddenly to her, held out his hand. "Let me see his gift. He is not a good man—barely a man at all—and I won't have him harm you by some bauble."

He would wrest it from her if she did not give it. She

watched his fingers heavy on the delicacy of it, said, "His ships are under your name, and you take a smaller percentage than the captains who would otherwise be transporting his cargo. You nonetheless turn a profit, and of course he does by a wide margin."

"If I thought you would ever be faithful to me, I would dress you as a boy, call you a foundling, and raise you as an heir." He shoved the box back at her. "Empty but for red velvet and the smell of sand. Cheap, if you ask me, but not dangerous. You never look so happy over my gifts."

Lilly turned and placed the box on a shelf, hoping the rigidity of her shoulders would not reveal too much of her thoughts.

"You didn't when you were a child, either." Frustration entered his voice. "He is the get of some monstrous fire bird, you know."

"I gathered something of the sort." She flinched back when he raised his hand, but he only ran his fingers through his hair then strode out, slamming the door behind him.

She put the blood-stones in the new box, then removed them, thinking: They would not be safe, would they? If Nikolaus ever found it locked, he would know it held something as valuable as a heart.

The tumbled pillar kept its height for a month, two; the gulls and the secrets of the waves met her, but not her oldest friend. She avoided Mary and the town and did not make her appearances in Nikolaus' study, too wrapped in her waiting for her absent friend. Her stepmother arranged a dinner for the two of them at which she felt ashamed of her own behavior, twitching, eating little. When she abruptly rose to leave, making apologies that neither of them would believe, Mary followed her and, catching her hand, gently laid it against her rounded stomach.

"I'm hoping for a girl. A baby half-sister for you."

"I know." Lilly caught up her sense. "Oh. It's not—"

"I understand." No one could really accept such a petty emotion, though.

Or perhaps Mary could, and Lilly projected her own fault. Nonetheless, she could not tolerate the thought of another thinking her so small. "Please, understand. This house has never been a comfort to me, and recently—recently it has become less so. I will be going soon, and I don't want you to ever believe you or your child is at fault."

Mary looked levelly at her, letting go her hand. "Nikolaus talks when drunk. I know why he's driving you out. So: Did you just lie to me, or do you really believe it?"

"Why blame the child for the father's sin? I'd be bloody-handed myself." Hesitant, she touched the curve of her stepmother's belly again, watching her face. "I would like to know my sister, and not by halves."

Mary cast her arms around Lilly, and more from surprise than affection Lilly returned the gesture. "Whatever you need," the woman said. "It is a horrible thing. Did he—I'm sorry, but I must—" She took a ragged breath. "Was your mother's death arranged?"

Was it worse to consider yourself the wife of a murderer or a bigamist? The thought seemed silly after it passed through Lilly's mind. "She's not dead at all. She left."

"*Oh.*" Mary laughed shakily, let her go. "Well, that's not so bad as I thought."

Lilly returned a wry smile to her. Then, hesitant: "Anything?"

"If it's about finding that boy who has left you, I know ways of tracking that would make him regret ever to have stepped foot away from you. My brother needed such help once, you see." She laughed. "Don't look so surprised! Your father calls your friend *he*, and you are always out. Wise, though—I gather you have known him a very long while, and look at you, still mistress of yourself."

Lilly considered how she might disabuse this belief yet found herself asking, "By what means?"

"Such that not even the end of the earth is far enough. You— you will be going anyway, so it's all right to tell you, isn't it?" At Lilly's nod, the other woman touched her hand again. Seeking comfort or offering it? "My brother lost his flocks to a tribe of dog-headed people who drove them far, far away, across hardpan that left no tracks at all. So he went to the Old Crone mountain where the troll lives and asked for directions."

Lilly nodded; such things were known. "Just like that?"

"Well, of course not. Who doesn't charge a price? Hers was reasonable, though." Mary tapped her lip. "I don't remember it, though. He only told me once. If he weren't on the other side of the kingdom I'd surely ask him for you."

"But you know the directions?"

"So eager! You worry me." Mary shook her head. "Will you wait a few more days? I'll write down what I know and give you the instructions then, but I'd like to think a while to make sure I have everything right."

Lilly hesitantly brushed her lips against the other woman's cheek, an affection that she did not know quite how to give but felt necessary, given the circumstance. Mary certainly looked pleased despite the worry line between her brows.

"So." She clasped her hand with Lilly's and dragged her back towards the table. "Now that we have that sorted, will you stay for dessert?"

She went to Nikolaus' study the next evening and he did not mention her absences; there was guilt on her heart and fury in the twitching of her hands. The topic of the moment was the advantage of height—"You're tall, like your mother, that's good"—and how to ameliorate the effects of drink. "Know to look sloppier than you are. It keeps people from pressuring you to drink dangerous amounts."

The topic of her room and its neatly packed-away things did not come up between them, nor the Mare's freshly shod feet or the saddlebags packed with all provisions but food. They had not quite reached her birthday, but she thought he would let her go with his monetary blessing. Failing that, Mary would pass on some of her own funds; she had hinted at such and Lilly understood the gesture would be as much for her stepmother's sake as her own. A storm in the air oppressed them both; those on ships caught the worst of the ocean's moods, but those on the shore knew them just as well.

When she rose to leave, he reached into a drawer and dropped a clinking bag onto the desk. She took it without so much as a nod, not able to articulate what this meant; he did no more than watch as she left. It was a more amicable parting than she expected; she hoped they never learned how its reverse, a reunion, would go.

Tomorrow she would leave, then. The thought of not taking

the time to wait once more for Octavius drove her out when she knew better, a lantern swaying in her hand with the knifing of the wind, the jacket tugged close around her neck. The rain struck before she even reached the end of the tame beach, yet still she went on. At their old place, the best place, where the ocean lashed like a penitent against the rocks, she sat on a boulder she had often perched on while listening to distant tales or the kraken's ruminations over what she thought of as the common ways of humankind, where she had sung for him and described the town and the folk in it.

A gust and lurch brought the waves high enough to catch her across the chest and arm; sputtering, she shrugged off the jacket before it could soak down to her skin. The rain was not so heavy nor as cold as a wash from the ocean; still, it would force her back to the chateau. Again the water swelled and she cried out in protest, but her fingers were numbed, and the jacket tore from her grip.

What use this loss? What use this whole vigil? Years ago Octavius learned not to look for her when the weather turned so sour. The hours that had passed were ephemeral, uncountable, meaningless; they might have been minutes. Yet the rest of the world knew them as hours. When she reached the house, Mary opened the door before Lilly could fumble the handle into turning and dragged her inside, making horrified noises about how wet she was, and did she know the lantern wick had been blown out?

"I'm leaving tomorrow," Lilly said, and: "You do have the directions for me?"

"Yes." Mary's arm felt too hot around her waist. "Come on, let's get you somewhere warmer than this drafty hall."

"I'm trouble to you." She startled when that won her a laugh.
"I don't—"

"No, not quite trouble. I'll miss you being in the house. Even
your low moods are interesting, do you know?" She opened the
door to Lilly's room for her. "Do you need help?"

"I'm fine, really." She stood silent, acquiescent, as Mary
snatched up a hand towel from beside the basin and wrapped
it around Lilly's hair, keeping it from soaking her further. Toe-
ing off her shoes—she would have to dry them by the stove
and pack them tomorrow—she allowed her stepmother to go so
far as unlacing the more complicated knots then turned, catching up her hand. "Thank you."

"Nothing worse than a wet lacing and cold hands." She
shifted her weight. "By tomorrow, you mean—?"

"Early. Earlier than the marquis stirs." She raised an eyebrow
as Mary reached into the pocket of her evening gown.
"You . . . ?"

"Have been carrying it, yes. I didn't know how urgent your
leaving would be." She moved to hand it to Lilly, then shook her
head and set the note on the table, pinning it down with the
brush. "There. Will you go with my luck?"

"If you offer it." She raked her hair back from her face, salt-
sore eyes watering.

"I'll have a servant bring you a basin of hot water, too." She
rubbed her hands together, fidgeted. "What should I wish for
you?"

Lilly crooked a smile. "I know I wish *you* the best."

"Then I wish you the same: swift travel, swifter resolutions.
Go with my love." She clasped Lilly's hands, let them go. "I
hope to meet you again someday."

Not unless your husband is dead. Lilly nodded, instead, then— "Mary."

She turned, hopeful.

"I have something for you. It's a present—one made to me very recently, and which means much to me." She took the little box from its place atop her dresser and proffered it.

Mary whispered, "I know what this is. I can't have it. It's an apology."

"Perhaps you mistake it for some other box—it's from Saleem, the sheik. We've been long acquainted. Friends, even." As the woman still did not reach to take it, she took Mary's hand and closed it over hers. "Here. It's too delicate to travel with me."

The woman accepted it, then, turning away—perhaps she thought Lilly did not see the tears glossing her eyes. There was a dignity and a respect in not crying at such a parting; her voice thick, she said, "Godspeed," and seemed to be running when she left.

Alone, Lilly shucked the rest of her clothing and tied back her sopping hair so that it would not drip on the directions she read by candlelight. *The Auroch Mountain*, it read. *This is how you get from here to there.*

When she left with her horse and supplies, Mary waved from the doorway, and Hannah watched from a window. She did not see her father anywhere. The road was long; she turned to it.

The Auroch Mountain looked like the long, heavy slope of a bull's body, peaks upthrust on one side like massive horns. The troll's haunt could be found on the thick neck at the end of a road, said Mary's neat handwriting, *and following it up* Lilly came first to a village with thatch moldered green and an omnipresent smell of chickens. Stopping at the local inn, she asked the man lounging on the front porch, "How far to the troll's home?"

"Why would—" He considered her face. "It's another hour's ride up the path."

"Thank you." The Mare surged forward beneath a touch of the heels.

"She eats young people!" the man shouted after her. "Children and horses!" He did not feel this point important enough to pursue her with it when she continued on without sign of having heard.

The trees stooped low over the path as it led out of town. Leaves lay thick on the packed earth, muffling each of the horse's hoof-falls; autumn came soon and deep this high in the world. Lilly tried not to think of a mountain with a serpent coiled around it, and whether her mother might have returned to the village below the place of her first lover's death. How had the corpse been disposed of? The story should have told.

Such thoughts made a poor rider of her; when the Mare came to a stiff-legged stop, she was thrown forward in the saddle, which sent the horse jibbing to the side. Whispering apologies, Lilly dismounted. A cloying-sweet and sticky smell muddied the air. Tying the Mare lightly enough that she might pull free if her rider did not return, Lilly continued through the woods on foot.

The clearing at road's end was hazed in odorous smoke and half-hidden by piles of refuse in which horse's heads and iron shoes dominated. The cottage beyond was tumbledown within

the arms of a weather-torn wall. This was a troll that did not
want company—and that was, in fact, a comfort. The ones
who lived in castles of confection tended towards anthro-
pophagic hungers. As she came into the rancid yard, a flock of
chickens looked up from their pecking, and a hip-high rooster
all black and garnet-eyed stretched his neck at her, the spurs on
his legs far too prominent. She edged around him to the door
stoop, keeping a leery eye on the bird.

She should have kept an eye on the door. It was flung open
and caught her shoulder, staggering her back. There were windows, incongruous glass, all on the walls of this squalid place; it
provided plenty of light to see the mistress of the house. Vast,
taller by two heads than Lilly and three times broader, grey-
eyed, grey-haired, the latter straggling around her head in a
dandelion tuft spray. Her face was cragged as cliffs were, and
set into it were three crimson eyes: two like rubies where a human's would be, and the third squinting from her brow.

In a voice that would have suited any cranky old woman,
she said, "I don't trade for souls. Scram."

"I'm not here for that, ma'am. I hear that you locate people."
Stories suggested that one did not make too broad an offer to
any magical creature, and Nikolaus had told her to let others set
the price of items one did not know the cost of and to haggle
down from there. To hell with them; she had little to lose. "I
wish to make a deal."

"What else do you have worth trading, human woman?"
She extended a gnarled, clawed hand to tap the silver that
clasped Lilly's jacket at the throat. "I do not require wealth such
as you would consider it: not gold nor goods nor favors."

"You are lucky beyond measure if there is nothing in the

world that you want, ma'am." The hens clucked behind her. "I offer all the resources I have—my abilities, you understand, my willingness to work, to give—and in return but one thing."

The troll raised her eyebrows, third eye squinting further. "Not often does someone make such a broad offer. I see in your eyes that you know it to be foolish. What do you want? That unpretty mark off your face? Maybe a prince for your bed?"

"No, ma'am." What had she sold? "I fear my friend is lost at sea."

The troll drew back. "I cannot revive the dead. Would you regret being led to a drowned corpse?"

"I do not fear him drowned, ma'am. He is a kraken, you see." She took that hesitation for some qualms with the task. "He is dark, dark red—almost black—and his body is about the size of two standard rowboats set side by side. Will that help you find him?"

The troll smiled with blackened teeth. "Oh, we are something of brother and sister, me and him. It will not be so much trouble. You have merely startled me. And what do you offer me? Anything?"

"Anything that is mine, ma'am."

The troll traced the edge of the birthmark with her claw, expression thoughtful. Then she tangled her fingers in Lilly's hair and tore it free. Lilly recoiled, hearing her own pain-noises. Reflex wanted her to kick but reason said, *You agreed to this.* She knew the hair would not grow back again. Besides, the troll's hand clenched on her shoulder kept her still.

"You could lay down," the troll offered, "for the rest I want is deeper."

The rest? Lilly hesitated, which the troll took for a prideful choice. The troll's claws snapped out and rent her dress from neck to hem, and as her hand came up in a reflexive gesture to cover her breasts, Lilly thought—said?—*goddamn*! Then she dropped her hands to the side, fisted, and waited. Careful, now, the troll lay her hand on Lilly's belly. Her last coherent thought was, *There is no more orientation; she must be holding me somehow. Why would it matter if I were not upright?*

The troll slit open her abdomen, tearing muscle and tissue and membranes into two flaps to frame the viscera beneath. *Be, hell, oh god, no.* Lilly touched the edges of the mutilation, as if to indicate the pain that wracked against her spine and say, *Can you believe this?* She would have fallen if not for the hand on her shoulder; she felt that if she could only fall the soil would have taken in her blood and guts and self, and it wouldn't hurt anymore. The troll plunged her dirty claws into the glistening mass—and what terrible things hid beneath tender skin, mounds like monstrous slugs blued by veins and covered over in a newborn's gloss of blood. It should have been no different from a pig's insides, except that it belonged to *her*. Lilly sobbed open-mouthed; this could not abide silence.

It would have been somehow a less awful violation if more violent, but the troll hummed as she rummaged among the organ meats: prodding aside a greenish knob the use of which Lilly didn't know, running a finger along the ridged coil of bowels. Even a farm animal's eyes dulled before the last of its blood pumped onto the boots of the butchers; where, Lilly wondered, was her mercy? Where, for that matter, was her blood? Her hands, dry, clasped the edges of her flayed body.

In a voice that broke twice, Lilly said, "While I hate to impose, you might go about your business somewhat faster, you son of a bitch, *please*." Her teeth chattered. The rooster crowed a warning to his hens.

The troll laughed and shoved her hand deeper, down into the cradle of Lilly's pelvic bones. For a moment she held in her palm a red lump, rounded, trailing from it two arched protuberances with clubbed ends, and—made visible as she lifted it upwards, triggering a deep ache—tapered on one end into a ridged length of tissue. Understanding, Lilly groaned in protest, arms rising to cross over her chest in a futile gesture of self-protection. The troll clenched her fingers and *pulled*; continued upwards, claws raking, knocking aside Lilly's hands—

They would not inflict that pain in Hell, for even Satan knew what sinners deserved not to suffer.

Lilly became conscious of herself crying, head hanging forward, staring at the butchered remains of her body. The troll weighed in her free hand the lump of hair and organs and flesh she had taken. Something pink and fatty distracted Lilly—she grasped after distraction; she did not flinch as fingers touched her again.

What a cheat, she thought as the troll pinched her blouse closed, did up the buttons, and pulled the bottom edge so that it lay flat along the planes of Lilly's—chest. Pectoral muscles. Then the creature crouched, drawing a claw through the middle of Lilly's skirts, giving each half a smart tug. Lilly stared down at the trousers which resulted from this process, somehow most befuddled by this. She didn't hurt anymore, it occurred to her. The tailoring must have doctored the flesh beneath. Magic made as little sense as she expected it to.

The troll stood, shifted her burden of meat from one hand to another, and reached out to squeeze Lilly's throat. The strands of hair caught between her fingers felt stark as metal wires. Perhaps she cut off the breath in the throat under her grip. Lilly took no notice, as she did not breathe for panic anyway.

The creature now withdrew into her doorway and looked upon her work with eyelids lowered in self-satisfaction. She wound Lilly's—the material between her hands like a skein of wool, and said, "*Now* I shall find your kraken."

"What—" Lilly coughed, surprised at the depth of her own voice—androgynous more than masculine, surely, but not *hers*. With an effort she managed not to whisper. "What, exactly, have you gained?"

"These things, obviously. Somewhat useless and meaningless to me in the normal course of things, but I happen to want a child. Not personally, understand, but for a friend." The troll smirked and held up the organs. "The hair is for me. Consider the pants and voice as gifts. No one would have believed you were girl *or* boy without them. Wait here, these shouldn't be in the open air too long."

Lilly stared at the door, with its peeling paint and a hatchet mark at its center, so abruptly shut in her face.

Then she *knew* it, the ache in her abdomen and chest, and the pain alike to stitches across what might crudely be termed a wound—Nikolaus Rosa, she suspected, would have been obliged to harm the particular captain who let her overhear *that* term. Pains all wrought across womanhood. Her hand went to the clasp of her shirt and froze there; what could she do, out in the broad day and with the damned chickens staring on? The damages—changes?—could await later inspection.

The strange sounds and sulfur smells from within the troll's hut could not budge her from her place frozen on the stoop, but eventually weariness did what common sense could not and she sat upon a tumbled portion of the wall. The birds watched still, but left her to hunch around herself, feeling the alteration the troll had made—more than the pains, she felt as if she'd lost something like a promise, the knowledge that certain paths in life would always open to her, even if they were no better than becoming wife, nun, prostitute. She thought, *I wish I'd known this would happen. I would've been lewder, I swear.*

The reemergence of the troll jerked Lilly onto her feet; she held up a rag of scarlet cloth in one hand and a shiny black glove in the other. "Here. Look."

"I hope there's more than that."

"Don't be sharp, girl. Well. Whatever term you want. This is just the physical evidence of the spell." She tossed it among the hens, then watched with a pleased smile as they tore it apart with a great seething of feathers and cackles. "Your kraken is in the cages of a circus master, one Gero Alt, who encamps upon the land of the dark-wife, waiting for her hand." The troll held up a gnarled claw. "No, that's still not all. I have a map."

Lilly grasped the map without much conscious effort and inspected it; the leaves seemed to shift and the mountains to jut from it; the path she was to take glowed in red ink. Distracted enough to loosen her tongue, she asked the troll, "Are you much inclined to injuring people? Say, a child born of a detached womb?"

"That's never been my goal." The troll tilted her head, creaking like stones. "Why? Do you feel injured, that you would ask me such a thing?"

"No, ma'am." Discomfited, altered, *hurting*—but not injured within the terms of their deal. She glanced down at the map, then tucked it into her belt. "Pardon, but I feel a certain obligation to what comes of my body."

The troll waved aside the issue with her gnarled hand, driving Lilly back another step with the gesture. "Because you have given reproduction as a gift to me, I will not have to steal it. Though I said I needed no favors, that *is* one. Theft leaves a stain. Perhaps I owe you more than the gifts I have already given." She bent her head down, and spoke in a lowered voice, as if she confided a secret, or broke a trust, when she said, "The dark-wife who men call Ermentrud will smell the magic on you. Her method of temptation is lust, and if she does not eat you outright, you might as easily use that against her as be consumed by it." The troll stilled for a moment in thought, a smile at the edge of her mouth. "The dark-wife conquers, collects, consumes. Despite her methods it is passion she wants, not flesh, and you are a prime cut."

"Thank you." For a moment she had hoped that the basest parts of her body having been removed, such a creature of sexuality would not want her.

"The flesh is all of a piece. Oh, and don't bother keeping the rags in your pack, they'll just get in the way while you're looking for other things." With that last advice so much more pragmatic than the rest, the troll subsided back into her lair, leaving Lilly to the hens that were fighting over the last scraps of glove.

Lilly held off as long as she could, riding down from the troll's hut, but halfway down the mountain she resigned herself at last; she straggled down from the saddle and went into the bushes at the roadside. She had known straight off that she hadn't been given a man's parts in compensation—there had been one time in town when a drunk reveler got pushed from a tavern with his trousers around his ankles and her mother hadn't turned Lilly's head away fast enough. She would *have noticed one of those, and in fact felt somewhat gladdened simply by the fact that the troll had made her no such extravagant gift. Yet women were made with more than nothing, and she felt uncertain, not knowing what it would be like to see and feel her new lack.*

Though it took some effort, she managed to go about her business without catching a direct look at herself.

Afterward, she stood beside the Mare with her hand on the packs, considering the rags and skirts. She could sell the latter, of course, and the rest—it could wait. The map showed a long road and it was best not to delay.

But the night had no care for human concerns. At the foot of the mountain, darkness forced Lilly to camp where a blackened circle of stones spoke of previous travelers caught in the open. With a fire struck to life, she watered the Mare in the stream which trickled just outside the firelight. She knelt to wash her hands in the chill waters, sighing as the tacky roaddust peeled from them. In regards to peeling—she ran a hand across her scalp, wincing as sunburnt skin flaked onto her shoulders.

The Mare settled, the water called again to Lilly. It had been too long since she last bathed, but once divested of boots, the rest seemed insurmountable. Over her shoulder the firelight imparted a special wild darkness to the night. Gazing down upon the sky's reflection in the stream, she tugged off her jacket and shirt, then with clumsy fingers negotiated the ties of her trousers.

Muscles knotted in the cold of the water, but some deeper discomfort dissolved. She negotiated her own body like a stranger's, careful where her hands fell. Careful, even, of her own stare. What she saw, she attributed to the moon: that blueish goblin light must surely have smoothed out shadows and made plains of more complex geographies. The troll couldn't have left her so few curves, unless she had adjusted the very angle of the hipbones while Lilly hung unconscious in her grasp. Perhaps even her chest—

Lilly palmed water over her head, forcing herself to feel that baldness, and with gritted teeth, she killed her denial by palming her own chest, flat as a child's. Or as a man's, she supposed. After washing her hand as if at the touch of something disgusting, she made herself inspect other territories, and found with a strange disgruntlement that the hair of her head was not the only that the troll had stolen away. Lilly hesitated, loath to be caught at self-exploration, fearful to continue for reasons that had nothing to do with someone *else's* discovery. She knew what *should* exist, the folds and hollow.

What should have existed no longer did; she snatched her hand away from the flesh as smooth and featureless as that of a sanitized classical painting, and wondered if she should think of herself as *it*. But—no. The troll had said theft left a mark, and so Lilly would not steal from herself. She came out of the water shivering, glad not to have the heft and chill of wet hair across her back, tonight; glad enough, almost, that she could believe she did not regret the loss of it. Naked she went to stand by the fire, drying, regarding herself.

———

Three days of travel brought her to a town large enough to boast a market where she purchased a hat, supplies, and replaced women's clothing with men's. The merchant with whom she exchanged skirts for trousers didn't like her face and clearly didn't think she'd come by the garments any honest way; he scowled throughout the process, so she made sure the transaction favored him as an incentive not to cause her trouble.

"Where're you going?" he asked. "Not much down the way you're traveling but abandoned fields and hunting lodges, boy."

"I . . . I have some task to do. In that direction." Her answer was perhaps more inarticulate than he expected. Her mind had tripped badly over the term *boy.*

Sympathy softened his face. "Here, boy," he said, gruff, and handed her another shirt. "We didn't get things hashed out quite equal."

It was the first time she'd been taken for an idiot, and though it stung somewhat, she supposed at least she'd benefited from it. Stuffing her new supplies into the Mare's saddlebags, she nodded to the man and then left him and the village behind her. Only much later as she walked the Mare across a part of the road so damaged by oak root and past rainstorms did it occur to her that her face—her birthmark—had only been a part of the man's re-action. He had seen it but not dwelt on it; it did not matter so much if a boy were ugly, after all. Lilly squinted up at the sun as if the horse cared whence came the prickling of her rider's eyes.

The red line faded to grey as she followed its directions. She won-dered, sometimes, what would happen if she should stray. So she did not.

———————

Three days into a thick woods where strange animals called, Lilly crested a hill and looked down upon acres covered over by dozens of circus tents and trampled by the men who moved among them. At the heart of the ruckus stood a dignified old manse, gothic beside the gaiety of the striped circus tents. When Lilly reached into her saddlebag for the map, she found it transformed into a blank piece of paper.

A strange figure alone but for the falcon on her wrist and the massive stallion she rode astride stood at the edge of the camp watching the circus men as a bird would the hare in the field. A shudder ran up Lilly's spine. The dark-wife, the troll called this woman: Ermentrud. Lilly sent up a prayer that she need not utilize the troll's advice. Was this not the sort of creature that God would gladly answer appeals against?

The rider wheeled her horse hard enough to make him sit back on his haunches and drove the animal hard back to the manse, scattering circus men. From the heart of the camp emerged a man in a coat the color of a torrid summer, his hands raised in supplication. Lilly shuddered once more, and dismounted to tie the Mare and go down on foot. She had spotted a cluster of cages from her vantage. She might break the lock of a cage with a mallet, steal a key—whether by force or craft, she would free Octavius.

Through the tents all gaudy and the wagons with their yokes rested on the beaten-down dirt she strode; she passed individuals far more startling than herself—and at least three more androgynous—and thus she suited the place enough that none questioned her.

She reached an enclosed crescent formed by iron-barred cages. A male lion huffed; something with the beautiful sleek body of a doe and the head of a snake twisted to glance at her, but did not cease to pace. And *there,* the long coil of black flesh corrugated with spikes and suckers. She must have run, she folded onto her knees at Octavius' cage, she said his name far too many times; her hands shook as she spread them across the bars—small ones, set close together, to keep him from reaching too far out.

"Lilly?" He stirred, rolled to level his eye on her; it was sunken, dry.

She could not tell if his sluggishness came from uncertainty or illness; heart-sickened, she scrambled in her pocket and pulled out the shark's blood-stone, held it up to him, pressed it against the only limb within her reach. "It's me. I've come to save you."

"I know it is. You look different. But I knew you would come. Who else would it be?" He curled the tip of his limb around her hand, cold against her fingers. "Besides, you have such a distinctive sound." When he moved, skin sloughed from him in greyish lumps.

She brushed her fingers against his skin and found it dragon's-skin dry and rough. "I'll get you out of here. Give me a moment. What *happened?*"

"I have something for you." One of his limbs uncoiled to display a dirty scrap of dark cloth. "When they first caught me they did not expect my strength, and with the ocean's own voice I tumbled from their ship and went at fastest pace, their barbs in me, and me dragging them. I knew you would help, should you be able, and I went towards you." He pressed the cloth—her jacket, the one her mother sewed for her—against her hands, and it was stiff with salt, ruined, but nowhere torn. "A great storm settled over the water and the humans could do nothing against me, hunkered against the swells, and still I dragged us on. At last we came nigh to the shore and this came to me. I reached out for it, knowing your love for it—and because I knew I was close to you, and needed to feel the sign of it. Then the captain gave brave orders, and nets came on me. Some of them lost their lives, but not to me—to the waves. They dragged me aboard, but I held to this. I've treasured it."

"Keep it," she said. "Octavius, I was *there*."

"In retrospect, Lilly, you really wouldn't have been much help." He gave his strange laugh, the wind in a conch shell. "But you're here now. *Now* you can help."

"Yes. Let me try—" He released her wrist so that she could tug futilely at the lock.

"I didn't tell you the beginning, though. Men in a ship with harpoons and a girl who laughed when she did not shout for help—I thought it was in play, but the words were not, and I couldn't risk that. She reminded me of you, Lilly." He hissed in remembered fury. "When they caught me up, I could not kill them without being a monster."

It took a moment before memories ten years old, fuzzy and fond from her childhood, could resurface: she remembered, though, her first and only interdiction on Octavius' behavior. She bruised her fist on the metal door of his cage.

"I am worth fifty gold ingots—that much did the circus master buy me from the captain for," he said into the silence after the blow. "Lilly, is that good?"

"Well enough for common goods. But you're worth far more."

She cleared her throat of the unaccustomed deepness her fierceness drew up from her lungs and into her voice. "I need a mallet. Or a hatchet."

Arms caught her from behind, looped under her armpits, and locked behind her neck. Lilly flung herself forward, to the side, struggled to kick and bite and claw—managed even to twist her elbow into the muscular man's stomach, though she caused no effect by doing so. Octavius screeched, an awful rising gale-wind sound that made the man shout, "Hey!"

Silence followed. Lilly hung, dead weight, sullen and gulping air, while Octavius pressed forward against the bars, the tips of all eight limbs strained through the too-small spaces between.

"All right," said the man, his voice a thin whisper. "What's this about a hatchet? Got something against the kraken, boy?"

"No." She near choked in horror at the thought. The man spun her around, bruising her skin meanwhile in a way that might have been unintentional; he had kind eyes.

Octavius, wriggling still, said, "This is the one I spoke of so often, the one who would vouch for me. Friedrich, if you would please—"

"You haven't power over me," said the man, "no matter however polite you are. Monsters lie, and when they do not lie they are sly. Another word for freedom is death, and this one must want to die, hurt as it is. Anyway the master's orders are to turn deaf ears on them."

She clenched a hand around his wrist and glared with all the hurt she saw in Octavius' sores. "If orders will not allow you—" sharp bitter words sought to intrude, *to be compassionate* or *to see that a person is here tortured*, but tact was too ingrained in her for such foolery "—to act, then I will speak with the circus master. If you would free me, sir, or else escort me to him, I would be grateful." Friedrich looked uncertain; desperate, she asked, "Please?"

Bulging muscles shifted across the strongman's shoulders, neck, forearms, like tense ropes keeping a ship's sails high. "What for?"

"I would make a deal with him." She held up her free hand between them, fingertips held over his chest—as if she _could_ push him away. "I would pay any price for the kraken."

"Sure, boy." The strongman looked down on her with pity. "He won't give up his star, though. Not for gold or jewels." His hand covered Lilly's shoulder down to the collarbone when he braced it there to steer her in the other direction.

"I _will_ be back!" she shouted to her friend, which made Friedrich frown, confused.

Lilly disregarded him, because Octavius called her name in reply, low and mournful and sonorous as the soft rush of the tides. The man asked, "What's it want with a flower? Something you said?"

"No. Its meaning is subtle, friendship-wrought."

Friedrich took her to the heart of the camp, the scarlet tent, and at its door-flap the man of the torrid summer coat. Close by, he was tall, broad-chested, cockerel proud. He almost managed to make his mismatched gloves look intentional.

"Thank you," Lilly said to her guide; then she stepped out from under his hand and asked, "Mr. Gero Alt?"

He turned with a flare of coattails and a turn of his cane through his hands, but the best showmanship in the world couldn't hide the sag of his jowls and the bags under his eyes.

Inspecting her closely, the circus master said, "Indeed. And you are . . . ?"

"I'm L—" *Lacking an alias.* She coughed, as if nervousness caught in her throat. "My name is Lyle. I have a favor to ask."

"A favor," Mr. Alt repeated, flat.

Lilly supposed a man did not amass fortune enough for such a large circus by being openhanded, but she had paid enough already and would not be the first to mention equal exchange. "There is a—a creature in your possession, a young kraken. Would you consider giving him up?"

"Not for love or money. What kind of favor is *that*?" Her glare lowered his brows. "It's the only new beast I have, and my old patrons won't be pleased if I return to them with nothing novel in hand. I haven't had the time to look for anything good, of late." Scowling, he looked older yet. "Where'd you hear about it, anyway?"

"A friend," she murmured, and broke eye contact to look over his shoulder—at the manse, and the dead land all around it. She saw no servants, no workers. "If it isn't too personal a question, Mr. Alt, what brings you here?" She made herself smile when the sourness she had already caused closed off his features. "It was a considerable distance to ride." Oblique comment, real meaning—*I am invested in this.*

That gave the man reason to consider. "Well. I *am* busy." When she nodded her agreement, he continued, "But it doesn't take so long to tell—Ermentrud, the woman who owns that manse and all this land, is a great lady and a widower. I mean to have her hand."

The troll told me as much, Lilly thought, frustrated, *and how am I to use that as leverage?* A tall, spidery man was approaching with a purposeful stride; she needed to pry the price of Octavius out of Mr. Alt soon. Otherwise she would be forced to break the kraken free, an idea she loathed for its impracticality. "A great lady, Mr. Alt?"

"She doesn't answer to the King's power. What else would you call her?" The spidery fellow haled him, and Mr. Alt twisted around to wave and shout, "I *know!*" Then he turned back. "Look, boy. Lyle. I can't sell the thing for gold, so you might as well go on and—"

"What else might I buy it for?" The snap in her tone was not appropriate for supplication. At least she did not follow it up with *Tell me or I'll steal from you.*

It got Mr. Alt's attention, anyway. "Well, I suppose there's one thing you could find me." He waved off the other man's attempt to speak to him, smirking at her—the smile of a man condescending to a child. "Up in the mountains yonder is a tailor who spins magical coats which make the wearer appear however he wants. Get me one of those coats, and I'll give you the kraken." He flared his hand, and the smirk flourished into a showman's grin. "That's nearly free of charge, isn't it?"

"Yes, Mr. Alt. I would be glad to do so, if you gave me better directions. And—might I ask what this has to do with Miss Ermentrud?" If it did not have to do with his ambition-love, Lilly doubted Gero Alt would uphold his side of the deal. Obsession cared only for itself.

He waved towards the hill crest. "It's somewhere up the ways of the peaks of the Three Crones. I don't know anything else—you'll have to ask around. I heard about them when I was a lad and have been imagining acts using a coat of illusions ever since. My queen asks me for a show, and I could give her *such* a show with one of those." He shooed her, then. "Off with you, boy. Sooner gone, sooner returned, eh?"

Lilly heard him chortling with the other man as she began the trek back through the tent-pocked landscape, head turned to the mountains again. Before she left she crouched beside Octavius' cage and told him, "I'm going to the mountains for a coat to buy you with."

"Now I am only worth a coat? What value I lost!" said the kraken, teasing, and laughed when she sputtered in response. "Thank you, Lilly. I will wait for you."

Lilly reached through the bars to brush her fingers across his drying skin, thinking, *This is not the last time we shall see each other.* It could not be.

The Mare whickered greeting as Lilly met her at the crest of the hill. From the saddle she looked back on the tents and wondered if guile and nightfall would serve her better than the deal she struck in sunlight, after all. Whatever the morality of the theft—fifty ingots of gold embodied in the flesh of a friend—she knew she would never feel guilt for it. The impracticality of it plagued her, still. How did one sneak an ill kraken from the midst of ten-score men loyal to his enslaver?

The Mare's restless movement jostled her free from fruitless mental circling. She had been raised a canny and stubborn creature, not a soldier whose strength lay in the body, so let her be the merchant. If naught else a magical coat ought to be easier to steal than a kraken. She presumed it would weigh less. Lilly turned the Mare with a touch of the reins.

Ermentrud blocked the mouth of the woods, her stallion snorting beneath her.

The horse had a delicate immensity about him, an air of the unreal, but his rider outshone him. Her dark eyes reflected the universe and the cupid's bow of her lips promised a taste of it. Though wrinkles enough to make her a convincing widow webbed her face, one did not need to imagine her younger to see why she would be desired. The signs of her monstrosity only added to the temptation: how she balanced on the saddle as if she might lunge at any moment, the smile like a panther scenting blood. A myth come to life. A predator dressed as an impeccable woman.

Gero Alt would die by her, for he was only a man.

Lilly only hoped for the time to find the coat and trade it for Octavius before Ermentrud consumed her prey. By his words, Gero Alt viewed her as something fragile that might break beneath his ardor. Not so: the fecund curves of her body bespoke a strength to birth an entire race, not as Eve but as Lilith did. No man would plough her under.

"You shouldn't be so pensive," said the dark-wife; she spoke French not as a language of diplomacy and trade, but in its incarnation as the tongue of lovers, throaty and sensual. With a touch of her hand the stallion came forwards; the Mare pulled at the bit as he loomed over her. She was no more accustomed to being short among her own kind than Lilly was. "It ruins handsome things."

The dark-wife did not flinch from Lilly's choked laughter, and that frightened her; it was an ugly noise. Did the clouds draw over the sun, or only the shadow of Ermentrud over her eyes? Those words had not been empty flattery. She wet her dried lips and mimed misunderstanding, saying, "Pardon, ma'am. I won't sour the view further."

The Mare stepped forwards at the touch of Lilly's knee, trained to overcome fear in the name of loyalty, but without visible command from his rider, the stallion kicked out with his heel, driving the other horse back. By the quiver in her sides the Mare would have bolted if she were a lesser animal, and Lilly would have bent low over her neck and dug her heels into her sides, encouraging. No such flight was afforded them: the stallion moved his delicate feet close enough that Ermentrud's calf brushed hers, nothing like the awkward knocks riders' knees sometimes suffered.

"You think that I am mocking you?" She smiled when Lilly flinched. "No. I must be frank. I have never seen a suitor such as you."

"I'm no suitor." Giddy with a tightness in her chest she thought, *Marked and bald and neutered as I am, what a suit I would make!* The leather of the reins ground into her palms, a reminder of the world which existed outside the musk of the dark-wife's perfume.

"Is that so?" Ermentrud reached across the space between them and stroked her fingers along the dark skin of Lilly's marked cheek. It seemed to hold an honest fascination to her, much as a cat come to investigate a noise in the kitchen without yet knowing it meant to eat the mouse who made it. From this close, it became evident that where humans had hard edges and the architecture of bones, she was fluid. It made her no less beautiful as her mouth opened around a conspiratorial smile. "There are roles other than suitor that a man might take towards a woman."

 humans.

Thing, boy, even suitor—all terms Lilly could comprehend applied to herself—but *man*? Startled, Lilly failed to react as the dark-wife's fingers slid down to trace the bottom edge of the birthmark, across her chin and the edge of her jaw. In those places, skin not muffled by the thick flesh of the mark, she could feel the cool of Ermentrud's touch. Those fingers slid to the back of her skull—which seemed somehow the most intimate of gestures, fingers touching what eyes didn't—and Lilly opened her mouth to protest—

Her words died on a yelp as Ermentrud dragged her close; Lilly clenched one hand around the saddlebow to keep from falling beneath the horses' hooves.

Against her mouth the dark-wife's lips pushed plush and firm and smooth, and Lilly's hands convulsed, though she could not move otherwise; could not, until the dark-wife's tongue— heat and wetness and—and it washed out the ice woven into her muscles so she could jerk back, near losing her seat on the Mare. Her lips stung, as did the scratches left by the dark-wife's nails. "You—no." She did not want conversation on the point. "Let me pass, ma'am."

"Let you—" The stallion threw back his head with an angry snort. "You *will* stay with me. What kind of man would leave me? What boy, even?" She pushed the curls of her hair back from her face and tried to smile. "Are you afraid? You don't have to worry about the circus master's jealousy. This land knows its mistress."

Down below, Octavius rotted in a cage. No heated mouth mattered more than him. "No. I must go." Lilly wet her lips— flinched—felt her cheeks burn as she muttered, "I will come back."

"You're not so easy to tempt as other young men, are you? Well, return *soon*." She reached out again, but not for Lilly's face or throat; she stroked her hand from knee towards crotch, a fire through the cloth of Lilly's trousers. "Return *very*—"

Lilly threw herself back in the saddle, panicked, thinking that if Ermentrud groped much further—well, she did not know quite how the conversation would go, other than to a dangerous increase in attention. The Mare tried to answer the command, hooves sending stones skittering down the steep slope of the hill's face, muscles bunched from neck to haunch as she fought to keep from falling. A broken neck would leave less of a mark than the pleased noise Ermentrud made.

The stallion moved aside, and for the moment his rider kept her counsel. Lilly felt the acidic roil of bitter gratitude that she would thus be let free, and steadying the Mare urged her forward.

"When you return you will think it for whatever quest drives you. Yet the hidden parts of you will know that it is for me that they come."

Lilly clenched her teeth; what good would it do to call back, *I have no hidden parts*? Once out of sight she scrubbed the back of her hand across her lips.

Lilly learned how to ask questions at crossroads, where signs pointed her towards the villages of Kleindorf or Luttenheim or some such, but gave no indication which way lay the road straight up into the mountains and which turned or ran back to the ocean. Because those she asked prefaced their answers, almost without fail, with inquiries as to why *she found herself headed upwards, and grew taciturn if she demurred an answer or stuttered out a bland lie, she learned how to say, calm and plain, "I search for a coat of illu-sions." That excited people, made them talk more; thus did gossip serve her as a map to the tailor, though one writ over by strange beasts and mistruth.*

A grizzled old man propped up outside an inn in the foot-hills seemed a good source of information, but he answered her query with a vulgar hacking snort. "Magical coats? Ridiculous! Nothing but the master bandits up that way, lad. Better turn back now rather'n have your throat slit one side to the other for chasing stupid rumors."

"That's not right," interrupted a young man with saddlebags slung over one shoulder and a tentative smile on his face. "I mean, there *are* bandits to worry about, but Mr. Nadel has a workshop that turns out fantastic sorts of things—it's up in the Three Crones, isn't it?"

The old man replied with another snort and turned his face away. "Yes, it's up there. That tailor is a Devil worshipper, granted, but his tricks *do* work."

The young man's eyes twitched to her birthmark, almost wistful, but from inside the inn a voice called for him and he withdrew. He called back over his shoulder as he left, "He lives on the middle mountain—up one of the old roads, I should think."

The forest turned gnarled and strange with massive boul-ders all covered up in moss soon as she ventured onto the old ways of the middle mountain. She led the Mare over the dirt of a road unsuited for mortal, domestic feet, and both of them trod carefully. Given the environs, she startled only a little when there dropped down from its perch on one of those boulders a strange blind child, an albino, sex less determinate than her own, who demanded she share a portion of her noon meal with it and mumbled mad phrases into her ear while they sat eating.

The Mare grazed quiet beside them, and Lilly trusted the horse's judgment. For her fortitude she was rewarded when the child turned the animal's head back the way they'd come, one reedy arm held out to point down the path. "The mountain of the felled master bandits lies *east*." It wrinkled up its nose with a grin. "You want the newer road than this, Lilly. Turn left at the next crossing down."

Lilly made a solemn thanks at which the child laughed, then urged the Mare quickly back down the path. It was a far easier ride down than it had been up.

On the newer road she found a dirty woman peering down into a hole in the ditch; Lilly pulled up short, unsure if she should offer help, and made her usual inquiry. The woman, without lifting her head, said, "Don't go that way, honey. There are bandits there—the master bandits." Now she looked up, expression turning sour as her gaze flickered across Lilly's face. "But if you must, the Devil's tailor is at the end of the road."

Lilly suspected that she would find the tailor when she found a person who both gave her precise directions and referred to the man by name; until then, she gave her thanks and left the woman to her strange pursuit. As expected, in the little village of Hofburg the single townsperson who deigned to speak with her, an old grizzled farmer with half his fingers gone, raised an eyebrow and asked, "You mean *Nadel*? That damned fool lives in Gertburg. You want to go back the way you came and turn down the road the King put in thirty years back—the one with the good cobbles, because the people in Gertburg with all their monies mattered more to His Majesty. Not now, of course. The road's not safe."

In shuttered Gertburg she found the tailor's shop with scissors and thread hung over the door. It was a disappointing place to end such travel: it was once a fine old farm manor, but the town had crept up around the tailor's workshop, and it now stood in an incongruous huddle, hemmed on all sides by smaller shops. Most of those were empty but for cobwebs and weeds sprouting through their stoops.

Mr. Nadel's workshop seemed little more alive with all its windows closed off by draperies. She pounded her knuckles sore on the old wood door and won nothing; so she turned to the fierce snarling bear's head which served as the building's knocker. With this she persisted.

After some minutes the door wrenched inward and filled with the body of a middle-aged woman, tall and squared, a deep scowl across her dusky face. Lilly stepped back, took in the woman's raggedly done-up hair and the peasant's crucifix nestled atop her bosom, and thought, *I see no magic here.* No magic, and no bent and gnarled wise man, as *Mister* Nadel had been described. But—hopeful, she asked, "Mrs. Nadel?"

"No," the woman snarled, and tossed her head so that a hank of hair all shot through with iron grey came down into her face from its bun. She loomed out of the doorway, black-clad—Lilly had not seen that at first, dark clothes lost in the dark of the closed-in parlor. "I'm Frieda *Reiniger*, which I will *always* be. Now, do I look open for business, boy?"

Lilly, although not short—she'd learned that anew, traveling—felt her shoulders stoop against the force of the woman's physical presence and anger, but she made herself meet the woman's eyes, and asked, "Pardon me, Miss Reiniger—but *is* there a Mr. Nadel here?"

"Lord! Will people ever stop pointing towards my home with his name in their mouths? He's been dead these five years." Miss Reiniger's lip twitched in an animal snarl. "Good *day*."

Lilly caught the door with a flat hand before the woman could slam it shut, and although the bones of her wrist shifted under its weight and heat rioted across her cheeks for the well-deserved incredulous look she won for it, she did not retreat. "Ma'am, he *did* make coats of illusion?" The woman paused in attempting to shove the door closed. "Please, do you know where their like are made now? I have a dire need for one."

That won her an open door. "No, there's nothing like." Pain wrenched her face askew. "And I've . . . I've run out of the material to make them." She did not lie well; it seemed Lilly's face did not, either. "Are you all right, boy?"

"Quite all right." Trusting that Miss Reiniger would not shut the door, she rubbed at her sore wrist. "Where might the coats he made be found now?"

"I made them, too, until three months ago." She would not go on until Lilly nodded agreement. She swept her loosened hair back behind her ear, the calluses on her palm and fingers ample proof of her claim, though certain of the marks seemed bizarre for a tailor to wear—pale, smooth, like a baker's burns. "Every client holds onto them—in life, in death. If I gave you the names and homes of our old clients you might go grave-robbing, but I won't allow it."

Where will pity get me? Lilly asked herself, the tale of it lodged inside her chest—and answered herself, *To Octavius.* Pride thick as burs in her throat, she said, "The coat is the price set on the freedom of my friend."

"The King's justice doesn't allow for slavery." Miss Reiniger snorted—at herself, it seemed. "Which you know, and doesn't matter. What's it, then? Does a noble have your friend—or clergy, maybe? Oh, is this a girl?" Her eyebrows raised as Lilly shook her head to all the options, and her voice became sarcastic. "It's not about a girl, sure. Are you vagabonds, then, that the King doesn't care who sells you?"

Lilly twitched her jacket straight—had, at last, conquered the habit of attempting to smooth down a skirt she no longer wore. "If you will not believe me, then I must go. Thank you, ma'am, for the information."

"No, no, I won't mock anymore. How far have you come for this? —There's more dust than skin showing on you." Miss Reiniger tapped her nails as rough-edged as herself against the frame, then with an abrupt motion stepped back from the doorway. "Come in and rest a moment, then, since I'm sending you away with nothing. There's little enough on you as it is—flesh or goods."

Dignity cried out that she leave, but Miss Reiniger's gaze had caught on the leanness travel had afflicted Lilly with, and the prospect of decent food overrode any nobler instinct. An hour spent here would not make her quest for another garment of illusion any more or less futile. "Thank you." Uncomfortable with herself, she stepped into the tailor's parlor.

It was all dust and dark and the strange washed-out feel of a space no longer lived in. Miss Reiniger gestured Lilly to follow her down the trail of footprints that led across the room without a blush for her housekeeping. Through a door no less plain than the one in the entry—it had been a *very* wealthy farmer who built this—it seemed they passed not into another room but another world, a rabbit's warren of hallways and small rooms clothed in vivid wallpaper and wall hangings, in every open space a bolt of cloth or silver-edged shears or a knot of thread stabbed through with a needle.

It was intimate beyond any other house she had known; it brought her up short for long enough to catch Miss Reiniger's attention. The woman toed a half-finished garment on the floor out of their way. "Sorry about the mess, I suppose. I haven't gotten much business since—since the coats ran out. Kitchen is this way—how about tea? You look like someone who appreciates tea."

"Do you often say that to vagabonds?" Lilly asked, too dry; the drip of humor was wasted, anyway, since the tailor looked perplexed. "You asked if I was—"

"Oh! Well clearly you're a sophisticated type of vagabond." Miss Reiniger frowned down at her, swung open yet another door and gestured Lilly in ahead of her. "I'm not going to defend myself, boy. Be clever again and see if I won't throw you out. What's your name, anyway?"

"Lyle, ma'am." Lilly oriented herself in the crowded room— there a squat iron woodstove with battered kettle atop, here a water pump, on one wall cabinets and the other three sheepskins, and in the corner a roughhewn table and chairs with scarlet cushions worked with gold thread. In such a room it was difficult to settle oneself out of the way, but she made the attempt.

Most would have taken the moment of making tea—water in kettle, kettle to boil—as opportunity to pause, breathe deep, consider; not Frieda Reiniger. Even as she shuffled cups with chipped rims into a stable geometry on a tray with the honey pot and cream pitcher, she began to speak, and turned at intervals to catch Lilly's eye, looking for acknowledgement, reaction. "Do you know—? No, you can't, you came asking for Hans. Well, after he died, his grave got dug up, and what business I didn't lose for being a woman alone, I lost for the bad luck of *his* desecration. Then the few still interested left once I couldn't make the coats anymore. Flies all of them, and magic their honey." She shook her head sharply and murmured something lost in the rising shriek of the kettle.

"Ma'am?" Should she help with the tea? She didn't know the courtesies for this situation.

"I said: Lyle, what are you willing to do?" Another lie, but a fruitful one. Miss Reiniger dropped down into the seat across from Lilly, slow and careful. It was a movement of the very old and those whose joints had become inflamed. Once done wincing, her expression came around to aggressive again, daring any to comment on this weakness. She drank her tea without cream or honey or lemon. "Are you willing to be involved in a matter that involves desecrated graves?"

"I'm willing to work with what is magic, ma'am, and consider that a greater risk than any of the dead."

Miss Reiniger chortled. "Oh, you've known a fae creature or two, have you? Well. I told you a lie, just now."

The tea was as much a comfort in this irregular place as when drunk from fine porcelain. "It *doesn't* involve graves?"

"What did I say about your smart mouth? I see the honey pot hasn't sweetened you any. I meant what I said *before* that, though I suppose it doesn't have much to do with the boneyard, either. No, it wasn't that the grave got dug up. Hans dug up and I dug down, which is a different thing entirely. You . . ." Miss Reiniger thumped her cup down on the table, sloshing hot liquid over the edge. "I've been holding this a secret for half a decade, and you sit and stare at me with no more surprise than if I'd said, *Oh, the weather was fine today, wasn't it?* How could you?"

"Pardon, ma'am." Lilly reached for a terry cloth she could see on the counter just behind her, offered it to the woman. "I have had a very long few weeks and am quite run out of shock." Silence descended as Miss Reiniger mopped tea from her hand; Lilly finally ventured to ask, "What befell him after he came up from the ground?"

"Why, we put our coats back into production and all was well. See that tin? It has biscuits. Take some, boy. No, do. You're no use to me if you faint before I can tell you what I want."

Lilly put aside her weak attempt to observe atrophied manners. These were better than she expected, lemon-bright, hazelnut-rich, and savory with her hunger. "Then?"

"Then the master bandits rode into town and went pillaging one end to another, their eyes on this shop, this house. They wanted two coats of illusion—but we only make them when they're ordered, and we hadn't gotten an order in a year. They cost too much. We did that on purpose, because they cost us, too." Her eyes slid shut, but the gesture did nothing to hide her pain. "They took him because he said he was the key to making the coats. Not entirely a lie, but not entirely the truth, either. He needs me to bring together the cloth."

Lilly washed down crumbs with the tea; felt throat-clogged yet. "I am sorry, Miss Reiniger."

"Thinking of your lost friend, are you? Put the kettle on again, my tea is cold." This time, she used the boiling as an excuse not to speak; when Lilly sat once more, the woman was clear eyed. "They have him at their camp, and someday they must realize he is not making coats."

"You want him back, and in return will give me a coat. Yes?" Lilly stood. "Could you tell me where—"

"I tried! Do you think I would not *try?*" Her shout gave out to a rough whisper. "I marched militia there, I chose to bare my secret and my scars for him, and those damnable bandits and their auguring witch and their men drove back two dozen men. I would have gone alone after that and flung myself on their bayonets. I went through hell for Hans and I would again—but I can't die for him. He would follow me down to the pit and belabor me right along with Satan for being such a fool."

"Miss Reiniger," and Lilly's voice sounded like her own, for a moment, not the voice before the troll, but the one she had before Octavius disappeared. "I am glad to carry out the task. I will go forward with it regardless, but it will be easier if you set my feet on the right path."

The tailor met her eyes, grimaced. "Oh, sweet Mary help me, those are words only the foolish or beloved or young would say. Which one are you? How old are you?"

"I don't see that it matters."

Miss Reiniger came to her feet now, and her power was of the sort that kept birds in their flocks and fish to their shoals: the need of like to answer to the need of like. "I want to know how guilty I should feel."

"Old enough to care more for a friend than the dangers ahead." Lilly thought: *I must deal with shorter people, or I'll get a crick in my neck from all this earnest staring upwards.* Irrelevant, that, but better than crying for her next goal being so close and yet held just out of her grasp.

"God save you, boy. Let me tell you how to get there," Miss Reiniger said. "I'm already damned, you know, but this will be a greater black mark against me than any other. First you go down the way you came, and you take the first fork to the right, where the road is wider but less traveled. Then you'll see the tree."

She found the tree where Miss Reiniger had indicated, an old dead oak with pennants of dead flesh. Bodies desiccated to leather and yellow bone, their clacking against each other pricked the Mare's ears. They must not have any smell left, *Lilly told herself, and forced herself not to draw rein. Mushrooms made fairy-circles beneath their gnawed feet, and she only had to duck a little to avoid them; she'd been wrong about the smell, but theirs was a musty, attic odor, not the abattoir stink she expected.*

The path beyond was weedy and low with branches, though with enough headroom to ride, and in the dirt were crisp-edged hoofprints. Birds did not sing here. *More than a bandits' path,* she thought, resigned.

She learned, in the next instant, that though there was enough room for a rider on a walking horse, if that animal reared it meant one's head in the branches. She felt the blow to the back of her skull as a burst of light and directly after the ground pushing air from her lungs. Then the pain of it came, of the fall as much as the bruised skull; she blinked away starbursts to see the horse's head thrust down to her, eyes rolling and ears pinned, quivering with the readiness to strike out with her hooves. Lilly grasped the animal's mane to drag herself onto her feet, leaning on the Mare's neck and breathing hard. Winded.

She met the eyes of a creature that her mind could not at

first parse: red strands of tissue, the gloss of black hair like raven's wings, and eyes sea-green. A woman—skinless. Small and nude and each little change showing in the bunch and flex of raw meat, the ridges of belly, a fluttering of the chest under greasy lumps of fat. Her teeth were fine as pearls, exposed and framed by a ring of muscle, and her eyelids were delicate pink scales with long lashes. She glared, perhaps. Bare, the human face became difficult to read. Perhaps not human. No regular woman could have kept that hair so straight and untangled in a forest, a smooth drape down to the knees except where it clung damply to shoulder, thigh.

Lilly closed her gaping mouth and said, weakly, "I am called Lyle. Ma'am, I'm here to make a request."

"A *request*?" A blue vein which wended across her temple bulged, then she threw back her head and trilled laughter. One hand, delicate long bones and white tendons, came up to hover over her mouth. The nails were sharp and slender as doctor's needles. "Did the dead men not speak loud enough?"

"I heard their chatter." Lilly turned and spoke soothingly into the Mare's ear, stroking the animal's nose. "They said, *You must have a good cause and a willingness to pay any fee.*"

"The fee is death, boy." She came forward with the forthright, elegant stride of a confident woman, faltering only once when the bones of her knees shifted and audibly clicked. "The bandits want for nothing."

Her voice sounded too much like her father's when she answered, "I am not here to offer *them* anything." Lilly would have words with Reiniger for how offhand her "auguring witch" comment had been—and Lilly insisted to herself, *I will have opportunity to tell her so.* "What I come for is not a thing they will sell to another."

The woman stepped around the horse's haunches. "And what would you offer *me*?"

"You have a need." Hands tight on the Mare's mane—might she vault into the saddle now and flee? But one did not run from predators. "Or you would have said the same of yourself as you did of the bandits." She took a deep, choked breath as her last chance to take flight—her quite possibly illusory chance, but it had been there—died with a last step forward. "I come for the tailor's corpse. What—"

When she touched Lilly's wrist, the bones of the woman's fingers were distinct as rings of gold, the flesh hot and moist. "Do not mistake me—my mood is not so swift to change as this. But I favor whoever means to remove that damnable thing. Its noise is enough to drive a deaf man mad—but your taking it is not the price I will charge. How well do you climb?"

"Well, ma'am." Lilly thought of clambering over sea-wrack. *So this is not quite a lie.* "Why must I?"

"You might say that I am on a quest as well—for my beauty." When she laughed, all other sound cowered from the air. "My skin is a pennant on the branches of an oak, and I will have it." The woman pointed back down the trail, and for a moment Lilly thought it meant, *You have pleased me enough that you may go*; but then the woman crooked a finger. There came a shambling, hesitant noise, like—

Like a dead man walking through underbrush. Some noises could not be compared to others. He clasped a soldier's cap in a hand with most fingers shortened by weather or the picking of crows and came knocking to kneel before the woman; tilting up a face with cobwebs in its sockets, he wrenched a tooth from his own mouth and dropped it into her outstretched hand.

Lilly knew enough to raise her hands defensively, but the woman easily slapped them aside and grasped Lilly's jaw tight, forcing it open by the joints and pressing the tooth down her opened throat with thumb and forefinger. She tasted of copper and rosemary, awful knowledge to have; and when she clamped shut Lilly's jaw to keep her from spitting the thing out, the strength of that hand crushed to gagging. The skeleton fell back to unlife; the Mare pulled away snorting as her master's hand dropped lax from her neck. And Lilly thought: *Did I make this choice when I spoke to this creature, or did I already make it when I walked into this wood, or even before, when I promised my kraken his freedom?*

It did not matter which; though she could regret this, she was beyond penitence. She swallowed the tooth and coughed, wretched but released.

"I am Gottschalk the Witch," said the woman, "bound by the loss of my skin to these bandits you seek to steal from. It is up a tree at present. You will fetch that and take away the tailor and we will have completed our deal, you and me." She squeezed Lilly's biceps, made a derisive noise. "I think you are lying about being able to climb. Be that as it may: you are bound here, now, and cannot go outside the sphere of my influence."

Lilly coughed again; dizzied, she asked, "Wherever the birds are silent?"

"Precisely." Impatiently Ms. Gottschalk gestured for her arm. "Come, I must hand you to the bandits like I do all their toys.

They might kill you yet, but I do not think so. They are lonely and they trust me to bring them sweet things."

The Mare snaked her head around Lilly's shoulder and considered biting the witch; Lilly caught her by the bridle and pulled her straight, cocked an elbow and tried not to think hard about the fluid that began to soak her shirt wherever the witch pressed against her. She was so *small*, this woman who brought a dead man to his knees and gripped no weaker than the vice of torturers.

The cottage Ms. Gottschalk directed her to was disorientingly quaint, set in a field of long grass spangled in buttercups and the neat lines of a small late garden of squashes and potatoes. A stable flanked it on one side, a shed on the other. Reared over it there stood the monument of a dead oak; from its topmost branches hung something moth-white and innards-red. Incessant, creaking, the song of the spindle and the thread suffused the whole of it.

That was quite a distance to climb.

A man straightened up from the garden; tall and muscled, he might have been some woodsman who lived by grouse and deer, except that he was well-dressed in linen and leather and a scar deeply puckered his cheek.

He smiled friendly enough. "Now, dear lady, since when did you bring mice to me? You're not normally so squeamish that you need a man to torment these things to death."

"I—" Lilly grunted at the impact of Ms. Gottschalk's elbow in her side as the woman disentangled herself and stepped forward, hands propped on hips, expression all distaste.

"I tempted this soul into the forest." The pads of her cheek muscles twitched; a smile? "Lately you demand far too much attention of me, so I got you a pet."

Lilly drew herself straight and said, "I am Lyle, sir. So long as I'm here I would be useful."

"You expected sweeter things from a witch-trick, I imagine." He laughed, all humor and no sympathy. "That's why I like our lovely Gottschalk: she is all surprises. And look what she brings me! You're ugly as sin—that face. But I'm one to talk." His attention back to the witch, he asked, "Will you be offended if I take this pet behind the shed and shoot it soon as you are out of sight? I promise to say it took ill and needed to be killed for mercy, if it will keep peace between us."

Ms. Gottschalk shrugged. "It would displease me."

However much he *liked* his lovely lady, the idea clearly did not put the bandit off too sorely. Lilly felt the violation of the witch's fingers in the soreness of her mouth, the lingering herb taste, and knew she could not flee; so she put away her panic for some other time and asked: *What can I offer him?* "I was on my way to the city."

"So are most." He swung the hoe up onto his shoulder, and the gardening implement, of a sudden, looked a weapon. "Or, the poor country lads are, which you are not. I don't want a liar, Gottschalk."

There—harshness. The witch spat at his feet. "Where is my servant?"

"Hassling the corpse. Take him away, witch. He does little good and I'd hate to put bruises on him." The bandit stepped aside to let Ms. Gottschalk walk past, which she did with slow dignity.

Lilly met his eyes, grip white-knuckled on the Mare's reins, feeling how the animal wanted to bolt. "Sir, I never claimed to be a country lad. I'm a sea-trader's son and on my way to make a fortune."

"Your origin and purpose—"

She spoke over him, fighting to keep her voice level. "For I have something better than any bean-plant or squash in this garden."

"Not difficult." He was most disinterested in her pitch; his hand tightened on the hoe's haft.

One needed a story to sell something, but visuals helped. Props distracted the buyer, too, which seemed most beneficial when said buyer was currently focused on one's death. She snatched the blood-stones from her pocket and held them forth to catch the light. "Here are gems borne of the moonlight and shark's blood on the surface of the sea. When planted, they will grow a hundred times their own weight, nurtured by rock and starlight. Tell me, what court lady would not adorn her throat and ears and fingers with such a stone?"

"I'll grant you *that's* interesting." He had been playing with her, for he took no more of those sliding steps but covered the distance between them in two wide strides—*another* tall stranger, for she was not short and he towered over her— and whisked the blood-stones from her hand. "Warm," he said, startled, "and they do have a nice shine."

A man who would sacrifice the innocence of his hands to the blood of victims for the sake of coin *would* have that need she saw in his eye. Not for profit, no; nor for the things that money bought. The sight of it was enough to inflame such a lust, though never enough to dull the wanting's edge. Her father took advantage of this sort. "They will come up by spring, sir.

But only if I plant and tend them, for I know the trick of it, and it is no easy thing."

He tilted his head. "That creature has the worst habit of beating whatever is weaker than her, which is most things. Look at that black and blue coming up on your throat!" He shook his head, held out the blood-stones. "Take them to plant, then. You had me at the first hint of gold—and you knew it, you damned trader's brat. It's not me who will kill you on principle, though, but Ignatz. Ignatz Kunze. He'll be home from the hunt soon enough."

"Yes, sir." She accepted the stones; imagined their reproach seeping into her palm. *Who may touch us but you?* None should; but there was a need.

"*Sir* is such an officious term. I'm Ivo Duerr." He caught her roughly by the shoulder and led her down the path. "In back is a stack of wood to chop. I want you tired. Good runners are tedious." He crossed behind her to take the Mare's reins, clucking his tongue when the animal startled. "*She* will be well cared for. What a fine animal—stolen?"

"No, sir, unless a gift of guilt accepted is a type of stealing." She liked to think her father was guilty, anyway.

With another amused glance—it had been a rhetorical question, probably—he pointed her around the cottage. She found his willingness to let her wander puzzling; what was to stop her from going up the tree for the witch's skin now?

Around the corner was another circular yard, a stack of logs ready to be hewed close by the cottage's back wall, and in the shadow of the dead oak her goal. His foot on the pedal was swollen as a drowned man's flesh and the rest of him hung bloated from a body that might have belonged to a blacksmith, not a tailor—in life, anyway. He spun his own forearm for thread; when he swiveled to glance at her with filmed eyes, his chest was revealed to be quite hollow. In a ring around him stood three men in rough garments and blood-rusted coats, each leaning on a long gun, and each with eyes blanker than Mr. Nadel's. They were not alike to each other as brothers, but as a man and his reflection in a mirror. Statues would have acknowledged her more.

If I induce vomiting now, will the tooth come up, and will it matter? She shook the thought from her head, glanced once at the witch's skin on its macabre perch. To work, then; she grunted at the weight of the ax as she tugged it from the block, only to set it down again because she could not hold both it and the first log she propped up. The first swing came hard, awkward; soon enough she had a workable technique and it did not feel so much as if she would jar her arms out of their sockets. It seemed hopeful—for a little while. She knew of Mr. Duerr's leaving by the sound of horse's hooves headed away from the cottage and allowed herself to slump over the ax handle. If she had hair it would be sweat-matted, and she tried to feel glad for being bald.

Always the tailor worked with that omnipresent creaking, a futile sort of temptation; Ms. Gottschalk had been wise to bind Lilly to the land. Left to her own she might have gone mad and made her attempt at freeing Mr. Nadel long before success was possible.

A sodden, earthy smell clogged her nostrils, and she spun about, near tripping on the wood she'd lately chopped. Before her stood a dwarfish creature, burrs and worse in the hair that reached past his shoulders, dirt smeared over skin, clothing indistinguishable from a sack used to haul manure. Yet his gaze—*camel-eyes*, she thought, recalling illustrations all long-lashed and darkly thoughtful. And she realized: *just a boy*. "You are the witch's servant?"

"And you're tonight's dinner." His voice was high and nasal, faintly accented. He crowded close, standing on his toes to shove his face aggressively towards hers—which brought the top of his head to the level of her chin. By God, he *stunk*. "That is, if they don't put you on the spit for a midafternoon supper. I saw you looking at the tailor. It's not the first time someone has come for him."

Lilly resettled the ax in her hand and stepped around him, back towards the pile of unhewn wood. "You would risk Ms. Gottschalk's anger?"

"Better anger than success. Anger goes away." His heels were loud on the packed dirt; how had he snuck up on her? "But I have an offer. I can get you out of here in a snap and then you can run like hell to whatever you've got out there in the wide world. Like—go questing. You look like the type. Isn't that nicer than dying? Because she *will* kill you. She kills most things that come into her hands. No patience, see? It is not at a human pace that she is meant to live."

"You might say that I'm already on a quest." She turned, gestured him aside. "Pardon. I need to get back to work."

He stood with feet wide-planted. "I offered nicely."

"You did. But—"

His heel snapped hard into the back of her knee, and in the cognizant moment before the fall she thrust the ax away from her, disinclined towards being disemboweled on its blade. She came down hard on her side, thinking into the blackness: *Why are so many around me unnaturally strong? No mere boy, after all.* When his hands closed over her ankles she kicked out and he relinquished one hold only to clamp both hands on a single leg. Dragged through the dirt like so much offal, she fought to turn on her side, lost a nail scrabbling for traction in the dirt. Her skull bounced over a rock and again her vision went strange, hiding a moment the grotesquely fearful expression on the witch servant's face.

With a last yank he released her and bounded some distance away; she would have glared if not for the dread in her gut. The spinning wheel did not sing anymore. She got as far as her elbows before one of the men swung his bayonet close enough to tap her on the nose, the point wavering as if he would carefully choose which eye to plunge it into. They were facing *out*; not to keep Mr. Nadel in, but intruders away. The tailor was quite well secured by a manacle which bound his far foot to an eyebolt driven into the oak, she saw.

That detail could only command so much attention. "By no purpose of *mine* am I here," she said to the men. "Do you not see that?"

The bayonet stilled, though still the man who held it remained blank-faced.

"Please, if you raise your weapon, I will stand and back away. We need have no quarrel." She wished she had taken the time to glare at the witch's servant before; now she could not move, and it would be a shame to die without some protest against her murderer.

"Sorry," the servant called, "but you'll break everything. What's taking so long?" His voice cracked with irritation.

Ponderous, the guard once more planted his weapon on the

ground and returned his stare to level. Lilly scrambled back, nothing in her head but *survival* and the awareness that she could escape. Pains edged onto her awareness, bruising on her rump and back that made this backwards scuttle a brutal business; with a grunt she shoved herself to her knees, and from there to her feet. She touched the back of her head, wincing to find it lumpy with a goose egg already, and turned on the boy. "You—"

He looked at her with all the white-eyed, nostril-flared panic of a spooked cow.

"You bastard," she said, the word rolling odd but satisfying off her tongue. "What did I do to *you*?"

He stared a moment longer, and answering her first question about him, blurred out of existence with a puff of dust and the sound of air shutting in on itself.

Well. After some consideration, Lilly returned to work.

In the end the ax haft tore her hands raw and with a bow to necessity she abandoned the woodpile. The shadows grew long and the chill obtrusive, so she went around to the front of the cottage where the bulk of the building formed a windbreak. For a while she leaned against the face of the cottage, comforted by its warmth, then she stopped to consider *why* it should have that heat, fingering the close-fitted stone, squinting up at the spotless eaves. Unnerving but not so unnerving as a tooth in the gut, by which standard Lilly decided all things of magic could be neatly categorized. She eased down to sit with knees drawn up as the mountains swallowed the sun.

At this elevation the familiar constellations held bellyfuls of little stars, numerous as the bubbles in champagne. Caught dozing under them, Lilly startled badly at the commotion that raised up in the cottage behind her. The door banged on its hinges and out flooded a dozen copies of the men who guarded Mr. Nadel, two carrying lanterns, three shovels, and the rest with stacks of burlap sacks in their arms. Fighting the urge to chafe her numb hands—it would be a terrible way to burst blisters—she watched this parade with a curiosity intense enough to taste, and no contortion of her mind capable of reasoning how so many had fit into the small building in silence, these hours past.

A thirteenth emerged a beat behind the others and veered towards her.

Having lately been menaced by such a creature she lunged up from the ground only to find herself confronted with a wool blanket, rank with lanolin and promising warmth. She took it with a "thank you, sir," and as before raised no response. This one held a butcher's knife in his off hand, such as was used to carve joints from an animal's body. When he turned away from her, Lilly settled the blanket over her shoulders and once more slumped to the ground.

The sound of men and horses startled her awake some hours later, to judge by the risen moon. She struggled to her feet and hesitated with her hands clasped on the blanket; folded it and tucked it under one arm in an attempt to regain a touch of dignity. She saw them before she became visible in the light of the lanterns their men held up to either side of the procession, and thus caught an unguarded moment between the bandits: Mr. Duerr leaned far over to press an arm around the neck of another man, a bearish fellow, and kissed the corner of his mouth. An innocent would have called it a brotherly gesture.

The men went around the side of the cottage towards the

shed, but the bandits halted in the yard. Mr. Duerr looked at his partner, and the latter looked to her. He had a scholar's inquisitive eyes and the short-cut hair of a clergyman; for the rest, he looked what he was, as rough and deadly a creature as nature never produced. "She's brought us no mouse." Preacher's voice, that, deep as a well and carrying.

"I never claimed to be thus." Lilly stiffened her neck that she did not appear to look *up* at him. "She captured me for to be your servant—"

"Plaything," Mr. Duerr put in, idly; his partner scowled.

She would not think of it. They had each other, had they not? "—and I will serve that function so long as it takes to convince you, gentlemen, that I should be freed. I don't expect mercy of the witch."

"Clever of you. Ivo tells me that you tempted him with a pair of stones." Mr. Kunze came down from the saddle, a cue that Mr. Duerr followed. "He's often a fool for pretty things."

Lilly disapproved of the double meaning there. "It does not take a special foolishness, sir." She held forth the blood-stones again. "It—" She closed her fist over them as he grasped her wrist, the blanket tumbling into the dirt as she raised her free hand to protect herself; but after the initial shock, she registered the firmness but not *cruelty* of the hold.

"Open your hand." His eyes were blue, like the last fragment showing through a soot-stained painting, and the darkness on his clothing was blood. "*Now.*"

She laid it flat, the stones in the dip of her palm, and flinched at his taking one of them, not for fear what he would do but shamefully at the pain of her blisters. Most of them had burst before she stopped.

He turned the stone in his hand; sighed. "You've never worked a day in your life, have you?" He dropped it back into her palm, let her go. "Get inside. There's a cabinet to the left of the door where we keep bandages and salves, and on top of it is a basin of clean water." He frowned. "Have you been inside already?"

She followed his stare to the blanket on the ground. "No, sir. One of your men brought this to me."

Mr. Duerr, in the process of kicking off his boots and shrugging out of his equally sodden coat—had that blood on his mouth and cheek come from Mr. Kunze's hair when they kissed, or from their victim?—regained interest in the conversation. "Horace? He's not ours. That's uncommonly kind of him. You shake your head. One of the *automata*?"

"They are clockwork?" She glanced to where they had gone. "That's a great comfort." She caught two blank stares for that. "Well, it is far less disturbing an answer than one woman birthing so many children alike."

"It's new to me that any would think fae magic less distressing than human monstrosities." Mr. Duerr shook his head. "I'm going around back to clean off this mess. Coming with, Ignatz?"

"Sirs." Lilly met Mr. Kunze's eyes. "Does this mean you will not kill me?"

He snorted. "Are you a servant of Gottschalk?"

"I am servant to myself, sir." She smiled thinly at the surprise on his face. "I am quite fond of life, and I have it from good sources that she will kill me, someday."

He nodded; and turning away, said, "Tend to your hands, boy."

She stood waiting for a musket shot—did bandits not play tricks?—frightened, now, as she had not been of Mr. Duerr.

But it did not come, and as they turned the corner of the cottage and went out of sight, Lilly bent to pick up the blanket; she rubbed her wrist, where bruises would show, come morning.

When she opened the cottage door, food-smell and the warmth of the cabin's wide sooty hearth breathed onto her. Lilly stared into the fire-lit hominess of it, at the rough wooden furniture, cloth partitions, a gold cross on the wall, and the grey-nosed cat which lifted its head to stare at her as she entered.

Folding the blanket and setting it aside, she went to the cabinet Mr. Kunze had described, admiring for a moment its craftsmanship, then somehow unsettled by the way the supplies were arranged as if to be quickly taken up in an emergency. With these in hand, she sat on a stool next to the fire; there she saw to her palms.

Or, *tried* to. The bandages tangled and hung in sagging loops; the salve smeared the cuff of her shirt. She startled halfway off the stool at the sound of heavy footsteps, only to be gently pushed back down by the automaton who had approached. He knelt and took the supplies from her unresisting grip; she was less willing to let him hold her hand, but though his fingers were loose around her wrist she could not break his hold. Foolish of her to resist, anyway; he made quick work of bandaging them.

"You don't even know how to bandage a blister? Well, you'll be skilled at it before you leave here." Mr. Kunze stood in the doorway of the kitchen, having lifted the partition aside and secured it to the wall.

Past him she could see the accoutrements of a kitchen, woodstove and utensils, and Mr. Duerr carrying a smoked ham from the pantry. Her stomach made a dramatic noise, and she might have laughed at herself, in another place.

"It is not only your hands that are scuffed—how did you fall?" He spoke with a distant, evaluating curiosity, drawing her out to speak rather than indicating an interest in her answers. He hoped to make her nervous enough to slip up; she supposed it was a comfort that he cared to test her for evil intentions, as it indicated the chance that he might let her live.

Lilly took her hands from the automaton and mumbled her thanks, although she got no more response from him than she would have a clock. Without acknowledging his master, he went into a nook set aside from the living space through which she glimpsed a bed. Lilly had no such luxury of escape; she glanced up at the bandit, flinched away from the questions in his eyes, and found herself staring at the stained and scraped surface of the table at the room's center like a dog unable to meet its angered master's eyes. "Horace took exception to me." She paused, but preferring that he speak rather than her, she asked, "What is he, sir?"

From behind him, Mr. Duerr answered, "He's the witch's work. She normally prefers inhuman servants. He was a mule— now he's a mule in a boy's body. We wanted the animal for work and she turned him into that. He still has a useful magic about him, but she's jealous and won't let us give him orders."

Lilly made an inarticulate noise of interest, unsettled by the thought of the witch's preference in servants; what did that say of how she perceived Lilly?

Mr. Kunze said, "I would think even he would be easier to command than our automata. Yet you seem familiar with our servants. Where do you come from that you are so quick to hand out orders?"

"I did not order him, Mr. Kunze." For this she met his eye that he might see the truth in hers.

She heard his footsteps on the floor, and he must have thought she lied, because something sharp underlay his voice when he said, "No? Then what—"

Mr. Duerr interrupted him from the kitchen doorway with, "*Dinner.* Shall we leave Gottschalk to feed you, Lyle? After all, it is by her hand that you are here."

Lilly could hear the mockery in his voice; she might have felt thankful for the interruption, otherwise. "I will make my own way if I must, sir."

"And have you steal from the cellar while we aren't watching? That seems inconvenient for us all." With a laugh, he put a plate onto the table in front of her. Though it held considerably less than he had prepared for himself and his partner, there was nonetheless enough meat and roast potato to fend off a fainting hunger.

When she looked up into his face to speak thanks, her attention caught on his water-slick hair; he must have bathed himself in the stream despite the cold. Perhaps spilled blood remained an unpleasant companion no matter how familiar it be. She said, "Thank you," and it sounded sincere; she could see that it surprised Mr. Duerr.

Mr. Kunze set down his own plate and bent his head, ignoring what must have been a familiar gesture of mockery from his partner. Though shocked a moment at that murmured prayer, Lilly lowered her eyes to the plate, shaken by the irony of the gesture—ironical for herself as much as for the bandit, she supposed.

The potatoes were spiced with rosemary; she once liked the flavor, but for now she ate the meat first.

After that they did not speak, quite as if the meal were their last, or food held some special significance. Used to Nikolaus' rambling oratories at meals, this left her troubled and fidgeting. The quiet of the night outside crept in among them as they ate, held at bay by nothing but the gentle crackles of the fire. Distracted by the task of forcing down the distasteful potatoes, her attention wandered from her silent dinner companions.

"So," said Mr. Duerr, and laid his plate on the table. "How much did she pay you for this farce, Lyle?"

Lilly put aside half-finished what would, perhaps, be her last meal, and rested her hands on her knees before she looked up to meet Mr. Duerr's gaze. He had his chin on his interlaced hands, posture forward, like a man who expected a good show but knew the end already; Mr. Kunze, in the chair beside him, leaned back, all shadows but for the firelight glossing his eyes. "She let me live." Mr. Duerr arched his eyebrows, and Lilly tried to steady her voice when she said, "Then bound me to her service—I cannot leave her domain." She smiled, strained. "I *would* have run and spared you having to feed me."

"He is leaving out details," Mr. Kunze told his partner, voice low and soft and steadying. "She would not do us the smallest kindness without her own interest behind it, and there is no ambition in her but to foil us."

How old this friendship, Lilly wondered, and how many times strengthened in hardship? Surely Mr. Duerr heeded that warning, eased back from her, his interest banked. She drew forth one of the blood-stones from her breast pocket, the one with the golden light at its heart; the one wrought of mermaid's blood. She rolled it, smooth and shimmering, across her bandaged palm, to put its splendor on show. "Mr. Kunze, it is with this that I convinced Mr. Duerr to let me live a while longer. I do not doubt that the witch will use me then discard me—is that not the way of the magical?" *No*, she knew, but doubted that these men could detect the lie. "In truth I would rather serve your interest than hers—and if you wish that I enrich you while I stay, I am glad to pay that little for my freedom."

Mr. Kunze took the stone from her hand, holding it up to the light that the fire might catch in its heart. "How much is this worth, then, that you will give it away so easily? Where does it come from?"

"It is worth less than a life but more than a diamond," replied Lilly. "I learned how to grow them—"

"*Grow* them." Mr. Kunze did not phrase it like a question and reached towards a pistol laid out on the sideboard.

Mr. Duerr restrained him with a hand on his wrist and a sidelong grin. "No, wait, I'll listen to this." He snitched the blood-stone from Mr. Kunze's hand, playfully holding it away from him. To see a killer smirk like a child satisfied at winning a game struck Lilly silent; then gathering herself, she lied.

"I learned to grow them from the Sheik Efreet." Her palms sweated but her voice kept steady. She could feel the stone birthed from the shark's blood as a weight against her heart, and thought, *If they kill me, they will take it, too.* "This man is a merchant who deals with my father in spice and fine goods of the eastern empires. They often gift each other valuable things to keep their dealings sweet. When I lost my father's—" She looked down, stalled by the bitter taste of truth in her mouth. "When I lost his regard, I thought to find my fortune elsewhere. A witch did not factor into my plans, sirs."

"She plans to kill you," said Mr. Kunze, with as little rancor as sympathy, then sighed. "I don't believe you, Lyle." He turned to Mr. Duerr, and sounded tired when he added, "This all tastes of lies."

Mr. Duerr grinned, of a sudden, looked into his cupped palm where the blood-stone lay. "You're right. Who's ever heard of something *magical* like precious stones growing out of the ground?"

"When has our witch ever let live what would be easier to kill?" snapped Mr. Kunze, fierce, low, none of his attention on Lilly, now; the frustration in his voice was not for Lilly.

That was a useful fact; a smart merchant would have known not to be so bald with their emotions. "She seemed desperate." Lilly ducked her head under Mr. Kunze's glare, willing to be submissive in the face of death. "As if she has tried something on her own, but not been able."

It took her a moment, in the silence which followed her words, to recognize the emotion on Mr. Duerr's face as fear; he hid it well behind an ironical little smile, but his hand went white-knuckled around the stone in his fist. Mr. Kunze leaned back again, hand over his mouth, and she could not interpret that—not fear, she thought. Perhaps exhaustion, or his face found that expression when in repose, from long use. He seemed a tired sort of man.

Lilly felt the potential of the situation heavy as the premonition of a thunderstorm. "I will tell you what Ms. Gottschalk

asks of me during my time here, and in the spring I shall have
the blood-stones for you—I ask only my life in return, sirs."

"You could tell us how to grow the stones now and leave the
problem of Gottschalk to us—we can order her to take her spell
off of you. Think about it, boy. You'll have your freedom *so*
much sooner that way." Mr. Duerr bared his teeth at her, feral as
hounds, unhappy to have lost the advantage, collared with his
greed and his worry.

Lilly flinched when Mr. Kunze laughed, did not feel at all
comforted by the amused, resigned glance he gave his partner.
"To think I believed you would be a dull and bothersome creature to dispose of. You shall sleep in the stable loft. There is
bedding there from our last servant."

"Yes, Mr. Kunze." She got to her feet, paused. "I will need
the blood-stone, Mr. Duerr."

"Of course you do," he muttered, and put the stone into her
outstretched hand; for the moment he hesitated in letting it go,
she could feel the pressure of his fingers through her bandages,
and remembered with a painful lurch the blood on his shirt. A
killer's hand, over hers; and her making deals with its owner.
She returned the blood-stone to her breast pocket and dropped
a bow to the bandits. Before she could decide what would be
appropriate to say to them in parting—did one wish a good
night to such men?—Mr. Duerr waved her off, and she went,
back into the crisp dark of the night.

In solitude outside the door, she pressed her fisted hand to
her mouth for a long moment. She did not think of herself as
someone who lied—or, well, not *this* sort of lie, not so cold-
blooded and convoluted, surface things couched on deeper
promises she never meant to fulfill. She did not cut harsh deals

with master bandits. Lilly thought of Octavius in his cage, touched the blood-stones over her heart.

"You are *ballsy*," hissed Horace from the shadow beneath the bandit's shuttered window.

Lilly laughed, clamped her hand over her mouth; if the bandits could hear her, they probably thought her mad. For a long moment the hysterics bubbled painfully up her throat, and she thought she could see Horace's incredulous look despite the darkness.

He forged on despite being obviously put off, whispered, "It hasn't even been a day, and you're already double-crossing Gottschalk?" He huffed, annoyed; had doubtless not meant to phrase his words as a question. He stood, stepped away from the window—perhaps he liked the bandits as little as he liked Lilly, then, or he wouldn't have minded disturbing them.

"I'm—" *Sorry?* No, not after he'd tried to kill her. "—not going to confide in you." She turned her back on him, and wished for something to ward him off, whether the ax or a stout stick she didn't care. She kept her eyes on the sliver of lantern light which showed through the gap of the stable door, which seemed of a sudden farther, with Horace at her back.

"You could," he called after her, sudden and rough. "I *know* things!"

She listened for the moment when he followed her, but when she reached the stable door and looked back over her shoulder, the yard was empty. With a shiver she slipped into the horse-scented warmth of the place. The Mare snorted a greeting— Lilly paused to pet the animal's nose—and the bandits' stocky little horses watched her with wary dark eyes as she passed; the animal in the last stall—the light did not reach far enough for her to see it—made an awful wet rasp, ill or magic or mean. She kept herself on the far side of the aisle; dragged herself up the ladder to the loft.

It occurred to her that she might worry about the where-abouts of the last person who used the pile of blankets and hay as a bed; then called herself a fool to think they were anywhere but in God's hands. A lingering delicacy from when she had hair for lice to invade made her fold her jacket for a pillow; the sound of the ocean in the blood-stones carried her down to sleep.

She woke with a violent bout of sneezes courtesy a wisp of straw, then moaned, curling around herself to enjoy a shameless moment of self-pity over the soreness of her muscles before getting upright and moving. The bandits had lodged her in the stable's hay loft with a pair of old blankets for bedding. Morning hunger did not make the witch-tasting potatoes any more tempting.

On the ladder, a stinging nip to her calf sent her gracelessly down the last three rungs, biting her tongue against yelps and staggering against the Mare's stall door. That got her a curious nudge from her own horse while she stared across the aisle at—well, a creature pretending to be a sway-back nag. Horses didn't have such eyes. The night before she had not seen it through the exhaustion and gloom. With less trauma she properly met the bandits' mounts, a pair of solid, scruffy animals with placid temperaments. That would be better around gore, she supposed. The last of the stalls contained nothing but eyebolts on the floor, at which she stared in some puzzlement before passing on.

Gone blinking into the day she near ran up against Mr. Duerr. He looked her over, grinned. "You look like hell. Here, have
some porridge. Then you need to fetch a bucket of water from the
well—here's the key—to take down to the lady." He pointed to
the space between two gnarled junipers that she supposed might
be the opening to a path. "After that, plant your blood-stones,
then weed the garden some."

Turning her attention from the steaming porridge to the
rusted key in her other hand, she asked, "A locked well, sir?"

"Open water draws things out of the woods." He shifted.
"There's a lot of blood in the soil."

"Sir," she said, and went around back to the well, on which
she perched as she breakfasted. It looked as if the morning
would be better than the night: the porridge was filling, thick
with dried fruits, and the well-latch and cover hinges better
oiled than she expected from the state of the key. Sighing as her
arms took the weight of the bucket, she took herself to the
trail mouth. Something moved in the branches overhead, a
staggering noise with nothing of bird or squirrel in it. Yet surely
the bandit would not set her a task only to kill her with it; they
were more direct men than that. Under the trees it was cool and
damp. Their roots made steps and tripping hazards alike.

Could the witch walk so long as this on her loose-jointed
legs? She must; the ground must aid her moving, anxious that
her weeping feet touch it no more.

A crash among the branches broke her from this mulling to
greater trouble; she brought the bucket up, ready to fling it at a
threat. When the witch's servant emerged onto the trail, scuff-
ing his bare feet sullenly, she felt uncertain whether the situation *didn't* call for violence. He tossed his head, shifting the

great mass of his hair over his shoulders. "Herself sent me to pick you up. *My bandits will think it funny to send her groping through the woods*, she said. You can't find your way if you've never been before." With that he turned and strode off, and if there was not such a difference in the length of their strides she might well have lost track of him.

"You made a quick enough exit yesterday," she ventured into the edged silence.

He snorted, rolled his eyes; it was somehow a more fearful than condescending expression. "Yes, well. I'm magic."

"All right," she said, not sure if she meant *that's fine with me* or *you're an ass but I won't harm you*.

He pulled up short. "Listen. Lemme ask again. You leave, we all live—big bonus!—and you don't need to lug that bucket this whole way each day."

She shook her head and waited until he began to walk again. "I heard your name from the bandits. Mine is Lyle."

"I have no idea why you're being friendly." He descended a mossy trio of brick steps, hesitated.

"There is no reason—"

"She's angry," he cut her off. "She's angry because I told her *Lyle looks more given with the bandits than you* and she's suspicious at heart and easy to turn vengeful. You still have time to leave."

The dark hollow before them framed a circular building, a hut of black brick; the stack stood smokeless, the garden a black carpet of rich soil. Lilly coughed on the sensation of nails in her throat, swallowed a bolus of cold air, and walked the path to the door. It swung open at her first knock, and in the cluttered gloom of that place stood the witch, her skin scarlet with the hard pumping of many blood vessels. "I have brought your water," Lilly said, "and an explanation."

The witch hissed from between those clenched, perfect teeth. "And you court them with these stones—why?"

"They will not grow, ma'am."

"They *are* magic." She raised a hand; a slap from her would be scarring.

Lilly lowered her head in submission—and to provide a less tempting target than her mouth or eyes. "Magic, ma'am, but not of the self-reproducing kind."

"He took a moment to come up with that story," Horace put in; he stood some ways back, wary, with a sour expression that said quite clearly he did not understand his own motivation in intervening. "It sounded convincing—too much so; real magic isn't ever."

The witch wavered, lowered her hand. In gripping the doorframe with the other, she had deeply splintered the wood. "Come in with my water, boy."

Obedient, Lilly stepped over the threshold. Strange silhouettes suggested esoteric objects littered on many small tables, a bed, the floor; the dark mercifully hid their details. She kept close behind the witch as they picked their way to a basin on the far side of the room into which she was directed to pour the water. Ms. Gottschalk made an impatient noise.

"Pardon, ma'am." Lilly set aside the bucket. "I do not know what is expected."

"The bandits must think it something clever to send you ignorant. No, that is not Kunze's game. Duerr did." She gathered up her hair into a twist atop her head, and though no pin was in sight, it stayed poised there as elegantly as any lacquered wig might. "Lift me into the basin, boy."

Lilly looked on the sponge that sat upon the basin's edge with a sudden knowledge. The smell of rosemary would cling to her hands. She had intended no part of her misadventures to reach Octavius, for it would grieve him to think her troubled in her search to free him. This, though. *This* he would hear about. Maybe by then she could make a jest of it. "Certainly," she said to the witch. "Before I do—ma'am, am I to engineer the theft of skin and tailor on my own?"

"Of course not, stupid boy." Ms. Gottschalk settled her hands on Lilly's shoulders, her stomach pulling taut in anticipation of being lifted. "Come tomorrow. I will have a gift for you."

Between a stand of peas and a tumble of fanciful squashes the likes of which she'd never seen, she pressed the blood-stones into the earth; they seemed to go dull, brooding, the ocean bounded unnaturally by earth. Lilly built a small cairn of stones over the spot, knowing she could craft a story of the agriculture of rocks should the bandits question the practice. If they disbelieved her—well. Not for a hundred tailor-corpses would she lose Octavius' gift.

Horace might travel as the wind, but his smell betrayed him. Lilly straightened her back and looked across a row of thick-grown squash plants to find the boy sitting with legs stretched out and a long stalk of grass in his mouth, steadily chewing. They eyed each other a while; he said, "There's a few potatoes ready to be dug up."

"I'll tell the bandits it is thus," she replied, and bent again to weeding. "Mr. Duerr directed me to work here."

"As if *this* is work. She's giving me more than you'll ever see."

"Is that why you tried to kill me?" She worked in silence long enough to believe that he must have gone, then heard him spit aside the grass blade. Straightening to arch her lower back, she looked again at his sullen expression. "You already told me, didn't you?"

"You'll change things." He heaved a sigh, bounced to his feet. "Well, whatever. It had to happen sometime. I still don't like what you're going to do in the meanwhile. *So* much work for me."

Better an ally than someone who would constantly pester at her. "Might I help?"

He snorted, disappeared.

And she realized: the question should have been *can I?*

Which might have been a question of her capabilities as much as the manner of the witch's exploitation of Horace's powers; Mr. Duerr wandered by not much later, and leaning over said, "That's not a weed."

She stared at the scraggily thing in her hand. "Oh. I apologize." She glanced at the greasy rag in his hand. "You've been cleaning, sir?"

"Something like that." Mr. Duerr pointed at a flowering thing which she dutifully plucked. "The truth is that we do all the housekeeping and cooking and growing and—well, *all* of it. The forest doesn't give willing. We would take on a servant if that hadn't gone so badly before."

She ducked her head to find more of the weeds he'd pointed out. "What of the automata, sir?"

"Oh, we told the lady, *Give us men who kill at our bidding.* And she pulls out this sack and takes all the teeth of the men we had killed and puts them in, and out jump these men, and back in they jump when we are done with them—I see that look. I asked at the time, *Is it not foolish?*"

"She laughed." Lilly could imagine the gape of that thin-cheeked mouth.

"Like a crow got into a nest of rabbits." Mr. Kunze came up the path from the forest, dusting his hands against each other. "The burying is done. The witch asked us, *What greater dominion could you have over them than being their death?*"

"That being as it is, *biddable to kill* is not *biddable to clean*. You must be most accurate when speaking with such a thing as Gottschalk." Mr. Duerr offered a hand down. "Before you kill more innocent plants, come in and I'll point you at the rafters. We're going to be out so you might as well knock down the dust then mop the floors. I *hate* doing that." He shot Mr. Kunze a pointed look to no visible effect.

His hand was rough with calluses, warm as any human being's, and his strength disturbing when he drew her to her feet. Not inhuman like Horace's, but it wouldn't take more than human power to overcome *her*, should it come to that.

"Your present." Ms. Gottschalk held out something black and glistening. *"It won't do anything, so act your part in this ploy well. I went searching through my collection for something disturbing. This is a preserved dog's nose. Somewhat preserved."*

Lilly schooled her face to the sort of calmness she once habitually used on unpleasant dinner company and accepted the thing, hair prickling at its greasy, putrid texture, the scent alike to stomach acid. "What am I to do with it, ma'am?"

"Say to them that I ordered you to feed it to the Nag. She stands guard over the best of their hoard, and among those items is the key to the tailor's shackles. I've long held a campaign of harassment against that *thing*, and they will believe I mean to use you against it. Another attempt should not alarm them so much as leave them aggravated at the necessity of moving their wealth." She paused, hands on her sopping hair, which she held still over the basin. "Help dry my hair, boy. And be gentle. I don't like to do it myself, for my hands leave oils on it."

Oils? Not so, but Lilly understood the dignity of the word choice. She took up the towel and pressed the length of hair, wary of tangles.

"Duerr was always too rough," the witch muttered. "It's a murderer's folly to think everything must be strangled and subdued. You, on the other hand, are competent enough."

Lilly flinched to find the edge of Ms. Gottschalk's scalp, worrying a moment that it would peel back even at a soft touch, though it seemed to be attached firmly enough. "Ma'am, to what extent should I make them believe me their servant and not yours?"

"Far enough that they trust you." The witch leaned back into the touch of the towel against her scalp, said, "Massage. Yes, just so. Do not go so far that I will feel it necessary to kill you."

The bandits reacted as Ms. Gottschalk predicted; it made Lilly wonder how many years the three of them had lived in these woods together, all that resentment and isolation boiling between them.

"Well, hell." Mr. Duerr rolled the thing across his knuckles like a coin. "I guess we'll have to feed it to the poor old beast,

or the lady will think you completely come over to our side
and—" He made a dramatic throat-cutting gesture with his
other hand. "Takes the whole thing off, she does, and some
more besides. It's impressive in a wretched way."

"Quit playing with that thing," Mr. Kunze snapped, and
gingerly took it from his partner's hand. "Come. There are
things we must remove and hide, first. How are your hands?"

"Healing, sir." She cleared her throat, feeling awkward over
this genuine concern. "What am I to do today?"

*Some weeks into her stay, Mr. Duerr asked, "Is it you that Horace
has been pestering?"*

The abruptness surprised her, but the casual tone didn't; the
novelty of her presence had worn within the month. She shook
her head.

"He's never left us alone this long. Well, maybe the witch
has replaced him." He laughed when Lilly blanched at that
and seemed to be content with the explanation, for he sent her
away to work then.

It seemed only she remained anxious of the passing time.
Ms. Gottschalk ordered no movement on their plot, except to
say one morning, clipped, *I do not know where they took the key.*
Later, when Lilly inquired after his absence, she was told, *Horace is more use than you.*

Mulch the soil, the bandit said. *You'll find the tools in the shed.*
What he did *not* warn her of was the fact that the dust-choked
mess within the outbuilding near rivaled the witch's, though it
was less disturbing. Over some metal obstruction she stumbled, and searching it out with fingertips found it to be a gun,

the muzzle badly bent. Carefully, she set it atop a nearby crate and toed her way deeper into the place, thinking, *Gardening implements must be within easy reach.*

She met the rake's tines with her toes, which vindicated the shuffling walk she had taken up; it only hurt a little. The spade proved somewhat harder to track, being leaned against the wall behind a bushel of variously broken bayonets, but with only a little scraping she foraged that from its place and escaped back into open air.

To find that Horace had returned; he stood staring mournfully at the cellar doors. He looked rattier than when last she saw him, a clamminess to the skin beneath its coating of dirt, a lambency of eyes that said *fever*. Had he not been squarer once, too? "Are you—do you need something?"

"I don't know why you're pleasant to me," he grumbled, trying to scuff a hand across his scalp only to be brought up short by its tangles.

She leaned the gardening tools against the wall of the cottage. "That means *yes*, doesn't it?"

"Maybe." He scraped at the ground with his heel, would not meet her eyes. "I don't like the cellar."

Patience. She had little enough work today. Somewhere nearby a bird sang, a simple three-note song that shivered up the back of her neck for its rarity.

Horace noticed it, too, head swiveling, nostrils flared. "Gottschalk said she would go to the bone-hung tree today. That bird'll be surprised when she gets back and the air goes to poison again." When Lilly gave no response but to wince, he said, "I *do* like turnips. Carrots. Radishes are the best. Apples too."

She hefted open the cellar doors and went down into the

dark cool. It was a pleasant room, smelling of root vegetables and glinting with the reflection of canned goods, an assurance of the sort of wealth that got one through the winter. Since she left the chateau, she had learned the preciousness of food. From a sack she plucked the least wizened of the apples, from another a good-sized bunch of radishes which she balanced in the crook of her elbow, and from a crate palmed three carrots. It seemed a paltry meal for a still-growing boy, but he'd requested neither meat nor bread.

His head had gone the other direction by the time she got back, towards the front of the cottage. He sneezed and snatched up the fruit and radishes from her arms, balanced them in either hand while eying the carrots. "The bandits will want you. They look a mess, blood streaming all over, shirts torn. Leave those on the cellar doors and I'll come back for them."

Lilly didn't quite throw them lest they fall in the dirt—not that Horace would likely mind, given he had taken a bite out of the radish without showing the least hesitation over its unwashed state—and went around to the door unsure how careful she should be. She stood on the threshold staring in at the scene: Mr. Duerr appeared well enough if blood-spattered, hands scarlet, hair dragged down with gobbets. The rag he pressed against his partner's wound dripped fatly onto the flagstones. Mr. Kunze stood uncertainly, his shirt a torn mess thrown onto the ground next to the cabinet of medical supplies, his shoulder—

She did not consider herself squeamish, yet almost turned away.

"Oh, it's not as bad as all that," Mr. Duerr said, chiding, and no telling whether he spoke to her or Mr. Kunze. "Lyle, get the whiskey."

Venturing back with the glass bottle—which went into Mr. Kunze's far hand—the frontwards angle showed Mr. Duerr to be right: the strip of flesh hanging down the back of the man's shoulder was a thin peel of skin and fat; the wounds it dangled from were gory but shallow. "Is there anything else . . . ?"

"Want to knife off that bit so he gets pissy with you rather than me?" Mr. Duerr patted his partner on the cheek when the man glared at him. "What? I'm sure our servant, who fumbles even the ladle in the porridge, is the steadiest surgeon in the kingdom." He grabbed Lilly's hand and, pulling it forward, pressed it against the rag. "Hold here a moment."

Mr. Kunze gave her a long-suffering look and took a swig of the alcohol, wincing as his partner did away with the strip of skin. Lilly wanted to ask if there was not some way to go about this in a more sensible manner than in the middle of the living space with each of the bandits filthy with mud and the blood of their victims, then reconsidered her priorities. There were scar tracks under the filth currently matting the hair of Mr. Kunze's body. Searching for some safe place to settle her gaze, her attention dropped to the leather thong around his neck, on which hung two keys quite similar to the well's. She glanced up into his face and found his eyes—glassy from drink as much as pain, now—steady on her.

"Gottschalk has talked about the key, has she? I thought so."

Lilly nodded, glanced aside. "I would have—"

"I don't want your excuses." He twitched, glared over his shoulder. "It doesn't need to be *trimmed*!"

"There's a bit of bayonet stuck in," Mr. Duerr replied, "so hold on a damned minute."

"You should be glad you're a fair hand at the tasks we give you," Mr. Kunze said, eyes tracking down from her face. "Or . . . "

Lilly fell back as Mr. Duerr dropped a thumb-sized piece of metal to the floor and indicated the rag need be held back so that he could apply salve and bandages. His leech-work done, he slapped Mr. Kunze's shoulder and said, "Go lay down. Lyle, new plan. Leave gardening a while and get a bucket of water and some soap, instead." He pointed at the floor. "Between the mud and the blood this isn't even a proper home anymore. Besides, you should get used to this. If you manage to stay around long enough you'll see enough of it. More in the spring—that's when the caravans go through the mountains, you see."

The dark of the witch's cottage never became comfortable, but walking across it no longer felt like quite so much of a hazard, now that she knew where the largest obstacles lay. It seemed the bucket got lighter each trip, too, though it washed as much of that ichor-slick skin as ever. As she poured it into the basin, Ms. Gottschalk impatient at her shoulder, she said, "Is the key like so, iron, without filigree? Then Mr. Kunze wears it around his neck, ma'am." She set aside the bucket, frowned.

The witch quivered with suppressed emotion beside her, a raising tension that made the air sickening, as that before a storm. Wary of Ms. Gottschalk's claws, Lilly stepped back, near fell as her heel came down on something that gave like an egg.

"Ma'am?"

With a feral, inhuman noise, she took up a glass bottle and flung it at Lilly, muscles cording on her neck. It struck the wall behind her at shoulder-level so that some of the fragments harmlessly struck her coat, but others lacerated her neck and naked skull. Her boots crackled over the shards as she stumbled back another step, hand hovering over the wounds, fearful to cut her palm on any glass still lodged in her flesh.

"I create what hampers me most, and *you*—*!* You are so *casual* about it."

Oh, how it stung; but the witch seemed to have spent some of her wrath in the gesture. Lilly spread her hands, placating. "What am I to do, ma'am?"

"You? You might drive a wedge between them—if they were not so closely partnered that even a fresh-faced youth could not break them. You might cut his throat—if I thought you could best him. Or steal it, if your hands were as crafty as your tongue." The witch turned on her heel, near slipping on the liquid that had accumulated on the pads of her feet. "I grant you'll be useful sometime, but now, *now* it does not feel thus."

Such danger here. "I am willing to try the skill of my hands—" She flushed. "My ability to steal. If I fail, what cost to you?"

"You could never take the key, free the tailor, and fetch my skin to me—it would be a foolish waste of this ploy, and the bandits will not let me repeat it again." She turned away. "I'll think on this. Lift me into the basin, boy."

For a moment Lilly considered attempting to walk out; never before had she felt her muscles lock against an action, and she could not determine whether it was the foolish pride or atavistic fear that made her loath to come near again to Ms. Gottschalk. Practicality overrode both. Accepting that the reward for her service was the blood soaking into her collar, she came forward to do this task as gently as before. It was as she lifted water over the witch's breast that the woman abruptly caught her chin, lifting her face.

"Do they let you feed them?" An eagerness flared bright in those eyes, the brightest thing in the room.

Rosemary, the scent larger than the witch's looming face. She thought it might be years before she could enjoy the herb again. "I—" She twitched, could not free herself; no use. "Sometimes, ma'am."

"But there's the trouble still of time. They won't be inclined to rest." That hand reached out to hover over her eyes, then to touch her scalp. "How often do they get drunk in front of you?"

Lilly eyed those needle points and considered if the urge to flee had been wise, after all. "Often, ma'am."

She dropped her hands, bent her head to have her hair doused. "Work, my servant, to make them even more comfortable with you. Get so close that you might be their bed-companion."

The witch's lowered head came no higher than her shoulder— a lie of vulnerability. "As you will, ma'am."

The witch straightened; asked, "Will you still dry my hair?"

Lilly paused, uncertain of why an order would be phrased as a request. Remembered again: some things were never vulnerable. Skinless, bound, the witch was still something to be feared. She never doubted that. "Of course."

"Yet you hesitated."

"It's no choice of mine, ma'am, and thus I was surprised at the offer. I will do what is needed." When the witch placed her hands on Lilly's shoulders, she lifted her out more from habit than any desire to see the woman free of the questionable boundaries of the basin.

The witch patted her cheek. "*Smart* boy."

———

Though she should have gone in and asked the bandits what they had for her to do that day, Lilly retreated to the barn loft to practice some physic on herself. The narrow space with its dusty sunlight had become something of a hiding place, somewhere the bandits did not tread. Tossing aside her blood-stiffened coat and shirt, thinking she would have to clean the lot, she settled cross-legged on the rough boards. It proved quite difficult to pull flecks of glass from the back of one's scalp, but she got along well enough with touch and careful pinching with her nails. They'd been long once, and clean—not so much, now. So it went.

"I thought I heard her throw something." Horace balanced at the top of the ladder, elbows on the edge of the loft floor. "How bad?"

Reflex made her lurch up an arm to cover herself before she remembered that her chest carried no shame; moving awkwardly as she wondered how to compensate for the gesture, she finally simply let her hands fall to her knees. Let Horace call her out on strange behavior—she would be in her right to laugh. "Just a small glass bottle. It was easy to sweep up."

"I meant *you*." He hauled himself up, standing on his toes to avoid the prickle of the straw. She did not know if he had grown more ragged in the last month or if his absence had made her forget the mats of his hair, the protruding bones and ripped shirt. Though she might be shirtless and him wearing two garments, she judged she could see more of his skin than he of hers. He did not make a prepossessing figure to have at one's back, but she allowed it.

"Scratches," she said, belated. "I just have scratches."

"With bits in them." He settled down on his knees behind her, his breath on her shoulder. His hands were fever-warm as he gently began to scrape the glass from beneath her skin. Perhaps it would have been more intelligent to rebuff him who had once tried to kill her, but this hurt less than her fumbling, blind attempts to do the same.

"You've been gone." Awkwardness—such a strange emotion. It brought out the inane in her.

"And you're shy," he replied, laughing. "You who are so brave with the bandits and witch mumble when shirtless in a loft. Oh, here's a *shard*. Stay still. That's the last, though."

"Thank you." She ran a hand across the affected area and grimaced when her palm came away bloody. Standing, she said, "I'm for the well to wash this off."

"The stream is better." He padded after her as she picked up her messed shirt to use as a rag and chose another from the small supply tucked into her saddlebags. "Sluices the blood-smell away. That's how I knew you were injured. I thought at first it might be one of the horses, so I came in to check."

She laughed, halfway down the ladder with him peering down at her. How to explain where her mirth came from? It helped to soothe the unease. "I could fetch something from the cellar for you. There's new cheese."

"I'd rather eat a pig's jellied foot." He clambered down after her, pausing a moment to scratch the Nag's cheek. She'd been quite sullen ever since the bandits took the hoard from beneath her hooves, forcing Lilly to dodge her teeth each morning. Yet Horace she tolerated. "I wouldn't say no to—oh, you know, turnips, that sort of business." He sighed. "It's too late in the year for greens. Wash first. You smell bad."

The stress of the day must be affecting her; she near laughed again. Would she forever be cursed by amiable conversations with those who wished to kill her?

She went down to the stream as he suggested, where he tossed pebbles at the tadpoles and taunted her for keeping her trousers on, for she merely bent down next to the water to wet her neck. "Are you a blushing maiden underneath those trousers?" he asked; she flicked water at him off the bloodied shirt then went back to scrubbing it under the water.

"The back of my head is already wet," she said, patient, when he flicked droplets back at her. Straightening, she slipped on her fresh shirt and hung the other over a branch to dry.

"Not fair," he muttered; he made a rough, grating sound which proved to be him scratching his scalp, much to Lilly's startlement. He grimaced at the attention. "It gets worse when there's water in it. I *did* wash for a while."

She settled back on her heels, eyed him. "Would you like me to cut it back some?"

"Duerr offered that, too." Horace licked his thumb, jerked up his chin, and cleaned away an area of dirt to show a pale, raised scar. "I thought *you* didn't have anything against me."

"I—" She stopped herself, took a deep breath; that kind of anger had no place here. "I wouldn't do that."

Horace shifted on his feet, nostrils flared, then: "Yes. All right."

She considered the knives in the kitchen, then chose the shed instead, finding a pair of shears that were not too much rusted. Horace eyed them warily; she said, "It's *very* matted. Sit on the stump, here?"

He sat, though so restless that she feared cutting him entirely by accident.

The spinning wheel stopped creaking; its omnipresence made

the lack of noise cacophonous. She looked up, startled and puzzled, to find the eyes of the automata and the tailor alike on her. For a moment she thought herself misinterpreted as a threat, the shears in her hand as—what? She'd walked by with far more threatening things: axes, and on one occasion a gun that Mr. Kunze had sent her to fetch. Mr. Nadel turned back to his work, after a moment, but the automata still stared. At least the pause had given Horace time to settle.

She took off the bits that hung from the elbow down first; then worked her way up, sawing through greater hunks of elf-lock with each handbreadth traveled towards his head. Dust billowed from them; halfway up she encountered a gold coin, and silently offered it over his shoulder. He put it in his mouth. Finally she had worked down to a span or so of hair and saw no way to continue with her clumsy tool; setting them to lean against the back of the shed—they would not be terribly useful for many things, now—she stood back to observe her work.

"I'm sorry," she blurted.

He spat out the coin, hands flying to his ears. "Did I lose one? Did you cut it off and I didn't notice?"

"No, no." He swiveled on her, and she blurted, "You're *tiny*."

He scowled, bouncing up to his feet as if this would prove anything. With the loss of the overwhelming mass of filth that he'd carried, he'd lost what little bulk he had, and—yes, she needed to bring up things from the cellar for him. Nor did she doubt anymore that what faced her was no human child. The loss of that fae tangle should have made him look less Ms. Gottschalk's thing, but it only emphasized those eyes, the shifts of weight and facial muscles that did not say *human*. He patted his hands over his head, expression losing some of its aggression. "It feels lighter. Still ugly, though. Like a dandelion puff half blown out."

Are you aware that your hair was roan under the mud? She shook herself. "I could get a knife from the bandits to trim off the rest. I might be occupied a while, though—I haven't done anything for them yet, and they'll have some cooking or cleaning or—"

"Proper little Aschenputtel," he said, kicking at the cut mass that surrounded the stump as if he found it threatening, serpentlike, now that it had been detached.

"Be that as it may, I'll get you something from the cellar, first."

She spent the better part of her day being badgered from one part of the cottage to the other by Mr. Kunze, who was both drunk and belligerent. The confinement necessitated by his wound left him in that state, and without Mr. Duerr's frequent anxious check-ins he doubtless would have gone out to do work, shoulder be damned. "Keep him seated," his partner groused, and meanwhile Mr. Kunze stared at Lilly in such a manner as said she could force no such thing on him.

It startled her, given how much time had passed, that Horace was waiting for her when she emerged; though she'd thought the likelihood of further barbering slim, she had tucked a small knife into her belt. The witch's servant did not even complain of the wait, but merely returned to the stump and sat expectantly. He leaned into her hand when she rested it lightly at his temple to steady his head for the more delicate work of shearing the last of his hair away. She ventured, while she fussed at some knots that lay close against the nape of his neck, "Does Ms. Gottschalk know that you are here?"

"*No.*" He whipped around, near losing an ear after all. "No, no, don't tell her, I haven't got anything yet."

Lilly held her hands up—such a different meaning, now, than when she'd fended off the witch's ire. "I wouldn't. But would you like to sleep in the stable tonight? There's an extra blanket."

He stared at her wide-eyed a moment, lips pulling off his teeth. "I don't *like* buildings."

"I noticed. But you went in earlier."

She stood close enough to see how he lunged into movement before he became nothing but noise and dust; shaking her head to clear the thrum of his flight, she sighed and went to get a shovel. The bandits had made it very clear that dead flesh should not be left on the surface overnight lest the forest encroach on the clearing, and by the smell she suspected the shorn locks counted as such.

She knew no way to foster intimacy but to excel at what she was set to do; in three days' time, she had brought herself down with a wracking cough. It terrified her; it felt like a wet, killing thing. The bandits met this with unexpected compassion. Mr. Duerr called her a fool and Mr. Kunze cooked up a rich broth, claiming his partner had a craving for it, though it seemed the better part went to Lilly. It became unnecessary that her usual chores be done, and Mr. Duerr took to carrying the water down to bathe Ms. Gottschalk each day that Lilly greeted him with a coughing fit rather than a good morning.

Though she spent much time by the fire in the cottage with fever and heat-shivers and much sniffling—which was to say, in closer proximity than usual to the bandits—it would hardly be reasonable to sneak up to their sleeping forms only to be bent over in a coughing fit.

The care proved well enough that the illness passed through her like a traveling guest; she knew herself recovered the morning on which Mr. Duerr shoved the bucket into her hand. That she trusted his judgment in the matter worried her a little.

When she returned, he had her help build a lean-to around the tailor. With the frame constructed, he sent her to fetch a ladder from the shed—and said, cheerful, "Up you go. I'll brace it."

Lilly resigned herself and took up hammer and nails; with the former clenched under her arm and the latter shedding rust into her mouth as she held them between her lips, she took the board Mr. Duerr handed up—and spat nails as the ladder jibbed to the side. The bandit laughed, said, "I probably won't let go again."

He did; when she had laid down enough boards, she swung her leg over the top of the ladder and took up an uncertain perch atop the lean-to. She felt her chances improved now that she depended on the strength of old wood rather than the man's fickle humor. For a brief while he refused to hand up another board, but the cold convinced him to cede the point.

"Sir," she said, for he showed visible signs of impatience and she did not relish the thought of finding her way down without a stable ladder. "Will there also be a fire to tend?"

"No, this isn't for his comfort—it doesn't even kill him to get iced up. Dead things tend not to, you know? But it does slow him down. You *are* useful on occasion. It's always hell convincing Horace to help us with this, though it was better than being up on that rickety thing myself. If there is to be a broken neck, let it be someone else's."

Though she could not put a name to the expression she leveled on him, it made him laugh. He laughed the more when the sound of a bough creaking with its load of ice made her flinch and look upwards; she frowned and cut off any taunts he might have thrown about cowardice with the question, "What of the skin?"

"Look closer," Mr. Duerr said. "It's been there for decades and isn't going to fall this winter."

She shivered, but not at the realization that the skin hung without the glistening of ice on it or the branch on which it was impaled, but at the tone of the bandit's voice. Rarely did she fear them, knowing that they would not kill without reason—but here she had touched on something which she did not understand. Did he think that she angled for an opportunity to steal the thing? She looked down at him, seeing paranoia in his mad-dog stare. "I am comforted," she said, "for I would not want the witch to get hold of it before I have my freedom of this place."

His expression eased; another man might have been embarrassed. "You done? Then get down here. It's too damned cold for lingering."

The wind nipped sharp today even with the sun at high noon. Lilly knew this quite well, being for the moment in retreat to the backyard, keeping company with the automata and Mr. Nadel while she peeled potatoes. From the cottage behind her came the noise of a fight all screams, thrown objects, and foreboding silences. Mr. Kunze, she gathered, did not feel his wound justified his staying shut in while Mr. Duerr hunted down the last of the year's prey. The last of the victims. *She need be careful not to fall into their coldhearted terminology.*

Something shattered. Probably the chamber pot. If God was merciful, it was empty at the time.

Lilly slipped the last potato into the water-filled pot and hovered a while at the back door, head tilted. The noises— were no longer fighting noises. Strange men. She put the pot on the stoop and retreated. The stables were mucked, the horses curried and exercised, she'd done what little work the garden required, and she would not take on tasks without a direct request so long as the bandits' favor persisted at its current level. When she had first arrived the upkeep of the cottage and its plot of land seemed endless; now that she could do them in half the time, she found herself loafing.

Perhaps I'll make someone a good servant someday, she thought to herself, wry; *there's gentry enough by the sea who would gladly take on a hand with such diverse skills—if the hand didn't admit where he developed them.*

One task she had set aside since morning, before the storm between the partners disrupted the household; Mr. Duerr wished her to take an iron coin down to Ms. Gottschalk. Sensing some greater significance in this gesture than she wanted to be involved with, she had gone about her other duties first. Cowardice—wisdom. Pulling the coin from her coat pocket, she turned it from one face to the other, on one a scowling king and on the obverse a startled-looking eagle. Huffing a sigh, she turned her feet to the path.

The shouts sounded at first to be an echo from the cottage above, but these were too high, too clear, bell-tones human voices never could reach. Lilly ran, and in running dropped the coin. She recognized a voice beneath Ms. Gottschalk's. Nasal— terrified.

She came up short at the trail mouth. Horace cowered a yard back from Ms. Gottschalk, who stood in the richly dead gardens like a queen on her throne, and in one hand upheld some small object. Her attention shifted, bit at Lilly's face. "You've come to disappoint me, too?"

Horace's eyes flashed panic, suspicion, and she knew he would strike out at whatever came near. Swinging wide around him, slow and careful and aware equally of the threat that each represented—a dog would bite out of fear, and its master kill for sport. "Mr. Duerr sent a coin. It is lost, ma'am."

A noise tore from her that sounded as if it might rend the fragile tissues of her throat. "*Always*! Those charms against magic—always he finds them on his corpses and brings them to me. Long ago he ordered me I must take all such things. He laughs when it burns." She snarled an offhand insult at Horace, threw her head back. "Where is it?"

"I lost it, ma'am." Lilly licked her lips. "I could find it again."

"Do you mean that you *might*?"

Do not, she meant, *find it*. "It's true, ma'am, that I might not know where I dropped it."

"Horace!" Ms. Gottschalk swiveled on him. "Do you think to sneak away?"

Half-risen, he allowed himself to fall back to the ground, resigned. His eye was blacked and nose running blood; scratches clotted with filth across his cheek.

Ms. Gottschalk held up the small object—a match—as if for the inspection of all present. "What happens when you destroy the locus of a spell? *You* do not know, Horace, or you would not bring me this. Are you enlightened, Lyle?"

"I—"

She cut the words off with a sharp gesture. "Of course not. Your magic-stink is all a victim's. To destroy the locus is to free whatever is bound within—in this case, many, many angry dead men."

"The automata?" Perhaps if she was led into talking of her plans, she would not pursue Horace further. Applying logic— *who should be faulted for his ignorance, him or yourself?*— seemed apt to get herself killed, perhaps with the witch's servant close behind.

"How did you think to get past them?" Ms. Gottschalk gestured once more at her servant, who cringed. "I set him to find what would remove the obstacle of the automata, and do you see what he brings me, Lyle? A cheap and useless—"

"I know of something else. A stag. He closes ways—if he should walk through a door, it is barred against any entry. His sinews would bind the mouth of the bag, but—but he is alive."

"Then kill him."

The boy shook his head. "You haven't ever hit me."

The witch lit the match against one of her needle-nails and flung it on the ground at Horace's feet. With a howl of fright he fled, three steps and then gone. The flame burned into the dirt, though it must be damp and an ill tinder, and onwards, sinking down into the earth, a perfect circle that glowed for a long while like a well to Hell before it passed beyond sight. Not gone out—no; it had not been the sort of fire that ever stopped burning. If it had fallen on Horace himself—

"Why do you sympathize with him?" Her voice was not becalmed, but sated with violence.

Lilly felt driven beyond the point of wisdom to the sincerity that sunk into one's head and, no matter how convenient tact might be, would not be shaken free until expressed. "He is the only one here who is not cruel."

"Don't think him an innocent."

"Innocence can be cruel, ma'am. He is not that, either."

Ms. Gottschalk shook her head. "Me, cruel? Perhaps. But do not judge, for I am not under your power—*you* are under *mine*. You offered yourself knowing what I am."

Lilly bowed to that, and felt herself dismissed as the witch turned away and hobbled into her cottage. It only left to be told if she could find Horace and see to his wounds as best she could. She regretted when she could not; nor could find him for days after.

Mr. Kunze returned to the cottage with a fresh-killed doe slung over his shoulder, her belly already flayed but feet and dangling head still attached. "How's your shoulder?" Mr. Duerr asked.

"You know," Mr. Kunze replied, with one of his rare teasing smiles. As ever, it disturbed Lilly to see such a gentle expression on that rough face. "Lyle." He nodded towards the back of the cottage. "Come here. Have you ever butchered an animal?"

"No, sir." She'd not meant to be caught sight of. That morning frost crackled beneath her feet, and it had been a slick walk down to the witch's; bad enough that she slipped, bruising her hip. It would have been preferable to do some less rigorous work inside. "I'll learn, though."

"If we teach you to shoot you'll make a proper woodsman yet," he said, idle, quite as if the implications didn't occur to him.

At a young oak in the back—and Mr. Nadel not at his spindle today, but weaving—Mr. Kunze heaved the doe head-down and hung her by the ankles from a hook Lilly had wondered at these last months. He gestured for one of the automata to come from the tailor's side. "You start like this," he said, pressing against the wrist joint of the forelegs and snapping them cleanly off, tossing them into the woods. "I give them back to the forest. Pagan superstition, I suppose, and ungodly of me—but I have less trouble than Ivo, who does not thus make an offering of the offal."

Lilly nodded, most of her attention on the doe's limply open mouth, her eyes like Horace's. She shook herself. *Its* eyes. A certain amount of distance from one's dinner did not make for a bad soul.

"We don't need the hide and we certainly don't need the little money selling it would get, but I'll show you how to do it properly." From his belt he took a neatly kept knife and cut circles around the animal's ankles, down through the inside of the thigh, and with a sharp tug pulled it with a fabric-tearing noise from the muscle. White connective tissue that reminded Lilly of Ms. Gottschalk—had it looked thus when the witch disrobed from her skin?—gave little snaps as its connection broke. With small, precise movements of the knife he trimmed the hide from the neck and flung it after the hooves. He winced as he did it— Mr. Duerr had been right to ask after the shoulder.

Casual, Mr. Kunze separated head from body, and laid that aside rather than flinging it. "I'll butcher up one side, now, and you'll do the other." He handed the cuts to the automata, who moved as quick and aggressive to store them in the cellar as he must when hunting gold for his masters. Lilly recognized the meat once it had been removed from the animal, stuff for stews from the neck and the tenderloins for grilling.

If she accepted the knife gingerly when he handed it over, it was to avoid touching him, and not chariness of the blade. He watched her awhile, thumbing distractedly at his shoulder, then left her to it with the words, "Good enough. Tell the automaton to take the carcass out to the woods when you're done. Don't forget to take the thigh bones for soup."

The rhythm of the work was soothing. She felt less becalmed after she looked up to find the head gone, nothing but a patch of wet dust left; her knuckles went white on the knife and her heart beat with the urge to run for the stable loft and hide a while. Only the thought that any beast in these woods with the desire to eat her would have done so long ago let her return to her work, and even then she shifted to keep the trees in view.

There came the unmistakable crash and thumping heels of Horace's arrival, the sound of his sitting heavily against the trunk. Something in it did not sound typical of him; and, turning, she found him ill-used. Though his face was clean of dirt, the blackness in his eye sockets and yellowing on his jawline was more filthy in appearance than ever before. Dropping the knife, she bent down, asking, "Are you—?"

"Bad enough to butcher her, but must you do it with a dirty knife?" For all the defensive words, he leaned towards her as one starved of comfort. Wiggling his toes and fingers, he added, "I've got everything working fine."

The knife needed to be washed clean of blood-thickened soil, and the pause gave her time to formulate an attitude to foster towards the witch's servant. She returned to her work that the question might be more casual—and perhaps not dodged, as most were—when she asked, "Would you like a poultice?"

"The swelling's not so bad. It's just gotten into the ugly stage." He remained silent some little while. "Don't you want to know how I got it?"

"If you want to tell." Did it not look like the witch's work? Yet, glancing back, Lilly saw no sign of claw marks.

He crushed a tick on his ankle, dug out the head. "The bandits stole me, but the witch wanted me when they brought me here, and so infrequently can they please her that they gave me up. But she changes what she gets—look at you. You were not soft when you got here, but you're hard now as well as sharp. You don't trust at all."

She'd begun to cut with the grain of the meat in her distraction. Correcting for this, she said, "I trust you."

"You don't. Don't argue, I hurt. Anyway. That's what they do, is steal. They very rarely give. I suppose that they are willing to share work with you shows that Duerr and Kunze are a bit fond of their little servant." He grinned back at her surprised expression, his eyes briefly forced shut by their inflamed lids. "The last servant they shot when she misplaced the cooking things. She was completely trustworthy, some cousin of Duerr's, but they couldn't stand that variation in routine."

Lilly paused a moment to shrug off her jacket, as sweat had begun to gather on her back.

"You don't want to hear about you. Fine. You're not the introspective sort." His foot jostled hers. "Do you know how they trapped the witch?"

"I've wondered," Lilly allowed, giving a hock to the automaton.

"They found her bathing with her skin hung on a tree beside the stream, and Kunze, being a clever man, fetched it up and forced her to strike a deal." Horace sighed. "I know how these things work; if she'd agreed to one wish or three or even a dozen, they would have had to let her go, but she became frantic and promised them as much as they could ask before growing bored of riches."

"They never will."

"She has made a stricter study of humankind since then. Do you understand the tailor-corpse? I can see by your look that you don't. He's weaving them those appearance-altering coats so that they can go back to their home village. They are rich in power, death, money—and near smothering from loneliness."

The ribs were proving more troublesome than Mr. Kunze had made them out to be. "Hence . . . hence me?"

"Maybe. You're pretty charming in your creepy, stoic way." He snuffled loudly, as if his nose might have been bleeding and gotten clogged. "It's going to rain. Sleet. It never snows here."

She turned, offered him a hand. "Will you go into the stable this time? You could borrow my coat, if you like."

He tucked his arms around his knees and merely stared at her, so she shrugged and returned to her work. After enough time for pride, he rose with a grunt and tugged on the garment she had offered. It would smell like ill-kept horse, she knew, but at least he wouldn't sicken himself for no better accomplishment than proving himself stubborn.

The sun dimmed with clouds that were like mirrors to the mountains, blotting the daylight until the air was heavy as stones. The rain, when it came, was gentle at first; its spatters knocked loose the oak leaves and dropped them onto her shoulders, her bare head, and spangled Horace's sitting form like parade banners.

By the time she stripped the last of the meat from the doe, the rain had become stinging, a presage to the sleet Horace said would come. Even the automaton hunched his shoulders against *that*, and when Horace almost fell in standing, she caught him under the elbow for fear he would strike his head against the oak. It surprised her how small she found the weight of him; surprised her more when he did not tug free but leaned harder against her arm, shivering and small against her side. He was using her as a windbreak. Perhaps the cottage would be a cleverer place to wait out a storm, but that required keeping near to the bandits until it broke; she made for her own hay loft.

At any time Horace might have escaped the weather with his magic. Yet he ducked into the animal-warmth of the stable with her, keeping close. She pulled away from him and went to the corner where they kept the tack hanging, where rags used to rub down the horses were kept. They were clean enough and she'd long since resigned herself to a constant state of grubbiness, anyway. Tossing one to Horace, she pressed the cold water from her face, neck, holding her sopping shirt away from her with a deep resignation. At least this one would dry up and be fine. She was down to two shirts altogether, and not given to the hope this wardrobe would last for long given the fates of the others.

"Here," she said, "you can hang your things over the woodstove." It sat in the corner and was more given to smoke than heat, but she liked at least to make the gesture. Handing over the spare blanket, she made her own way up the ladder, shucking her trousers and pulling on her looser pair before Horace had gotten up to the loft, scrambling a bit as he struggled to keep the blanket around his shoulders. Only then did she light the lamp's wick.

He made a noise of triumph as he managed a leg up onto the loft then burrowed down into the hay as if its prickles didn't bother him at all. "You're still shy. Do you have food?"

She tossed him an apple from the provisions squirreled away in her saddlebags—she would have to leave sometime— and settled herself against the wall, bereft of pillow and bed but perfectly tired enough to tolerate a crick in her neck for some rest.

Voice low, Horace said, "You don't *have* to be over there."

"Don't I?"

"No, you really don't. No one dies at being touched, particularly when it's for practicality's sake. Who raised you? What did they *do* to you?"

She prickled, glaring at the assumption.

"Well, prove it." He rolled away, back to her. Too loud to be sincere, he added, "It must be cold over there."

Lilly strongly suspected Horace was motivated by the desire to have a warm body close by and hadn't a care for her comfort. But it *was* cold over here. Besides, she'd faulted him for stubbornness earlier; why hold herself to a lower standard?

Among the reasons to avoid sleeping beside the witch's servant with a history of undesirable behaviors was being woken by fingers pinching one's side. She grunted, elbowing him; the sleet ticked off the roof still and the bandits were doubtless pragmatic enough not to expect her presence with the weather fouled.

Horace pressed his forehead against the space between her

shoulder blades and hunched down into the straw, grumbling. "I have something to say. I got beat up."

Lilly breathed out gritty-eyed annoyance. "Yes?"

"When I went to get the Buck of Clotting." He breathed out in an echo of her sigh, his body near rattling with the hugeness of the noise. "A prince's people guard him. I managed to draw them off to the four corners of the world, but they came close enough to strike me a few times. And it took so much to carry them that far. Feel, I'm so *skinny*." He leaned hard against her back, and she could feel the knobbiness of his ribs and hipbones.

She also seriously considered elbowing him away again before sense caught up with reflex. *A child,* she reminded herself; *a child or something with a similar understanding of touching.*

"You can go far with that ability of yours?"

"Wherever I like, with whoever I like. *Normally* people I like. I refused to ever take the bandits anywhere." He shivered. "Cold. I couldn't kill him, though."

Lilly unbundled herself from her blanket and spread it out over him, as well. The fabric of the spare blanket still separated them. "Couldn't kill him?"

"The stag. The Buck of Clotting." He began to make a harsh noise, a heaving, snorting sort of sob. "Gottschalk is going to kill me. Really. I thought she would kill me before—she *meant to*. She didn't know the match would fall short."

Lilly turned over and touched his shoulder, not at all sure how to offer comfort; she did not expect the boy to lean hard against her chest, quieted, but still shaking.

He whispered, "You offered your help, once."

She sold herself often enough to recognize this as a different business. "I did."

"It's to your benefit."

"I offered my help, Horace. What do you need?"

"There's no guards left." The low light of the lantern caught in his eyes, flame reflected in the glossy blackness of them. He hadn't been crying. "You just have to kill the buck. I'll take you to him."

When she put an arm's length of distance between them, he allowed it, but his nostrils flared, eyes gone white-rimmed—like a horse afraid of a predator. "How can it be done?"

"He closes the path he walks behind him. You have to get ahead of him to hunt him—and there's the trouble. Not only is it difficult to cut off an animal on his own territory, but then there's the antlers, too. He's in velvet, at least, so in being crushed you will have the satisfaction of knowing it stung a bit for him." Horace added, hopeful, "*Still* cold."

Lilly huffed. "You have my sympathy."

"Good! I deserve it." He wiggled under her arm and settled down again. "I think you were being sarcastic but actually meant that."

His boniness did not make him a good companion to share one's pile of hay with; if she were to judge from this, the pleasure of sleepy embraces was much exaggerated. "When will you be able to take me there?"

"Tomorrow. The bandits won't have anything for you to do with this much ice on the ground, will they?"

"Ms. Gottschalk's spell . . . The tooth—"

"Trust me. Bring a gun and a knife to get his sinews." He snorted again. "I don't want to be there, but I have to be, don't I?"

Lilly settled her arm around his shoulders.

Morning and the storm's passing came at the same time—
as did knowledge of Horace's absence with her jacket. Shivering she went careful-footed across the ice-slick front yard, and
on the stoop knocked her knuckles against the door to warn of
her presence. Mr. Duerr must have stood close by, for he opened
it, looking out curiously; said, "Damnit, Lyle, we might want
you dead someday but not by freezing. Get your ass by the fire."

"Sir." She did so, bracing one foot against the hearth to dry
her trouser leg where it had draggled against the wet side of the
front trough. Tone less willing than her usual, she asked, "What
am I to do today?"

Mr. Duerr laughed. "It's that nasty out, huh? Well, there's
not much worth doing when it's iced up."

She cast a glance his way and went without comment to the
kitchen, baffled as ever that she ate from the same stock as
the bandits; she'd been acclimated to a noble household where
the servants made their own simpler dishes, things cooked
in the margins of the bread-oven or over the coals after the
main roast had been done up. Yet these were common men,
given to no life but the one in which the townsfolk were aware
of their little differences but essentially equal. She'd seen that
in her travels.

She still resented somewhat the difficulty she had with manag-
ing the toasting fork.

"We should bake bread, but you still haven't managed to
make a decent loaf." Mr. Kunze emerged from the curtained-
off bedroom nook in a silk nightshirt and with his chin freshly
shaved, which gave him a softer appearance that belied the
grey in his hair. She idly wondered if he might be in his late
forties after all, and not the decade older she'd assumed.

"He'll run through our flour before he manages that one," Mr. Duerr said, pacing restlessly before the door. It reminded her of a hound whining to be let to roam. "If we send you out doing something active enough I'm sure you won't freeze." He paused, frowning. "Why didn't you come over in that jacket, anyway?"

"Horace has it." Caught up in liberally buttering her bread— she'd never appreciated the value of thus adding fats to one's food until she spent her days occupied in manual labor—it took her a moment to register the thoughtful silence this had generated. "Sir?"

"Hey, I could catch the little ass for you and get it back." He stood balanced on the balls of his feet at the door. "If you don't hit him around once in a while he starts in on trouble again. Poking the dead man with a long stick, that sort of thing."

"No, sir. I gave it to him."

Mr. Kunze came up beside her to slice his own bread, the angry-looking skin of the still-healing wound visible as the nightshirt sagged over his shoulder. "I thought you meant that. There's a coat in the bedroom chest, tucked beneath the other things. Take that."

She'd never been in their bedroom before, and went gingerly beyond the hanging—thread of gold, stiff brocade, worth as much as the Mare—to find it a simple space, small with a medium-sized feather mattress and a washstand to the side. A bag hung from a hook to the bed's right hand; it took her a moment to realize it must be the automata's. It looked bland enough to be a magical item. The chest contained mostly summer-wear, but at its bottom was a knee-length leather coat, supple and clean and deeply stained. The sleeves bunched at her wrists, but it fit across the shoulders. Mr. Duerr's; he must have been a young man at the time—*very* young.

"Oh, that old thing," Mr. Duerr said. "Right. Now we don't have to feel guilty about sending you down the lady's way. Don't break your neck, you still have to harvest those stones for us. After that, though—eh. Rest. Hem up those sleeves."

The bandits' property held no secrets anymore, and even the shed's once unfathomable contents were well known from much shuffling. There she knew of three different guns she could choose from, and took up the one that looked best kept. It had a weight and awkwardness appropriate to a weapon but of great concern in light of the fact that she'd never shot one. She had seen the bodies of deer and pheasants shot in the hunt, but never the act of shooting. At least Horace did not stand by while she fumbled through loading it; the horses were audience enough, with even the Nag craning her rough head to see.

Horace banged in through the stable doors with a defensive hunch to his shoulders and her jacket drawn tight around him. "I had things to do."

"I'm almost ready." She indicated the gun. "I can't shoot."

He looked at her blankly.

"Not *well*. I—know the principle of the thing." She leaned it against the wall, pinched the bridge of her nose. "But—damn!" She was a fool to attempt this. "The stag will have to be very close for this to have any sort of chance."

Horace went to the Mare and pulled bits of straw from her mane while she rested her head over his shoulder.

Lilly calmed herself; the stress of this need not touch him. "How close will he let me get?"

"I can put you in front of his nose." Horace glanced over his shoulder. "But I don't want to see him get shot." After a moment, he added, "Sometimes people ask him questions about things of the past. You could do that, like a trick." Horace held out his hand to her.

"Really?" She hesitated, clasped one hand with his, thought of priests as he closed the other over hers. "But you travel so fast."

He cocked his head at her. "You don't question that I move like the wind over the water, but you *do* ask why I can take you with even though we're only holding hands?"

"You have to draw the line somewhere." She tried to settle her breathing. "Or you'll believe anything a fool tells you."

"The fools are normally right. It's the scholars you have to look out for."

And he dragged her across forests, mountains, a place all glass and the halls of a castle and the silent mossy depths of a cemetery in which she saw only angels in tears. Heaving breaths like the winner of a race, he halted them a moment in a forest with somber time heavier than any sunlight could reach through, head tilted. The snow was heavy, the branches bare. When she would have drawn away, he clasped her arm under his elbow and dragged her deeper into that wood.

Nowhere did she see openings but for where he slipped them underneath the thorns of brambles and between the twigs of vast trees, and pausing them in an open stream, panting again, he gave her time to say, "This isn't a hunter's wood."

"It's the stag's." He cast her a troubled look. "He hears them

coming before they come within shot of him. Before that the
guards used to deal with them." He caught her hand again,
squeezed it. "I'll forgive you, you know. I don't think you'll
forgive yourself."

Once more they cast out, and came to stand on a log, solid
underfoot and new fallen, its roots thrust up towards the sky
like the hands of a beggar to heaven. Horace let her go, then,
and faded back into the undergrowth. This puzzled her until
she heard the strange, heavy-footed sound of trees moving aside.
She rested the gun across her shoulder, squaring her shoulders,
thinking, *He will talk and I must not waver.*

That which emerged from the woods could not be described
by the standards of a normal deer, nor anything but such myth-
ical beings to which class Octavius and Gottschalk and the troll
all belonged: as if this were closer to some ancient time when
man and beast were as one, and on his back he carried the first
human beings and taught them secret ways. He had the compassion in his eye for that, and the sadness. He flicked his ears
forward and eyed the gun on her shoulder with deep distrust.

She held her empty hand wide. "Please, it's not for you. I
must protect myself. I have a question, Stag."

The animal dipped his heavy head, great shoulders shifting.
"And what question do you come with?" He did not have a human's voice, but something of the tree creaking and something
of the ground shifting beneath one's feet.

And she could not bring herself to lower the gun. "You see
the past."

He seemed to smile at the inanity of that. She thought of
stripping the flesh from the doe. This life would take the will
to eat meat out of her if she stayed too long with it.

"I—" She couldn't lie to him. Slow, as if he would not startle, she shifted the gun down from her shoulder.

"Human," said the stag, "girl, why did you really come here?" The roots raised up to protect his chest and throat. Then he gave a trembling, mournful laugh. "Oh, I *see*. Selfish thing. Your past is a tangle."

Lilly stared down at the lowered gun in her hands then back up at him.

"You would do thus for my body?" His ears flipped back, forward, and the foliage peeled open behind him as he backed away. "Your attempt, at least, is not so earnest." The boughs began to close over him.

Horace struck the animal on the haunch, thus avoiding the flash of the stag's heels. This, however intelligent, was a prey animal still, and so the stag leapt over his own shield of vegetation. *Magnificent creature,* Lilly thought, and fired.

The stag's head jerked, blood spattering the snow; but he raised his face a moment later, nostrils dilated, no harm done but for a single split tine, its rich velvet torn. Lilly scrambled backwards, gripping the gun like a club, as the animal pawed the ground. She felt Horace's hands catch her hand in the moment before the world wrenched and they both came down on their knees in the yard of the bandits' cottage perhaps a yard from the tailor's guards. The ice had gone to mud in their absence; Lilly straightened, shaking off her hands, and asked, "Are you all right?"

Horace rocked back onto his heels, wheezing softly. "You're light. It's fine. I stopped in the wrong—" He flailed to his feet with a harsh, wordless noise, heels kicking up mud as he backed away.

Lilly let her elbow be taken by the automaton, wincing as her shoulder protested being pulled so roughly; from her other hand he took the gun, and she thought this must be the cause of his interest. Though that impassive face would not have communicated his intent either way, nothing of his gestures indicated aggression; whether they were ordered generally to disarm rather than murder trespassers or if the bandits' injunction not to kill her specifically had come into effect, she didn't know nor particularly care.

She cared more for why he offered his own weapon in turn. "Huh," she said, not her most intelligent commentary, and glancing over her shoulder to meet Horace's still-wide eyes, she accepted the weapon before the automaton took offense—or whatever might have happened should she have turned him down.

Horace came to stand with her between him and the automata, peering around her shoulder at them. "So you're a woman."

She fumbled the rifle, cringing as she caught it far too close to the trigger.

"S'fine." He jostled her shoulder. "Duerr told you about the deal, right? He probably told you the wrong wording. They said *make us the only men who our infinite men will listen to* or whatever, and Gottschalk—being, you know, a *witch*—took them at their word. So the automata listen to all women. Quite better than they do to the bandits."

Lilly cleared her throat, tried to find a way to say, *How could you think that when you have seen me shirtless?* The automaton cleaned the rifle he had taken from her and set it over his shoulder, taking up his place again. "Could you get one of them to the stag's trail?"

"Going to have one of them do your hunting for you?" Horace leaned against her. "I'm really glad we're alive. And, yes."

"Not my hunting, no. More like my dirty work. He *speaks*." And how different from Octavius was this person she meant to kill? She shook herself. "I'll ask—"

"If this were a fairy story," he said, "then the stag would offer to let himself be killed for his sinews, and when you took him up on the offer, he would emerge from the skin a beautiful, thankful prince. I never really understood that kind of story—if you know self-sacrifice will save you, why not do it earlier?—but it would be a lot more pleasant than this." He touched her shoulder. "Thanks for feeling bad."

She shrugged away his hand, not capable of the emotional energy it took to humor his need of contact. "Could you get him there today?"

The witch's servant heaved a sigh. "Yes. Make sure to tell him he needs to collect the sinews, too."

"Horace?" She pulled him into a hug, feeling awkward but knowing he would appreciate the gesture. "Ms. Gottschalk should know that you did all of this at great cost to yourself."

"Okay," he whispered. "I'm not sure it'll make a difference, but at least you won't get any credit. You were a little bit useless."

Drawing away, she turned and told the automaton his task. He held out his hands for Horace to take, and they were gone.

The next morning Ms. Gottschalk met her with the sinews of the deer dangling from her hands. "Horace has come through for us at last." The servant so named leaned against the cottage wall beside the door, expression closed. "Now we come to your part in this play."

Lilly dipped her head. "How am I to serve?" She felt cold; though there was no snow here, it was yet more bitter.

"See that the bandits are most horribly drunk—bring up their lonesomeness, or their deity, or their home. I see it in your eyes—I see by how you are never alone with him—that you are wary of Ivo. Smart, smart boy. Use that: make him look at you. That will rile them both, and Ivo will drink to distance himself, and Ignatz will to pretend he doesn't see his partner's jealousy. Such things will tear their hearts, and they will drown the wounds to heal them. Take your time—catch them at a vulnerable moment. Then, when they are abed and snoring, cut from each a hank of hair."

Lilly balked, remembering countless warnings against giving a magical creature the clippings of one's body. Shaking aside this reflex, she said, "Yes, ma'am."

"I would have Horace do it," she said, tone fond, and turned to rest her hand on his hollowed cheek. "He's done so well. But you still have that little problem with human habitations, don't you? And I'll not panic you today."

Quivering, he leaned back from her touch. Ms. Gottschalk looked briefly surprised, then shrugged.

"Will it kill them?" Lilly had that surprise swung to her. "Your spell, Ms. Gottschalk. Is it meant to kill?"

"No. I would not give you the satisfaction which is rightfully mine. It will make them slumber deeply so that you might go about your business. I will have you put it in the porridge some morning soon and we will at last conclude our deal."

"Soon," Lilly repeated, with an unexpected, quiet distress; and realized: *I am used to this life.* She shook herself. "I didn't expect that until spring."

"We work together better than I thought." She laughed. "You know, I thought I would kill you. When I first met you, and a dozen times after. But something stayed my hand. It must have been an awareness of fate. You, of all my ploys and servants and attempts to appease those bastards, will at last be the one to free me."

There came an ice storm, fist-sized hail and tree branches falling and no means for her to get from the cottage—where she'd been caught out when these clouds rolled down from the mountain— back to the stable. It had been early afternoon, then, and she blessed the fact that she'd already seen to the horses. Though they would doubtless grow restive at this change in routine, none of them had such bad habits as flipping their water buckets, which might lead to more serious troubles.

It did not occur to her that this would be an opportunity to intoxicate the bandits until she saw how Mr. Duerr paced, caged in his own home; with many a complaint about how much he detested the task, he suffered to settle by the fire—on the footstool which Mr. Kunze propped his feet on, as it happened—to patch torn clothing and darn socks. He went so far as to notice that her coat sleeves were merely rolled back rather than truly tailored, and saying, "You must have been spoiled stupid before you got here," he showed her how to sew. This struck her as the oddest event in her life thus far, watching those callused hands delicately loop thread through cloth, the scar on his cheek twisting as he squinted in concentration.

She tucked herself out of the way and made a clumsy attempt at imitating his skill, mucking up one sleeve terribly so that she had to pull out the threads and start again, and meanwhile the bandit paced once more. Mr. Kunze rarely stirred from the armchair by the fire where he read, but his eyes flicked to his partner whenever Mr. Duerr made some noise in rummaging through drawers or fussing in the kitchen. It took her some time to recognize those looks as concern. Evening came on slow, unknown; the sky would not tell the time even should they be fools enough to open the shutters and squint up through the hail.

The clock in the corner let out its cuckoo to sing the time, and thus they knew that dinner should be on. Though not hungry herself—after many days of work, one of rest left her with a strange, empty, energetic feeling—Lilly had been tasked with making meals and stood on reflex; Mr. Duerr waved her down with an aggressive motion of the hand and went into the kitchen himself.

Soon the cottage filled with the smell of venison and the radiant warmth of the stove; she shivered with it, made aware that it was not enough to make the room comfortable for one sitting back from the fire as she did. Though hesitant to cross Mr. Kunze, she nonetheless came forward to encourage the flames. Only then did she see that he read not any book, but the Bible. The worry lines in his face were sharply defined by the light—by the reflection of the words in the page.

He caught her looking. "Do you consider yourself a man of God?"

"I consider myself a man, sir, and leave God to Himself." She flinched from the way his stare hardened. "I do not presume to understand what I do not study."

He settled back, expression gone more thoughtful than angered. "And can you read?"

"Yes, sir." She stared, startled, at the Bible offered to her.

"It's not much to study," he said, and for all his fearsome moments, she had not before heard his voice so implacable.

"I would not take the holy book from you." This weak assertion broke upon his standing, pressing the volume into her hands. "Sir, I—"

"There are several copies here." He gestured at the case of books.

Mr. Duerr came in from the kitchen wiping grease from his hands, curious perhaps of the unusual amount of conversation; Lilly normally limited herself to monosyllables. Catching sight of the Bible, he grinned, a little rueful. "He's fobbing that off on you, too? Christ, the *genealogies,* what a bore. I do like David, though." He winked at his partner's scowl and turned back to the kitchen. There was no real happiness in his movement, just nerves.

Supper passed as did the rest of the day: short of words, nerves, companionship. Mr. Kunze took an unusually soft attitude towards his partner, and Mr. Duerr responded sharply. She would never get a better opportunity than this, she thought, and yet knew better than to speak while they ate. After she cleaned the dishes, she came back in with the tea things—the brandy bottle beside the honey pot. She cocked an eyebrow at the bandits.

Mr. Duerr laughed. "Wonderful boy. It's a brandy kind of night."

As she swung the kettle on, the bandits settled in their favored spots, a pair of thoroughly scuffed old chairs with the padding many times replaced and redoubled, their feet both propped on one hassock.

Lilly had no intention of flirting with Mr. Kunze, having little trust in the witch's understanding of how the man would react—*that* Ms. Gottschalk could not know of him—instead she asked, as she basked with her face towards the comfort of the fire's heat, "Do you never get visitors?"

Silence came for a long while. Mr. Duerr asked, deprecating, "Does that seem likely?"

"Horace tells me there is only ever ice in the winter." She fed the fire a few twigs, critical of the flame.

"*That's* pertinent." Scoffing, still.

"We are company enough." Mr. Kunze was quieter.

And here she could cross a line, and knew that the witch would never have given warning if one existed. "Ms. Gottschalk tells me the tailor's task is to make coats that change the appearance of those who wear them." She swung out the kettle and poured water into her teacup; dark and honeyed heavily, it would with luck make her alert enough to avoid any serious faux pas. "Is it to improve your banditry?"

"Aren't we chatty tonight." Yes: there the danger.

She gave the most genuine answer she would ever proffer to the bandits: "I do not wish to go back into the cold."

Mr. Duerr laughed. "Finally we found what could break our stoic servant! Not sores nor cleaning the outhouse nor the witch's death threats could do it, but a little ice on the ground and he comes shivering in front of our fire."

Stiff, she said, "I'm from the coast, sir. There is cold there—wet cold. It's not this nipping nose-bleeding thing."

"Why, you asked." Mr. Kunze cradled his cup—full of more alcohol than tea, in truth. "It does not suit us to have so much in gold and money and yet nowhere to spend it. We imagined ourselves as living in luxury by the time we reached our middle age, when we were young men and yet fools."

"This place is our home," Mr. Duerr put in, and as Lilly shifted to feel the warmth on her back, he met her eyes with an earnest expression most unlike him. "But sometimes you want amenities more than you want memories. I rode into the old place, once—the town where I was a child. Where we met." He nodded at Mr. Kunze, smile passing over his face; reached for the brandy. "Well. Well, it looks so nice. I couldn't burn it down like I'd meant to."

Mr. Kunze sighed. "Which turned out for the best."

"Right, right. You see, when we have the coats we can escape recognition, so we can go home. It would've been terrible, settling down someplace that was completely unfamiliar." Something tense, uncertain, crossed Mr. Duerr's face. "You know, I've only ever lived in two houses—the one in that village where I was born, all dirt floor and thatch roof, and this one." He shrugged this off. "Well, we're going to buy a damned fine house when nobody can recognize us as the most notorious bandits on the inside of the kingdom's borders."

"Why—"

"Lyle." Mr. Kunze tilted his glass, watching the fire in it, perhaps. "Stop asking questions and I'll ignore the fact that you're here."

"Sir," she agreed, and settled back, savoring the smell of pine and roast venison, the tea held between her hands.

The bandits turned to other matters, but their conversation remained uneasy; she could trace the level of alcohol blurring their judgment by how emotional they became about their exploits, triumphs and failures alike, tallying the year's bounties and failures. There were more of the latter than she expected; it seemed the automata were not so reliable as the bandits played at, which explained the lack of their presence around the house. Mr. Duerr went so far to grumble, three glasses into the evening, "You wouldn't have been hurt if those godforsaken things were better made. Or should I say better ordered?" He laughed, mocking himself. "You can't blame a craftsman for an ill-made request."

Not long after it became clear that their drunkenness had hit an unpleasant level of stupor; Mr. Kunze pushed to his feet and gestured for his partner to follow. "To your loft, Lyle." His words slurred over each other, a sloppiness somehow embarrassing to hear from him. Always before he'd been self-possessed after imbibing liquor.

"Sir." She hesitated; she'd not meant to ask this of him, but— "Might I stay the night here?"

"Is it so cold in the hay loft?" Mr. Duerr snorted. "You've had no problem with it so far and I'm not sure I care if you do."

Fighting to keep her tone dignified, she replied, "Sir, I am afraid of falling in the dark."

He rattled a sick-sounding chuckle. "We're learning all about you tonight, boy. You can be scared after all."

"Stay," Mr. Kunze said, "and have breakfast ready for us tomorrow morning. Then you'll be chipping ice off of the eaves. The automata will help with that, but they can't be trusted with the most delicate work."

"My muscles thank you," Mr. Duerr said, saluting vaguely, and staggered to the bedroom, hanging briefly on the curtain as he lost his balance. That left it swayed partway open.

She returned the tea things to the kitchen and fetched the

sewing scissors, so lately discovered and most convenient, given she'd thought to use the same knife as she'd worked at Horace's hair with. She padded back to the fire and took up the Bible with the thought that it would help her keep awake to read some of the more engrossing parts of the Old Testament; the sound of a laugh cut off with a noise she had no name for left her blushing. She scrambled in a rather undignified manner back to the kitchen, where she blessed the storm for its raucousness on the roof tiles.

Weighing the Bible in her hand, she turned to the Book of Samuel. It had conflict enough to keep a soul awake in the reading of it, though she doubted a priest would approve her purposing the good book in such a manner.

Through politicking and foreskin-gathering and prophesying the hail turned to heavy rain; she read, *Jonathan said, Far be it from thee: for if I knew certainly that evil were determined—*

And was interrupted by the sound of a resonant snore; the weather had let up enough for her to hear noise from the other room. Setting aside the Bible, she stood grimacing from her bent position and crept through the cottage to the curtain of the sleeping niche. She thought of mice, of thieves, and found herself feeling no more proud of the second comparison than the first. Pushing it aside, with care that the firelight should not fall on their faces, her progress was briefly arrested by the sight of them. Their clothes were scattered on the floor, though she wouldn't have known them to be naked otherwise, for the blankets were thick. Mr. Duerr slept with his head on his partner's shoulder, hand over his heart. No—over his shoulder, where the wound was, as if protecting it.

She thought, irrational: *my parents always slept in separate beds;* and blinked away whatever emotion wanted to mist her eyes. It might've been anger as much as sadness.

She went slowly up to the bed, felt a fool as she realized she held her tongue between her teeth in concentration. Drawing in a breath, she held it deep as her fluttering stomach would allow and bent forward, taking from Mr. Kunze a clump of hair that lay against the pillow, and from Mr. Duerr a lock that rested across his forehead. The latter sneezed, and she stood poised, feeling the sort of terror that she could only recall from such times as when she'd nearly slipped from one of the seaside cliffs, and Octavius was not close enough to lend help in saving her.

The bandit settled; she withdrew.

Why should you loathe yourself for this act? Perhaps she should have been reading about Samson. She tied the hair with kitchen twine and put away the scissors, stopping herself in the last moment from slamming the drawer. The air of the cottage clotted in her throat. What claim could she have for leaving when she insisted on staying the night? Perhaps: I heard something from the horses. Yes.

Horace met her at the stable doors, glancing at the basket of variously preserved vegetables that she'd brought with her, and catching sight of her hands—scuffed from a fall in the icy yard—the witch's servant gave an incoherent grunt of annoyance and dragged her into the stable, to the stove-side stool. "You'll let all the warm out," he said. "Also, you look like a corpse that's seen a ghost." Then he used the ointment for the horse's hurts on her palms, careful to rinse out all the dirt first. Not until her hands were wrapped in bandages did she realize that his unselfconscious use of touch had been a comfort.

"I have the hair," she said, aimless. "And—damn. I left the Bible open on a counter."

"Have you slept?" He said it around a carrot—he'd been happy for the food once he tended to her—and had to repeat himself twice before she understood.

She shrugged. "I had to—"

He pointed with the half-eaten carrot up towards the hay loft. "Go on. Me and the horses will keep watch."

"I apologize. The horses—"

It took a single glance at Mr. Kunze's face for her to close her mouth against further words and to slip into the kitchen to get the risen bread dough into the oven. It was obvious from the fact that the bandit was up and about and miserable-faced to know that the alcohol was letting itself be known. It was not until she waited for Mr. Duerr in the kitchen to learn what he planned for the morning's breakfast and the time stretched too long for him to be taking a trip to the outhouse did she realize that his companion's mood had nothing to do with headaches and nausea.

The bread was nearly done. She edged out of the kitchen; said, "What—"

"Tea. Tea and toast, boy. I can't bear the smell of eggs this morning." He settled into a chair—Mr. Duerr's favorite. "I saw the Bible open."

"Yes, sir." She cleared her throat. "I never have read much of the older—"

He stopped her mouth with a glance. "Those are not the most illuminating passages of scripture."

She nodded agreement and mumbled something about the loaf burning. It was, in fact, perfectly done. Amidst the great stress in the house, she felt proud of that. Now: how to get past Mr. Kunze without being slopped with the man's emotional bile. Ms. Gottschalk would be awaiting her water and the locks of hair.

"Lyle."

She turned at the door, expression stiff.

"Ivo thinks you are afraid sometimes. He laughs at it. I don't. I see that you are careful, wise—a barn cat sort of soul." He heaved out a breath. "Leave the ice be and come in from whatever your business is when you disappear for hours. You will talk with me."

She stood in the face of these words and thought of Ms. Gottschalk's sly suggestions: that lonesomeness did these men harm. "Is Mr. Duerr all right, sir?"

"Oh, he's merely a madman." He said it with a tone of hurt long scarred over. "He won't stay still for two whole days, and he doesn't trust that I'm well." The man's lips drew back in disgust. "I *would* be with him—but sometimes, when you are asked to do something, your reaction is more important than the request itself. He worries that he has no—" he hesitated "—influence over me. So he asks me to stay here, and I stay. Do you understand?"

The man spoke of power; the bandits' relationship did not seem so knotted with it as had her parents', but she did indeed understand. "The witch, sir."

He waved her away. "Yes, yes, attend to the witch. I'll not see you gutted today."

———

*"The hair!" The witch grinned and shook her lithe form in a dance
more elegant than any snake-sway or cat-leap, more graceful than
the slow movement of clouds or the sun passing through the leaves.
"It won't be long, boy. It won't be long at all." She caught up Lilly's face and kissed her forehead, the press of muscle and bared
teeth. She paused. "Girl. I should have known—you ordered one
of the automata to kill that deer, didn't you?"*

Lilly stiffened. "It was Horace's work."

"Yes, yes, protect him if you will. I see you two bonding."
Ms. Gottschalk tilted her head. "He is *mine*."

"I am not—"

Ms. Gottschalk shook her head, hair rippling with the motion. "Don't be a fool. I know. It is my business to know the
heart of things and I see yours."

"Ma'am." Lilly stepped back on the excuse of half a bow,
flustered. Hoping that she might cut short the time she spent
with the witch, she said, "Ma'am, Mr. Kunze is restless today."

"So? Come bathe me. You'll have to wait until the water
heats."

Reasonable: as they spoke a scrim of ice had formed on the
top of the water in its bucket. She would have to find a better
coat for Horace, and decent pants and shoes if she could get
him to wear them; though he'd largely taken up the stable as a
new home, she'd not have him lose toes to the frost.

By the time Ms. Gottschalk felt sufficiently clean—Lilly
suspected it was the hot water on her cold-inflamed joints that
she really wanted—it was near time for the midday meal and
her stomach was rumbling pathetically. In truth she'd seen
that the back meadow had been sheltered from the storm and
heated by the sun, and thus meant to take the horses to it be-

fore facing Mr. Kunze and his reflections on love, but she had learned from her illness not to push her body beyond its limit. Besides, it would require she deal with the Nag, a task she detested. It involved being nipped too often and walking the animal in circles to calm her more than once in the short space between stable and meadow.

When she arrived at the cottage she was left to eat in peace—that being something of an inviolable law of the house—but as she turned to leave, Mr. Kunze asked, "How do you find the good book?"

"An occupation, sir." She turned stiffly.

"It was mine, once." A priest—yes. She'd known that when they first met.

All the same, it would have been well never to have the knowledge confirmed. "The horses—"

"I will accept that I don't frighten you more than that skinless bitch, but I rank above the horses, do I not?" He leaned back in his chair. "Come talk with me, Lyle. You have been odd lately—distant. You have always been reserved and wary, but I could see that this life held your attention. Not so anymore. Are you so eager for spring? Are you planning to run—even knowing the witch will catch and kill you, if you try? Or are you considering that myself and Ivo might not be your best bet?"

You are not, she thought, and said: "Sir, I have always saddened in the winter."

"Prove to me that you are no danger to us." He pointed to the other chair, and when she still hesitated, he snapped, "I'm lonely and worried. Did you need to hear the shame of it?"

She came forward at last. "I feared to acknowledge what you would not have me know."

"Lying or tongue-twisting." He flashed a feral, teeth-bared expression, the sort of thing a person might wear while he shot his fellow man.

"Honesty." She settled, one hand resting on her stomach as she willed the food there to settle. Mr. Duerr's favored chair stank of him; she sat awkwardly in it.

Mr. Kunze reached over and took up a glass from the side table. She hadn't noticed the whiskey, but now she could see it in his eye shine—and in the fact that he would admit weakness. On reflex she took the glass he gave her, but could not stand the stink. Nikolaus had been slave to such things. "I do not drink, sir."

"You will. Tell me something of yourself. We know your name, that you come from the coast, that you do not complain at work though you know none of it. But what more?" He waited through her coughing fit. "You never *have* indulged."

"Wine." The roughness of her voice made it sound darker, more masculine than she had become accustomed to, and she shivered. "Never spirits."

"Your voice is ugly with it. Fine. For conversation I will resign myself to speaking." He knocked back the rest of his own liquor, poured another. "What will you hear?"

Such a dangerous proposition. She knew already how he viewed love; to learn of his life, his view of the world. She wished him to be a stranger that she might not mourn at his death. "How do you come to banditry, sir?"

"I, or we? Ivo by poverty—he's the seventh son of a seventh son and never could get work. A self-fulfilling prophecy, he was called lazy for it, and he accepted the label because it meant he could lounge at the riverside and rest for long whiles on the church pews, staring at the depictions of the Savior's life on the walls." His gaze softened, looking at the past. "I met him there."

Damnit all, she thought, *that didn't work in the least to make him seem less a man and more a monster.* "How old was he, sir, that the townsfolk tolerated such behavior?"

"Seventeen, I suppose. Sixteen, maybe." The look he cast her admitted no wrong. "I met him there, and seeing an intelligence in his eye—a cruelty, but an intelligence—I taught him how to read. How, truly, to *feel,* as no one had before allowed him." He met her gaze. "The townsfolk would have lynched us upon our inevitable exposure."

"You worry for him." She knew; it shocked her at every turn. Always she thought of sodomites as sexual but not romantic; such a thing as rats that would couple with no consideration and part as soon as the act was done. This eagles' devotion— "It's a cruel world."

"Yes. Humans are a cruel race." His smile hooked to the side, showing yellowed molars, a blank space far in the back where a tooth had been pulled. By Mr. Duerr, she assumed; jealous of their bodies, the bandits avoided even the medical care of outsiders. "It is their nature—and we are among them, no worse or better."

She bent her head in submission to the idea, though not in agreement.

"But you asked how we came to banditry. Criminals already, when we found the witch—what could we do but bind her? But she cannot make materials from nothing, being an alchemist of sorts and not a pagan god. Thus she could not *create*

the riches we craved, but only give us the tools to gather them."
His eyes slid shut, remembering. "We did not know to order
her not to harm us, at first. The scars on Ivo . . ."

Awkward in the pause, Lilly offered, "She, too, is human."

"Yes, and more genuine than most." He looked up at her.
"Your voice clears. Have another glass. Why do you seek prof-
its? I've seen no greed in you, or else you would have dug up
the gold in the Nag's stall long ago. She would allow you, for
she lets you lead her."

"My father is an honest merchant if a terrible man. I feel it's
a family tradition." She brought her hand up to her mouth,
pressing, unsure how to speak a lie that she would be able to
hold to, to act on. Mr. Kunze was too intelligent and sharp-
eyed for something far-fetched. "I seek a means to pay for the
release of a loved one from bondage."

He laughed, a rare, roaring noise. "Oh! I almost like you,
but I cannot imagine the soul but such as ours that could see
past that mark on your face."

He had meant not *like* but *lust after,* hadn't he? Lilly could
recognize the tone.

"Isn't it always a woman. Poor boy—she'll leave you soon as
there's a better suitor, a prettier one. You'll have monies a while,
but that's never enough."

She bit her lip against laughter, surprised, thinking of Octavius in a skirt and bonnet, powder smeared across that bulbous
head. He would not need jewels; the sleek oil brightness of him
and the gold of his eyes would be decoration enough. A snicker
escaped her, and she was forced to say, "You misapprehend, sir.
He is a friend—a very dear friend." She met him raised eyebrows for raised eyebrows. "What cause do I have to be coy?

Sir, you still have not said why you chose banditry over any other profession."

"Nor do I mean to. Theorize if you will; you're smart enough to figure it out." He gestured to her untouched drink. "Don't waste that."

She looked down at it, more mournful than loathing; truth be told, neither the taste nor the burn of it disagreed with her, but on principle it was abhorrent. "As you will. But then I must see to the horses—the Nag, who you claim loves me, will surely sour if I let her stand in a dirty stall. Besides, she fusses if prevented from prancing around the meadow's edge."

"Showing off," he said, shaking his head. "She started life as a desert horse with a teacup face and a flagging tail. The witch demanded her, and we do try to please the creature, once in a while. She gave us back that—thing. I almost believe the Nag would let you ride her—you should. You *will*, because it suits me, though we've never tried but that first day, when she was whole, beautiful, spirited."

Lilly, with a flush of bravado, managed the whiskey in two more swallows, wincing as she did, and set aside the glass. "I am not sure I wanted to know any of this, sir. Do you insist I saddle her?"

"Oh, I didn't say she would accept the saddle." He grinned at her. "I have said: we are cruel. I know you think Ivo worse than me. But it would soothe so many worries if she threw you." Then, shocking, he winked. "But—no, I take back my words. I don't insist on any of it. If you think dying is your best option, do that *after* you have seen to the day's chores."

———

Lilly eyed the Nag, who wore nothing but a sagging headstall and looked too crippled for a rider, no matter how easily she moved. Mr. Kunze might well be seeking to kill her, Lilly thought. A ploy that would be too obvious to work, surely, if it didn't strike at something inflamed within her. Pride, maybe. Dignity. Fishing the woody base of a carrot from her pocket—and another, when the Mare demanded the first—she approached the Nag from the proper side, holding out the treat. There was too much teeth in the way the horse took the vegetable, but she allowed Lilly at her side with only a pricking-forward of the ears and a glance back.

The two of them had arrived at a détente when Mr. Duerr, learning that Lilly was strong enough to hold up the horse's legs, ordered that she tend to their hooves. Seizing the Nag's mane and placing a hand on her back hadn't been part of that acclimation; she snorted, arching her neck.

Well. This was *so stupid*, and Lilly didn't give a damn. Too long had others threatened her with a death outside her control; she seized at a brush with mortality all her own.

She murmured soft nothings so that the horse would know where she was, mindful of the Nag's own language: one ear cocked back to listen, but posture still loose. Lilly mounted smoothly, arms and thighs grown strong enough to do so; her calves pressed tight against the horse's rib-ridged flanks. The Nag's back was precisely as uncomfortable as it appeared, and she felt a flash of gratitude for her blank loins.

Under her the horse jibbed, shaking her headstall as if she thought it might have become bridle and reins without her noticing. Lilly glanced towards the other horses and found the Mare staring intently at the scene, nostrils flared, head down.

Then the Nag gathered herself back on her haunches, warning enough for Lilly to tangle her fingers in her mane.

The animal's smooth-footed canter around the edge of the pasture was not quite what Lilly expected. Twice the animal's stride hitched, back straining to straighten, and then fell again into the comfortable stride. Her neck, so slender for that heavy head, arched as best as it could, and her tail flagged proudly. Lilly ran her hand across the animal's shoulders.

The Nag promptly surged onto her hind limbs. In the moment of falling, the thought that this had been quite an elegant movement occupied Lilly's mind. Then she struck the ground, air gasping from her lungs, back flaring with pain—but nothing broken. She'd fallen worse the night before when she slipped on the ice, for here she'd come down in a moldering pile of leaves and damp earth. Stirred by the Mare lipping at her ear, Lilly stood; in the midst of shaking rotting plant matter from her clothing, the Nag demanded another carrot of her.

Triumphant, mournful, Lilly patted the creature's nose and moved on.

When she returned to the cottage, Mr. Kunze saw the dirt on her coat when she hung it by the fire to dry. Raising his eyebrow, he said, "You didn't even hit your head, hm? Well, that means you can cook." He ran a critical eye over her hands. "After you wash up. I don't like horse hair in my meat." There was a strange humor in his voice; drunkenness alone couldn't account for it. She should have kept their conversation impersonal.

Crossing the cottage to the kitchen, she leaned forward, listening; that was not the sound of sleet, but of dripping ice. Sweat slithered down her neck, stimulated by the stove heat and the lingering fear-pleasure of riding the Nag. Glancing back over her shoulder—as if Mr. Kunze were coherent enough to protest—she opened the shutters just wide enough for a slither of cool air to touch her face. It was a beautiful day, crisp-clear and cold but not bitter. The autumn here had not been so pleasant.

In the near distance hooves sounded, accompanied by the clockwork tramp of the automata. Mr. Duerr returning; good. It would keep Mr. Kunze occupied.

She rinsed her face and hands in the basin set aside for that purpose—quickly pulled the shutter closed after, shivering as cool water dripped across her eyes and cheeks—and went to the doorway of the kitchen to ask the bandit if he wished anything that required slow cooking to be put on for the evening meal. The hooves were audible from here, too, coming fast up the garden path. That was odd—normally the bandits went around to the stable while the automata stashed the bounty for later sorting. If the horses were ridden up the main path, their hooves churned the packed dirt to mud.

The door was flung open, shuddering, and the bandit came through, but before him staggered a girl—a young woman, small—her dress torn, dark hair muddied, face tear-streaked and stark with her staring black eyes.

Shock held her still; shame scalded her cheeks. She looked to Mr. Kunze—surely he would object?—and felt no more proud for it. Surely she did not have such loyalty to these men that she would condone the abduction of a woman—but then, how many had they killed before, out of her sight and thus pushed to the side? Why did she mourn the Buck of Clotting and not those uncounted dead?

She gathered other thoughts to muffle her reaction to *this, now.* Her shock broke with Mr. Kunze's voice. "A hostage? What a strange season for one."

"They knew the secret routes—money-lenders! But I caught this one and delivered a note by automaton to let them know where they should wait to trade her for their money."

When the woman turned as to run, he casually caught her shoulder and shoved her down to her hands and knees. In her familiarization with the bandits' foibles, Lilly had forgotten her first impression of them: immovable, undefeated. She had felt Ignatz's blood between her fingers and seen Ivo staggering drunk, since then; had seen them curled together, sleeping. Even so—how could she forget?

"Our servant has a problem!" Mr. Duerr grinned, a jackal caricature of his face, the excitement sexual in the manner of stories used to warn girls away from sailors. "Or are you bothered in some other way? Should we let *you* deal with her, Lyle?"

Never before had something brought to her face such an unbridled expression of disgust. It must not have suited her, for the woman looked up at that time and promptly cringed, turning her face away from Lilly's with her eyes narrowed to unseeing. Of course: the birthmark. It had been so long, in the company of rough men and a skinless witch and whatever one could call Horace, that she had let its significance slip her mind.

"No response, Lyle?"

No: she thought of this place as *home.*

"Really, I'm going to take this as a *yes* if you don't say *no* soon. I knew you got along with us for some reason, and here we are with a revelation, a—"

"Don't bait him." Mr. Kunze pushed himself from the chair with the slightest of wavering. "Lock her in the stable." He made no response as his partner casually kicked their prisoner in the stomach when she tried to rise. "Where will you stay tonight, Lyle? Will you go down to the witch's, perhaps, or hide here in our cottage?"

"I will sleep in my usual place, sir." Pride spoke for her.

Mr. Duerr grunted with surprise. "Well, well. Maybe we should keep you around, after all."

"Or will you attempt to free her?" Mr. Kunze stepped across to the captive, seizing her arm to lift her to her feet. "I would feel personally obligated to hunt you down and kill you."

"I'm not a playing chip," the woman insisted, and flinched when Mr. Duerr stepped close to her.

Lilly stepped towards the fire, thinking of the pokers. "I have been your servant long enough that you should be able to predict my behavior, sir."

"Here!" Mr. Duerr caught up the woman—she looked so *small* next to him—and shoved her into Lilly's arms. For a moment there came the resigned thought-sensation that they would both tumble back into the fire and be given an agony of flesh to match the pain of fear that twisted the girl's face and knotted Lilly's stomach. Not so: her body new-built by labor felt unfamiliar when the girl's weight did not move her. Reflex made her catch at the girl's arms when she stumbled; so close, she recognized that fury, not fear, lit the face turned up to her.

Mr. Kunze gave his partner a displeased look, but to Lilly said, "Follow me."

The woman checked her expression—sickening, Lilly thought of a dog worried that it would be beaten—and went along meekly towards the door when Lilly turned her to it.

Outside, the evening was still beautiful.

The eyebolts of the empty stall were designed to take the chain of manacles. The woman struck Lilly clumsily in the side, bruising her elbow worse than Lilly's ribs. Mr. Kunze took the hostage then and bound her; the manacle key—so innocuous an item!—made a noise loud as a musket shot when it turned in the lock.

He caught Lilly's shoulder as he left, leaning in as if he might say something, but he left without a word, the stable doors thumping closed behind him. She would have preferred a threat, something to give shape to her inchoate horror.

Lilly turned away from the girl, though to have such a hateful gaze on her back dragged at the will to do so. At the foot of the ladder to the loft she looked up into Horace's face, his eyes curious and expression unalarmed. Skin crawling, she went to the rag pile and found one clean, wetted it, and stopping again at the base of the ladder said, "My blanket, Horace, if you please."

Catching it when he threw it down, she went again towards the hostage, imagining with discomfort how frightening the sound of her boots on the boards must be. Yet the girl met her eyes; she did not cry any longer.

Miss, I'm only complicit, Lilly thought, and fought down a grimace. Crouching, she offered the wetted rag in one hand and the blanket in the other. "I'll get you water, too. And—would you like—?"

"I would like to be set free." Her voice was brittle, but she snatched up the rag, roughly scrubbing at the worst of the grime on her face. "Failing that, I'll know who you are before . . ." Again, that defiant stare.

Lilly shook her head. "Before nothing."

"I'd still know who you are." She dropped the rag to the side with a wet slap.

Though names seemed besides the point, she was not given to refusing what requests the girl had. "Lyle."

"Lyle . . . ?" She yanked, restive, at one of the chains.

"Nothing more. Of nothing and no-one's son." She shrugged. That would prove simpler than saying, *Lilly Rosa, daughter of Nikolaus, lately made an androgyne.*

"Nothing—that's the only answer you have to give. I should have known." With a rough gesture she pushed the shawl from her shoulders, throwing the sopping thing against the side of the stall. "Well, Lyle—let me tell you this: I am—"

"I don't—" Lilly cut herself short. She hadn't the right to escape knowledge.

"I am Judith Meier and I will see the law take your head, if ever I get free. Your ugliness and name paired will be infamous, hunted, bounty-stuck. Yours and those—those—"

"Would you like their names, as well?" That won Judith's glare, though she'd not meant to be cruel. Lilly pushed herself to her feet, making of it a backwards movement. Judith flinched. "I won't offer an apology, Miss Meier—cannot. I have no sway over them."

"Then why do you live?" Again she moved against her chains; she would make raw meat of her wrists doing so. "Everyone knows that the bandits here are ruthless, rabid."

"I allied myself to their witch and with her support offered them something that they cannot get elsewhere." Judith looked hopeful, and Lilly meant to say, *wealth*. But that had never been true; Mr. Duerr liked things that glimmered, but Mr. Kunze would not have tolerated her so long for more of that which he had in useless abundance. "Companionship."

"Then I could . . ." Judith shook her head. "No, not that. But the witch—" She gave a bitter laugh. "No, I see by your face. If *you* detest her so, she must be a wretched creature."

"Not wretched—feral. And she has been a slave—" Lilly stopped herself. "You don't care about any of this."

"No. I—" Her voice broke at last, and she turned her face away to weep.

Lilly shifted her weight, glancing towards the doors. Even if the bandit listened with his ear to the crack, he would not be able to hear a whisper; and she knew Horace would not betray her. Leaning forward, voice low, she said, "I will strive to get you some advantage, though I can't help you directly. But you must give me time. Tomorrow they will plan to ransom you—and they will not—"

"No one survives them. We were so certain we had found a safe route—we paid good money for our guide. Who is dead, now. That monster recognized her and shot her, first. She screamed at the—the others, the doppelgängers. And what shall my family do, now?" In a flash of anger, she flung the blanket, though it made a most ineffective projectile. In respect of the girl's dignity, Lilly did not offer it back quite yet. "I thought you would violate me. Why must you abuse my mind instead of my body? The time and aid you promise will only delay the inevitable."

"*Listen.*" Lilly flinched at her own frustration; softer, said, "Your group is armed, yes? And if given a fair fight rather than an ambush—might they prevail?" She smiled, humorless, at the fierce and offended look that won her. "Of course. If you free yourself before the ambush is sprung and warn them—do you see?"

Judith held up her manacled wrists.

No promises, she told herself. "I will strive to get the key."

Horace peeked over the wall between the captive's stall and the Mare's, which stood beside it. "You're being damned stupid, Lyle. Again."

Judith sneered. "Another bandit's accomplice?"

"No, the witch's. He is innocent—sort of." Lilly shrugged at him. To Horace, she said, "Come, now. You should be used to it. Did I not help you?"

"Yes, but that's *me*." He flung up his hands, not understanding. "It's cold in the loft."

"Sodomites," Judith muttered.

Lilly offered back the blanket, unsurprised when the girl took it, practicality dominating pride. She thought, *If there were not other lives that depend on me,* but smothered the words. What comfort would they be to Judith?

In the long dark hours before dawn, Lilly sat cross-legged beside Hor-ace's sleeping form, the curve of his back firmly pressed against one of her thighs. The sound of the girl's sobbing splintered her thoughts; often through the night she would think, He has gained a little weight, *as if she need grasp after all evidence of her own goodness.*

The familiar swing of the stable door jolted her; Horace grunted and rolled away from her, settled again. Dawn being far off for any regular purpose, her mind went to the terrible possibilities. This could be Judith's people—they *could* have tracked her—in which case Lilly should not go down on risk of being shot. Or—more likely—Mr. Duerr intended to set aside his usual preferences. Quiet on bare feet, she went down the ladder, touched the Nag's forehead to hush her, and wide-eyed in the dark relieved only by the low glow of the lantern wick turned to its smallest flame, she padded towards Judith's stall.

Backlit herself, a darkness against the dark was not obvious until she had run up against a wide chest. She had expected some noise of footsteps, breathing, *anything*, to warn her, but shock did not muffle her violent response; she twisted away, far better able to strike with her elbows than she once had been but, crippled by relative size and disorientation, she found herself caught up and shoved into the tack room where the light was brightest, the walls clear of protective horses, two of which might well have taken offense to the cause of panic-sweat on her skin.

She wanted the strength of the Mare or Nag. She wanted not to be pinned against the wall, Mr. Kunze's face too close to hers, his breath hot and acrid and alcohol-smelling still. "I knew you would respond," he muttered, and pressed forwards to keep her from kneeing him, as she'd attempted. "I knew you couldn't resist the temptation of playing compassionate to a victim. Don't yell." His hand came up to her throat, and she gagged on the memory of the bruises it would leave as much as the pressure itself. "If you yell I swear I will kill you and Horace and this girl all."

When she could, she hissed, "You don't want Ivo to know?" That got her head shoved back, his hand up against her chin, the back of her skull ground against the wall.

But her hands were free; she clawed at his arms, thrashing as much as she could, neck muscles straining as she sought the opportunity to bite.

"I know that you are a woman." That stilled her a moment; he pressed his whiskey-wet mouth to her ear. "I've seen how the automata act towards you. That first night—that blanket they gave you—a man would never get that treatment. Horace squealed on you, did you know? Ivo grabbed him up that day, kept him from flitting away, and made him tell everything he knew about you. We wanted to make certain you weren't the witch's creature. What he said wasn't much but *I hate him I hate him,* but he told us about the automata failing to kill you when he dragged you into their circle." His fingers scrabbled at the front of her shirt, popping the top button, and he made a low, feral noise as she began to struggle again. "Do you think I will debase myself with your body? No, no, you've lied, you've goddamn gone around this place with gentle hands and passive face and subservience, and I've thought— I've thought— That's the way that young men act, isn't it? Young men who love—"

"It's not like that. You're not making any sense." Another button gone, and his hand on her chest. "Hell," she whispered, and it hurt, not a bodily hurt but one of betrayal. "Get away from me." She would not say *please.* She would not. He stayed there, hand pressed between where her breasts would be; she broke. "Please, sir."

He kicked her feet wide; she must have made too loud a noise, for his hand came over her face.

In the scuffle that followed, she caught the thong of the necklace he wore the keys on; tore it from him. If she did not die of this, she would have some payment. His hands were on her belt, forced her trousers down her hips; then he paused with thigh pressed against her crotch. She made a rough, hic-cupping noise, and bit, grinding the flesh of his hand between her teeth until he ripped it from her. She spat, snarled, "Are you satisfied, then?"

He backed away then, leaving her to sag against the wall; but when she would have bolted, he caught her arm, his face working through a series of expressions—disgust, fascination as his gaze traveled down her body, a strange sick look. All through this Lilly stood, panting but straight-backed, unable to wrench free; yet his grip only tightened, and the pain—

Ignatz said, "I won't tell Ivo."

Lilly spat to the side again, unable to tolerate the taste of grease and bile and dirt in her mouth. A moment later she wished she'd spat on him.

"What's *happening*?" Judith called, panicked.

A moment later Lilly and the bandit both jolted at a high, strange noise, something like a stallion's fury but so much weaker. From the direction of the ladder Horace flung himself forwards, expression all lips off teeth and wild eyes. He landed two, three blows, at which Ignatz but grunted—and knowing Horace's great strength, Lilly found a mind-blanking kind of terror at the thought that he did no more, but merely struck the witch's servant across the face, knocking him down. Rough—he had no right to sound as if he had been crying—the man said, "I'm done here. Done. This will be gone by morning."

Lilly watched him retreat, shaking with the thought that

she should *do* something; flinched hard as Horace came up on her left side and buried his face against her shoulder. Blushing hotly, she did up her trousers. Yet there was not disgust nor even curiosity on Horace's face, just a white-eyed anger still, and in his touch concern. It felt no more invasive than the Mare's nose on her shoulder would have.

Judith called out again, though her words did not register in Lilly's mind.

"He'll kill you for this," Horace whispered. "I can take you from here. The witch's power ends at the boundary of this place—that's why I could rip you from it. Let me take you."

"I need the tailor," she replied. "I cannot have come this far without doing what I meant to." She ran her tongue against her bloodied lip, wondering when *that* had happened. "I trust the witch to—"

His voice quavered. "Do you intend, still, to take her skin to her?"

"Of course. She's done no wrong to me. Well—nothing much." Lilly bent to fetch up the keys. Then she went around Horace to lean against the stall door behind which the woman's manacled form could be faintly seen in the dark, crouched, small. "You needn't fear, now. I have the manacle key. Tomorrow—you will not be able to both hide it and have easy access to it, will you? There are no pockets on that dress." She closed her eyes, thinking.

Judith said, "He hurt you," shocked.

"We are not a family, but masters and a servant." Servants. Not Horace, who would be strange to see and perhaps shot for his trouble; but— "The automata will do as you bid them, as I bid them. I will give one of them a key and order that he free you when you ask him to, that there's a double weight behind the command."

"But how will the bandit not notice the key missing?" That was a practical tone, calmed.

"There's another I can replace it with." Lilly shook herself, and went to get the well key that she might make the switch.

"I pity you," Judith called after her.

Lilly paused, foot on the bottom rung of the loft ladder. Had she been forgiven? Did it *matter*? Afraid of the answer, she held her tongue.

She met Ignatz with the well key and the one for the tailor strung on the thong, expression blanked. She held in her hand one thing that she sought, but they would get it soon enough, her and the witch. Mr. Duerr looked perplexed; asked, "How'd you get that?" Two automata shuffled past him towards the tack.

"The leather must have worn through." Ignatz hitched up a shoulder, casting his eyes to the side in guilt—for *this*, of all things, a small lie. His partner didn't notice, already leaned over the door to the captive's stall, grinning.

"Ready to look all ravished and pathetic for your people?" He ran an eye over the proud tilt of her head, the way she struggled to her feet. "Well, well. Looks like Lyle didn't take interest. I'm glad almost—wouldn't want to worry about *my* virtue, what with how often I'm all drunk and vulnerable around him, would I?" Laughing, he unhooked the chain from the eyebolt and dragged her to her feet by the chain. He gestured to one of the automata, saying, "Load her up on my horse when you have the lot saddled."

As she was led past, Lilly's eye was met by Judith's level stare, and with a shiver she thought, *This woman will not forget my face.* She saw in that expression more than loathing, now: pity, hope, that peculiar dislike of the indebted. If God proved kind, they would not meet again.

Ignatz murmured, "Do you mean it as a gesture of loyalty?"

"And why should I need to make such a thing?" She tried for dignity as she walked away from him, but she did not want to be alone with the man, and already Mr. Duerr was swaggering through the door. When she ducked out the door a step behind him, she got a surprised glance for her haste.

Several automata were occupied collecting shovels and sacks from the shed; Lilly glanced over her shoulder to ensure that she was out of sight, then seized the wrist of the one nearest to her, bringing up his hand. "I need you to take this key and give it to that girl, Judith, when she asks it of you." She gave it into his waiting palm, relieved that he took it; she took it as a matter of fact that this was the only sign of comprehension he would give. The automata were the least unnerving of the creatures she dealt with. "The bandits mustn't know."

The sound of their going held her in place; so long as they were within earshot, the option remained to throw aside her quest, her friend, and free this girl. Judith.

In the silence, she fetched the witch's well water.

She shattered the full water pitcher in the kitchen at the sound of a man's broken scream from the path up from the woods. With hands braced on the edge of the sink, she thought, I wonder if Ms. Gottschalk would punish me for one of them dying under a hand other than hers? *She scrambled out of the kitchen, pausing once to brush a sliver of glass from her heel; she forgot about the sting when she got to the doorway and saw—all of it. A dozen of the automata milled in the garden, one with a head gaping open on the whorled tissue of brain matter; on the path, perhaps half as many straggled towards the cottage's door.*

Two of them carried Ignatz in a sling improvised from one of the horse's saddle blankets.

Lilly scrambled out of the way, thinking, *I owe thanks to Miss Meier,* and: *I have never known someone who died before.* The man pressed a blood-soaked rag to his side, but that seemed reflex rather than awareness; his head lolled to the side, gaze wandering. He brought with him the stench of bowels; she recognized it from a buck that Mr. Duerr had shot in the gut.

Mr. Duerr ripped aside the curtain of the bedroom nook, gesturing the automata to lay down their master. They did so with the gentleness of machines, careful, not flinching when he moaned. "Out," Mr. Duerr snarled at them, then: "Not you, Lyle. I need human help. God help me. *Shit.* Get over here."

She did, steps stuttering when she saw how the blood made a rivulet down Ignatz's side. His chest still labored with breath, but that seemed more cruel than hopeful. Mr. Duerr caught her by the arm and dragged her forwards, shoved her to her knees beside the small bed, seized her hands. When he pressed them against the rag, she understood; played her part.

"Keep pressure like that—such small hands!" He touched the side of his partner's face, leaving a streak of blood. "You stay here, too. Please, please. I'm getting the witch. She'll fix you up." He ran, then; slipped and fell on the gore that dribbled onto the floor, but was as quickly up and away.

Something soft shifted beneath the pressure of her hands; an organ, she guessed, unmoored. She whispered, "I'm sorry that it ended like this."

He shuddered, eyes fluttering open.

"Mr. Duerr said: stay here. The witch will heal you." One proffered comfort to the dead who did not yet know of their end; decency required it. She considered removing her hands from the wound. Bleeding out would be a better death than the rot and belly-bloating that would follow such an opened abdomen, and something disgusting and wormlike in her heart said, *Why should you not let him die?* But this was not a choice of life and death as it had been to ride the Nag; a man stared at her with pain, glossed eyes, mouth working soundlessly.

She leaned closer; he whispered, "You gave me the wrong key. The girl got the other."

"I'm sorry," she said back; a lie, that. "Did she escape?"

He gurgled, eyes rolling back a moment. "Yes. Yes, damnit and done this." When he laughed she felt the shorn muscles of his stomach twitch. "Avenge me?"

Lilly remained silent.

His hand moved to grasp her wrist, wet and sticky. "See that I'm buried in consecrated ground." After a while his grip failed.

It took him another ten minutes to stop breathing, and some of those exhalations contained words. He spoke of God and Ivo and love and hate, but none of it coherent. She spoke back with the soothing half-words one used on hurt children and spooked horses.

For some time after his soul had gone to whatever place God felt fit for it, she kept her hands pressed to the body. Then she dropped the sodden rag and tugged open the collar of his shirt; the keys rested glossy-wet on his breast. Gently she slipped the leather thong over the man's head. Would it have been better to steal them while he yet lived, rather than to make herself a robber of a corpse? Foolishness. She stood, looked down at the gore that coated her to the elbows, and went to wash in the basin; around her neck she hung the keys.

She still stood with hands braced on the edge of the basin when Mr. Duerr came back; he dragged the witch with him, mindless of her stumbling, crippled feet.

Lilly met his shocked stare and broke down into senseless tears; knowing what that meant, the bandit still dragged Ms. Gottschalk into the bedroom nook. They spoke briefly, too low or too grief-clogged for Lilly to understand; she pressed the heels of her hands against her eyes and tried to make sense of her own reaction. She'd thought of killing this man—she had always meant to, for it was the inevitable conclusion of the witch's triumph.

She scrambled from the cottage when the sound of Mr. Duerr's sobs wracked the air. All so quick; the keys hung heavy from her throat.

Ms. Gottschalk effected an unnatural thaw; Mr. Duerr dug the grave in the still-hard soil himself, but he fetched Lilly to help lower the corpse into the ground. They lowered the shrouded body with dignity via a pallet and a pair of ropes, but no care could hide the fact that the worms and beetles would have free access to the putrefying flesh. When they stood for a long while in the cutting wind, Lilly volunteered herself to shovel in the dirt; Mr. Duerr answered with a nod and stepped away, far enough that he could not see his lover being covered with dirt.

When done at last, Lilly leaned against the shovel. Tired in body and soul, she could but stare at the mound of earth, though she wondered if she should have flowers or words to lay on the grave. *You were a killer and a bastard and I do not mourn your death, but I know that you were not a monster.*

"Did he say anything?"

While Mr. Duerr had cleaned and wrapped in linen the corpse of his lover, Lilly had made her decision with regards to the dead man's last request. She tugged the shovel's point from the soil. "He said he always loved you."

"I knew it would be that," Ivo said, fond and hurting. Then: "This was a stupid accident, you know? It's always stupid how a man dies. For the girl to appeal to the automata—" He grunted, like a man elbowed in the gut. Lilly recognized the noise from her struggle with Mr. Kunze. "Maybe—look at me, would you?" He reached out and turned her by the shoulder. It occurred to her, then, that he hadn't a cut or bruise or broken bone to show for the fight that killed his partner. "This isn't a job for one person, you know." He spat to the side, stared dull-eyed into a dark for which the sun had no remedy. "Though a partner's more work, and there won't be someone else who's—what he was." His voice faltered, shoulders gone taut, frightened of the implications.

"Oh," Lilly said, thinking, *You awful, lonely man.* "I am your servant, sir, until spring."

"And nothing more, you mean? You can dig up your damned stones and we'll never say another word about it." He gave a rough squeeze to her shoulder, bared his teeth. "We won't ever say one way or another if it was all a ruse to buy time."

It had been so long since the last mention of the blood-stones that she did not comprehend his meaning for three beats, four. "My blood-brother is enslaved. I must go to him."

Mr. Duerr rasped a laugh out between his teeth and turned his face away, hand falling. "So you want to play the savior, do you, all good intentions and desperate measures? Add a pinch of regret and you'd make one hell of a bandit, boy."

"Sir. The witch needs help back to her cottage." Her voice sounded wooden and low in her own ear.

"Yes, yes." He looked vaguely around, now. "I—I'm not fit company, anyhow." It probably meant *I am ashamed to be seen grieving.* *That* attitude Lilly knew from her father, in those drunken days after Anna's departure. She left him to it.

Ms. Gottschalk, after she spat on the soil—*crude spell,* she called it, grimacing—had staggered back into the cottage. Lilly expected to find her seated, perhaps tending to her feet; if asked, she would not have guessed that the witch would choose the soiled bed as her perch. Her swollen feet rested in a puddle of Ignatz's blood. Lilly asked, "Do you wish to return to your cottage?"

"Would you gag if I lay myself down on the floor and ran my tongue through this gore, looking for his warmth?" The muscles in her face gave erratic, unreadable twitches. "If I danced over his dead body, would you stop me?" The mockery in her tone bespoke frustration.

But not, Lilly thought, with *her*; the witch felt robbed of a killing rightfully hers. "Shall I help you to the grave?"

"You will regret the stoniness of your heart." Ms. Gottschalk held out her hand. "Come here."

Lilly stepped over her own bloody footprints, sure that the witch would not dispose of her; indeed it was with but a little prick of claws that Ms. Gottschalk seized on her arm and unsteadily came to her feet. Seeing how the strands of the witch's muscles contracted in pain, Lilly offered, "I could carry you, ma'am."

"My dignity," she replied stiffly, then laughed. "The rain has washed away my breasts and the softness of my cheek and my skin has flapped from that oak for these thirty years. You must wonder: *What dignity?*"

"I would never question it."

"Then carry me, boy." The witch touched the lapel of Lilly's coat. "But all the blood on me will ruin your shirt."

"The creek will clean it, ma'am." It was an awkward motion to get one arm under the witch's knees and the other across her shoulders, and worse still when Ms. Gottschalk pressed her damp arm around Lilly's neck, but—as ever—the woman was a weight no more than feathers. They were silent awhile, going out of the cottage and to the forest path. Once on that dark and rooted way, Lilly said, "Ma'am, I apologize. You made yourself clear with regards to the bandits' deaths."

"I know that this surprised you—even if you made it possible." Ms. Gottschalk's hand squeezed the back of her neck—a threat, or affection? "I would be more upset if you had slit his throat yourself. I do wonder, though, if it would have come to that. You nursed a new hatred this morning, and did not mourn when the stink of his death filled your lungs."

"No, ma'am. If she mourned, it was for the fragile stability this place has given her, which would now end." As she glanced down to negotiate a tricky slope, she saw how the witch's feet curled in towards each other, swollen, torn. "I will tend to your wounds, ma'am."

This time the hand at the back of her neck sent a clear message, claws scraping harsh enough to leave marks. "You are being solicitous to me."

She was. "I have conceived a new sympathy, Ms. Gottschalk. I apologize—I know you do not need it." Then, with an inelegant noise from far back in her clogged nose, added, "Besides, my lot is cast with you beyond all doubt, is it not?"

She was not sulking, quite, but she also was not doing anything, sitting on a rock out of sight of the cottage and holding her coat tight around her. The morning light was strong and she had not yet gone to the witch.

Horace made his loud-stepping way through the trees. His shadow fell across her, and after a hesitation he shoved a hunk of cheese stuffed into bread clumsily into her hand. Thereafter he settled with his back to hers and nibbled on a wizened turnip with less than his usual verve. "Eat," said the boy, "you'll be busy soon."

She looked at the food with stomach gurgling, at once upset and starved. Low, she asked, "Might you do me a favor, Horace?"

He leaned harder, but their strength was no longer so disparate that it moved her. "Sure."

"You agree so quickly? Hear it first."

He laughed. "If you feel the need to protect me from myself, sure."

"When I have gotten Mr. Nadel onto the Mare's back, might you lead her to the road? Then, if nightfall is close and I have not come, take them to the town up the mountain? There is a woman who lives there, Miss Reiniger, who will greet him gladly and make a coat in return—tell her that you come from Lyle . . . Lyle who is dead. She will give the thing to you. Then bring that coat to the manor of the dark-wife, to Ermentrud— I don't need to give you directions, do I? There pass on the coat to Mr. Alt, the circus master. *He* will give you a kraken, who must be returned to the ocean."

"A kraken," Horace repeated.

"A small one." She cleared her throat into that ringing silence. "And very friendly."

"That . . ." Horace gave a disbelieving laugh. "That is a long and strange favor, Lyle. And stupidly complicated besides—you say you are a merchant's child and yet you make *very* poor deals, though I suppose I can't say much about the worth of a small, friendly kraken." He heaved a sigh. "Try not to die. I don't really want to do it, but I'd feel obligated if you did. Gottschalk sent me to get you. She said not to bother with the water."

"Ah." They went together to the mouth of the path, but he stopped there and said he would wait for her to return.

Smoke with the scent of burning hair billowed from the door. Lilly ducked under the worst of it and went in, calling into the stinging gloom, "Ma'am?"

There came a low purr of words that her ears refused to understand, and the smoke fled as before the strong North wind.

In the square of light from the door stood the witch, bending over not a cauldron as tradition would have it; less traditional, a set of glass items that looked to be a scientist's were at hand, as well. She bent to watch moisture beading in the neck of a retort, eyes bright with a feverish greed.

"I spent my night separating Ivo's hairs from Ignatz's, but the sleeping drought is close to done, and today you might do your work." The witch drained off the liquid into a vial; frowned slightly.

Slightly. Since when could she interpret the skinless woman's milder expressions? Shaking the thought away, Lilly asked, "Is there something wrong, ma'am?"

"Oh, you have a fine sense for that—over fine. They call that paranoia, you know." The witch straightened, skimming her hair back over her shoulders. "You could have given me a bit more hair. Or I might have tired of sorting and left some with the dead man's." She rolled her shoulders in a dismissive shrug. "This will give you—*some* time."

"Some?" But the witch only turned away. Fifteen minutes— would that be a reasonable amount to plan for? It would have to be; she couldn't accomplish this in less.

The witch turned and tossed the sinews into her hands, adding more gently the heavy needle that would be needed to bore sufficient holes for them to be threaded. "I suggest you bind the men first, of all things, and take the bag with you. Wouldn't want them to come to Ivo's defense, would we?"

Lilly held them in her hand, then stuffed them into a pocket of the coat with the hope that Ms. Gottschalk had not seen the shaking of her fingers. "Can I not order them to stand aside?"

"When they boil from their bag to protect their home and long-time master, will you able to tell each of the thousand of them, *No, wait, I have orders for you*? Or—knowing you—*May I ask something of you?*" With a flourish, Ms. Gottschalk stopped up the vial and handed it over. "Don't delay. Go now."

There was a film of the witch's bodily secretions on the glass. Soon, Lilly knew from days when she arrived too late at the cottage, the witch would be gleaming wet with it, strands of the exuded substance hanging like saliva, her hair tangling against her body. She said, soft, "As you wish."

The path seemed long today—or her step more hesitant. Horace met her raucously when she emerged from the path, loud-footed and nervous, catching at her arm. She held him away, saying, "Can you saddle the Mare? Yes? Please do."

In her pockets she had the vial, the sinew and needle, work gloves. Everything else she owned was in the saddlebags of the Mare, as it had ever been.

The night before, Ivo had dragged the mattress into the yard; the forest animals—if they were animals—had come out and torn it, strewing blood-soaked ticking across the winter-sleeping garden.

Ivo slept curled in his partner's armchair, neck cricked, snores loud with lingering alcohol. The floor was clean, though in the corner there stood a blood-soaked mop and bucket of reddened water. Lilly took these out, first, then returned to put on the kettle, careful that it did not squeak. If the whiskey on the sideboard was the bottle she thought it, then it had been full the night before and was no longer. They had taught her the curative for hangovers before the first frost, claiming both that it would do her good someday.

You could almost call it kindness, magicking to sleep a man the morning after that much drink.

With a moan he woke when the kettle whistled; hands pressed to his temples, he rolled a red-eyed glare at Lilly. She murmured apologies, poured the cup—terrible, stinking thing, but sworn to be of help. With the addition of the witch's sleeping drought, it certainly put him out of pain.

"Oh, that's nice." He coughed, spat to the side. "But I thought I would go with the hair of the dog that bit me." He reached over, wincing as he turned his neck, to seize up the whiskey bottle; scowled when he found it empty.

"I'm afraid the dog is hairless, sir." She placed the cup next to his hand.

"If I thought you meant that less than seriously, I could be offended." He threw back a swallow of the curative, grimacing. "You know, the lady gave us this recipe. Sometimes I think— think—?" He gave her a blurred look, the muscles of his face fallen lax. "This isn't right." He reached out as if to strangle her, but she stepped out of range, and when he struggled to rise from his chair, his legs buckled. "*Still* her recipe, but a new one. God damn you. You—you're the witch's after all, aren't—?" With that, he slumped over, and she had to catch his shoulders to keep him from falling to the floor. The cup shattered, its content streaming across the floor. That meant he hadn't gotten even the minimal dose that Ms. Gottschalk brewed.

Fifteen minutes. Into the sleeping chamber she went, gagging on the scent of blood still on the air. The bag hung outside her reach—even Ivo would have to stretch his arm at full length to take it down. She stepped up onto the bed frame, shuddering when her boot peeled away from the dried blood she had unknowingly put her foot into. The memory of her hands against Ignatz's side, the first time—the last—dizzied her, made her grasp on the bag clumsily. It came down with a screech of the nail that held it; she fumbled the well-oiled leather, spilled it onto the floor. Its mouth gaped as if taking a great draft of the air, then the rest distended in bubbling motions. She half-fell from the frame, clumsy with panic.

Lilly brought her heel down on the fingers that were wriggling free of the bag's mouth, then dropped down to stop it with her knee. She fought to get the proper angle to drive the needle through the leather, but fell as a leg kicked through the too-small opening and caught her in the thigh. The thinness of the boot heel made the blow no less painful, and she escaped a vicious kick that would have caught her in the chin only by flinging herself back.

Six arms burst forth from the bag mouth, pinched at their base as small as her wrist and flaring out to the broad, stubby-fingered hands, the joints as yet flexible as Octavius' tentacles. "*Stop!*" Lilly shouted at them, and scrambled to her knees while those hands paused, fingers flexing against the floor. They began to emerge not with the writhing eagerness before, but a jerking motion—pushed from behind by their fellows.

She, thinking, *I do not hold it against you*, used the needle to pin down the largest arm, choking off the automata's ability to wriggle free—for the moment.

The sound of the front door crashing in twisted her insides, but when she started around, it was not the witch grown impatient or Ignatz's vengeful ghost—no. There stood Horace, every feature from his quivering legs to the whites of his eyes akin to a spooked horse, and his mouth forcing out the question, "What can I do?"

What could he? "Help me."

He gave her a distressed look and went loping towards the kitchen: to go out the back, perhaps? Would he lose his nerve so fast?

No. He returned with the cleaver.

She jerked this from his hand, feeling the wrack of muscles pulling against bone all through her body, revulsion at herself as she brought it down on the joints of the wrist, the elbows. Just like butchering a deer, in its way. The wounded arms whipped back into the bag—to heal, she hoped, in that stupid altruistic attitude she took towards these things—and when she'd got down to dismembering fingers that tried to crawl from the bag mouth, Horace finally got the sense to stomp down hard on the neck of it. It bulged behind this dam, and he said, "I'm strong, but only *so* strong."

She flung the cleaver aside and pulled tight the bag mouth with the sinews. It made her sick to think this, too, was a skill the bandits had taught her. They had not taught her well enough; as the bag writhed, her attempts to stitch it closed failed, the tendons loosening with each bulge of the bag mouth.

Horace caught her shoulder, tore the needle from her hand. "I told the Mare to wait until you had the tailor on her, and then where to go."

"What?" In an echo of their first meeting, he shoved her back, sending her sprawling, and with a grin, snatched up the bag and disappeared.

If it were self-sacrifice—

She couldn't think of it, not now. He had done this for her and to waste the gift would be a rebounding failure.

Ivo still sprawled slack jawed in the chair.

The Mare waited, neck arched, feet planted, playing at war horse, and though her ears swiveled and nostrils flared, she did not move away from the rankness of blood on Lilly's skin. Catching up the animal's reins, she led them around back.

The tailor's wheel sat silent, and the man himself had his clubbed foot braced on the ground, the withered one drawn up onto his stool. Beside him lay the great pile of thread he had pulled from his own body, and in the lanterns of his eyes dwelt an expectation. Around him lay three tangled, warped bodies: his guards, disconnected from their bag and thus destroyed. Horace must still be traveling in his swift-footed way. The Mare danced over them, snorting.

The key would not go into the lock. Spitting out a desperate blasphemy, Lilly stopped a moment, stilling when a papery hand rested on her head. She looked up at Mr. Nadel and determined that this was a very sweet gesture and one she never wanted repeated. Ducking away from him, she managed to force the key despite the rust and tossed the opened manacle aside. "Shall I help you up to the horse, sir?"

Creaky, that head shook.

"I will bring the Mare up broadside, sir, so that you can mount—no?" She looked at his snapping fingers, how he opened them as if to drop something onto the material piled beside him. *Oh.*

"Sir—" and she lost words. "Miss Reiniger has promised me—"

Again the snapped fingers, the gesture.

The thread had been coerced from him and doubtless he feared its misuse. Nonetheless, what of her? What of her quest? And when had greed so ruled her? "Sir, I wouldn't see you damaged." From her pocket she fished up a long match meant for lighting tinder in the fireplace, showed it to him. "I will light the threads, but shall I help you into the saddle first?"

At his nod she clicked her tongue at the Mare until the animal consented to stand parallel to the spinning wheel. The horse was alert but serene with a trust in her rider beyond what Lilly held for herself. The corpse's stump braced against her shoulder and his good arm wound in her elbow, she led him to the horse's side; then making a stirrup of her hands, she heaved him up into the saddle. He caught up a handful of mane, swaying, skin fluttering strangely over the opening that was his gut. Again he pointed to the pile of thread.

Some day I'll die for my respect of others, she thought, and striking the match flung it down, stepping far back from the conflagration that filled the air with roasting meat stink. Behind her Mr. Nadel made a crooning, pleased noise, mouth gaping, teeth and blackness and no tongue.

Catching the stirrup, she asked, "How well did you ride? I cannot come. The horse will take you where you need to go, though, and she is responsive. I don't doubt she will walk the road."

The tailor gestured her away, then knotted his fingers in the horse's mane, mismatched legs bowed tight around her ribs.

"God willing, I'll meet you there. Press your heels to her side and she'll go forward; shift your weight back and she'll stop. She's dressage-trained."

The Mare leapt forwards, away, and on her back the corpse cried out in unshaped words of encouragement.

Lilly tugged on her work gloves and scrambled up the side of the lean-to, slipping once on the ice; that put her within reach of the oak's lowest branch. When she first arrived in the bandits' forest, it would have been beyond her to fully extend her arms, haul herself up until her chest was level with the branch, and then fling a leg over. Not easy, now, but doable; from that solid bough, she could easily reach the one above. Even through the gloves she could feel the rough, scouring bark, and strange things wriggled away from her hands: the witch's hatred had put a malevolence in this tree.

The next bough hung too high for her hands to reach; puffing, she grasped the trunk and scrambled, grasped the crook of the branch as one foothold gave out, hauled herself up again, sat a moment. Her chest and shoulders ached; by the time she touched earth again, that would become the acid-hot pain of overwork. Not often given to pride, it surprised her to feel that emotion flowing into her chest with her next deep breath. Not without gain of her own would she leave this place.

As she reached again, the branch broke beneath her with a wet, moaning noise, and only her lunge for the trunk saved her. Down she slipped a yard, and the rough bark tore first her glove and then her hand, and the grubs she had noticed in the trunk, freed from rotting wood, were slippery on her ankles and wriggling into her boots. She kicked once, freeing her pant leg of the disgusting things, and after a cringing moment discovered that they did not bite. Or that they bit and anesthetized the wounds simultaneously. If the latter were the case, she should gather one up to nip her palm. She wasted a few minutes pressed against the trunk, cradling her injured hand against her chest, before she could summon the coordination to shift the opposite glove onto it—awkward but necessary—and begin her climb again.

The higher she ascended the more the oak moaned beneath her, and though she'd been neutral to religion all her life, she would have prayed then if it didn't seem inappropriate for a task done for a witch.

The next branch bowed most horribly, and she tensed; there was a heaviness on it, and twisting her neck, she saw her goal before her eyes: an unfleshed face, pearl white where not pomegranate red. The eyeless lids stared at her. Cognizant? The hands—hooked with black claws; those needles on Ms. Gottschalk's hands were not needles at all, but hardened quicks—swayed towards her, knocking against her shoulder without a wind to move them. They caught in her coat—would have dug into skin. She said, "I am *helping* you on your body's request," and the skin hung quiescent. One of those arms twined snakelike around hers as she jerked the skin from the skewering branch.

Its bloody side *burned*. Flipping up her collar to protect her neck, she dropped it over her shoulder, grunting at the weight, and began her descent. The oak no longer groaned.

She stumbled when she reached the ground, rubbing at her pectoral muscles, her cramping calves. Yet she had done this thing, and now had only to transport the skin and all would be—

She came around the cottage and met the bandit in the doorway. She scrambled back from him, but she needn't have; Mr. Duerr moved jerkily with both hands braced on the doorjamb, panting, his body all in spasms—but his face once more under his control, and the expression there haunting.

"If you ride hard now," Lilly said, "you will escape, won't you?"

"What does it matter?" His voice was bitter. "Who do I have? Not *you*, clearly. Not him. Not even the witch, if you get to her with that." He staggered from the doorway, fell to his hands and knees before coming within two yards of her. "I will—"

She bolted for the stable, thinking, *Surely one of the bandits' horses will accept me.* But she smelled too strongly of the witch, and they reared away from her, kicking at the stall walls and shaking their heads, froth on their thick lips. The only horse who did not react thus was the Nag. Lilly swung the stall door open—and, after a moment of thought, did so for the other horses, as well. They broke from the building, followed by Mr. Duerr's anguished shouts.

Lilly fitted a bridle over the Nag's head, but hadn't time to saddle the animal. Saying, "Don't throw me this time, please, please," she swung herself onto the Nag's back and pressed her knees into the horse's sides, urging her forwards. She took care that the witch's caustic skin did not touch the animal.

"Traitor!" the bandit shouted after her, though he had fallen to his knees again.

The Nag wheeled at a light touch of Lilly's knee, though the gesture had been reflexive, a holdover from the time she had spent riding the Mare. "Your kindness has been no excuse for your cruelty," she snapped back, "and I will not accept that I am owned by you." Again she turned the Nag, aware that the animal grew restive already. She must make good time.

The bandit would follow, she knew. His would not be so clean a death as his lover's.

The Nag balked a moment, realizing where Lilly intended to go, but she responded to a rider flattened against her neck, one who urged her to go on with heels and voice. At the front of the cottage the horse danced to the side, making feral noises most unsuited to a horse: at the stoop the witch stood, still as some macabre statue. Lilly patted the horse's shoulder and managed to dismount—or to fall off without injury, anyway. Holding the skin over her two arms, she approached cautiously, holding it up. "Ma'am."

As she'd ever expected, the witch could move faster than her usual shamble, no matter how she had been injured the day before. The bandages unwound from her feet as she moved forwards, trailing for a moment like a victor's banners; Lilly's arms had begun to shake with the burden, and for the witch to take it was a relief, though it came with claws scratching. She might not have meant to do it, anyway.

What followed could not be called *metamorphosis*, as a moth from its chrysalis, though it had something of that wet indignity; it was a sea-change, as she forced open her skin and hugged it to her body, and the skin as if glad of its owner crawled over the bare muscles and taut tendons. What that melding birthed was Ms. Gottschalk, still. Yet—more.

The beauty of the witch did not conform to that of mankind—she was lean, still, fatless on thigh and breast, but sleek, held-together, the terror of her articulated into a human flesh against which nature pressed, showing through the blue-green eyes, caught in the curves of her talons. This time when she danced she was not contented to do so on her own; she caught up Lilly's hands and turned her in a circle. Lilly scrambled with the memory of waltzes while the witch made deer-prancing, cat-leaping, spread-toes movements in the air, her hair not in the wind but part of it, the eddies around a raven's wings.

"Again I am woman of the moon," she said, "I am woman

of trees. Again I am all my power!" Though she stood no taller than Lilly's shoulder, her voice shook the mountains. Her hands tightened. "I'll reward you by making your death quick."

Lilly jerked back, despairing, and scowled at the witch's laughter.

"Now why would I do *that*? Silly thing." She released her hands. "I will show you how generous I can be. Where is my Horace? He should be here to see me. He has never known me whole." She shook her hair back over her shoulders and, glancing at Lilly's face, said with something akin to kindness, "Stand back on the stoop while I finish my business here. Then I will gift you with my gratitude."

Lilly backed away, considered turning her face aside. Too much of death wormed its way through her memory already, but she could not deny its sickening allure.

Mr. Duerr emerged through the trees, slapping away branches that would impede his path, tripping over the roots that buckled to catch his ankles. His breath heaved in his chest, sweat on his brow, a pistol in his hand. "*You*. You killed him. After all this time—"

"I had many allies," Ms. Gottschalk said, and strode towards him with the thrift of movement with which predators hunted. "Lyle played a part, and Horace. It makes the victory of Ignatz's death bitter to me, but not so much that I refuse to sup on it. Yours, though—yours will be mine alone."

Ivo thumbed back the hammer but didn't have time to pull the trigger before the gun melted to slag in his hand. He screamed, knees buckling, hand held far away from him; the smell of his metal-burned flesh stung the air. The witch caught him by the hair and dragged back his head. His met her stare, and for a moment seemed on the cusp of pleading. Then he whispered, "Our ghosts will madden you."

"No. I will make a servant of yours and dust of his."

Perhaps Mr. Duerr had some answer to that; surely his face twisted with terrible grief, a creature denied its mate. Ms. Gottschalk's talons dragged from throat to forehead, so light that the blood barely beaded before she gripped the top edge and ripped the skin free. Lilly should have retreated farther; from this small distance, she watched how the thin pink flesh of Mr. Duerr's eyelids fluttered before he screamed.

Ms. Gottschalk turned away from him. Behind her, the cottage crumbled to dirt, and somewhere nearby a lark sang. "What will I give you, my faithful creature?"

Lilly tore her eyes from Mr. Duerr's crumpled body—he'd ceased to scream, and now made only raw, guttural noises—to stare blankly at the witch. "Faithful . . . ? Oh. Mr. Nadel. I handled that already—that's where Horace is. You might say I traded turnips for this favor." She touched the witch's shoulder—so smooth, and *still* it had a faint sheen of oil—when it looked as if she would go up the path back to the bandit's cottage. "Ma'am, might I follow you, that I may dig up a piece of property I have buried in the garden?"

The witch laughed again. "I meant to kill you, once, and your actions convinced me to stay my hand. Now your actions incline me to a boon, and you ask me *this*. I might have made you a woman—or whatever it is that you really wear underneath that skin. Is it human, Lyle? Or are you bound unnaturally in this mortal flesh?" She clasped Lilly's hand like a childhood friend. "Never mind. I cannot make you less foolish than you are. Come along, come along, I don't find pleasure in

your grieving, and there's no other term for what I see on your
face just now."

"You're . . . You're quite cheerful, ma'am." She let herself be
led away from the scene of mutilation.

"I have got my skin back. Would you not be cheerful?"

On the walk Lilly never stumbled, but that seemed some
trick of the woman who dragged her along; for they walked at
a fast pace through that gloom, and the roots underfoot were
all different from the path Lilly had long since learned. Behind
them, the Nag followed at a distance, distressed perhaps to be
abandoned by humans after a life among them. At the bandits'
cottage, Lilly left Ms. Gottschalk—who was occupied in turning the yard back to a stand of oaks and woodbine—and went
to the cairn in the garden.

She threw aside the rocks and clawed through the dirt, frantic of a sudden that the blood-stones would be gone. She found
them, tore them free of the earth, saw that they were dull with
more than dirt. They felt a resentment—such a thing to sense
from tokens! Surely she had gone a little mad with the absence of
them; anyway, they warmed in her palm, and their light and
memories were at once intact. Drained now of vigor, she wandered back onto the cottage path. The witch startled her, caught
her hand in a firm grip, and Lilly at last realized that the woman
relished the fact that she *could* exert such strength on another
being. Thus they went around the land, the witch's gestures filling the well with mud and scattering its stones at random, pressing the slate back into the earth and raising the wood into trees.

Of the witch's work there stood, at last, only the Nag. Seeing the witch at rest, the animal approached and stretched her
head towards Lilly.

Lilly hesitated to impose on the witch—surely this mood must give out—yet she asked, "What of the Nag, ma'am?" She nipped Lilly's shoulder when Lilly took up her halter, but she let herself be caught.

"I should change it back, I suppose. It's so old it will crumble like the rest of this." The witch made a disappointed noise, looking around herself. "For so long-kept a prison, there was little enough in the way of bars."

Lilly nodded in agreement; though she took none of Ms. Gottschalk's relish in the activity, to see this place reduced to ash had hurt like a lanced infection: a sudden pain that gave way to an unsatisfying ache. "If it is all the same to you, ma'am, I need a horse to ride back to the road, and I will have her."

"She's quite an animal, isn't she?" The witch grinned, reached up as if to pet the Nag, who shied from her. "Oh, I did good work on this one, vicious and hideous and powerful."

Lilly bowed, unable to find words.

"You have one more thing to ask, don't you? Or will you have Horace carry you past the boundary of my land again?" The witch looked sly. "Perhaps I will gather him up and tell him not to come back. Wouldn't it be interesting, to come so far and die here in this wood?"

"Interesting, yes. Preferable—I cannot say that, ma'am." She hesitated. "Please, if you could null your hold on me—"

"Oh, please. You take me to be so wicked that I would not?" The witch ran both hands through her hair, smiling. Luxuriating that she could touch it and not have it stick, perhaps. "I took its power while we danced. It will trouble you no more—except in passing."

Lilly bowed again. "Good-bye, ma'am."

When she straightened, the witch had gone. It might have been a long time that she stood in that meadow if the Nag had not attempted to step on her foot.

Guiding the Nag took enough concentration that the simple pine smell of the forest took some time to communicate its message: safety. She rode outside the witch's circle of power, now, and a different woman might have sobbed in relief. She leaned down to pet the Nag in a gesture of affection only to have her face—the marked side, at least—cracked into the animal's neck. They had gone over the ditch and bracken which lined the road, and from the brown, grassy slope they were greeted by the Mare and Horace with very similar noises; the tailor, sprawled on his back beside the others, waved his arm. It might have meant thank you *or* hurry up.

The Nag wanted to bite, tense from the excitement, snorting at the other equine. Lilly slid from her back and made a limping way across the road, newly aware that a bony spine made a poor seat even for the least sensitive of bodies. The uneven sound of hooves following her bespoke the animal's strange loyalty, which was quite like—

Horace tossed himself at her, a flailing mass of stink and muscle and whuffling nose. She said something senseless and grateful, and had become accustomed enough to his habits that she responded by ruffling his hair; he often showed affection by grooming the manes of the horses and ever seemed disappointed at the baldness of Lilly's head. She stopped, asked: "Is that a tick?"

"Probably." He retreated a few steps, eyeing her up and down. "You're not dead—not even hurt in the body. Oh, except your hand."

"The oak. It's nothing." She squeezed his shoulder, awkward to instigate touch, still. "I'm glad. . . . You're bruised."

He tapped the yellow-black-blue that covered half his face. "I like your face so much I decided to make us match, see?" He laughed at his own joke. "No, no, don't frown. One of the arms got me in the face, but then I stabbed it a half dozen times, so I figure we're even. Once I got them sewed, I put them in the Mare's saddlebag. Still unhappy? You'll frown your lips off your face when you see my knees. I've never run and worked on something at the same time, so I landed horribly."

"I'm so very—"

"Don't say sorry. It was my choice." He slapped her shoulder.

What could she say to that? Hug him again? Swear some equal loyalty? She had only her acceptance of him, a friendship she associated with Octavius, and she did not know how to express it. The issue never came up before. "I would like to get up the mountain before dark."

The tailor grinned wide enough to crack his face—in far too literal a manner—and gestured at a flock of starlings as they passed overhead. The flight of birds, grown unfamiliar, was sweet to see. Now he held his one hand in a posture of prayer and tilted his head towards her—then to the Mare. He wanted a foot up, it seemed.

She could appreciate an honest man. "Horace, could you— Horace?"

"You said: *I* would." He thumped one of his callused heels against the ground. "Do you want me to go back to the witch?"

"*No.* I meant all of us." She gestured around at the horses, the dead man. "The witch would have you back, but I—I am not given to believe her a creature that would . . . You have a tick on your head, Horace. You shouldn't, and wouldn't were you cared for."

He scuffed his feet in the dirt, eyes intent on her. "You're very tired."

"Yes?" She smiled at him, puzzled. "Would being rested change my mind, do you think?"

"I think maybe you're not looking straight at things." His gestures now seemed almost to tell a tale he wanted heard: the look, the flared nostrils, the way he moved. "You know I'm her creature."

"Do you mean: You're a horse changed into a human, and this should put me off? Don't look so startled. Ivo told me." She arched her eyebrows at him. "Horace, my dearest friend is a kraken."

"Not a horse. A mule." He hesitated. "But a kraken isn't un-natural."

"Unless you are hiding gears I would not say you are, either." She reached out a hand, not surprised when he circumvented it to lean his shoulder against hers.

"The automata have gears. Does that mean you will throw them away?" He looked towards the Mare's saddlebag. "I don't even know what they will do with their masters gone."

You decide what to do with them, she wanted to say; *you had a greater part in trapping them*. But that would be cowardice. "They did not go mad when Ignatz died. Perhaps they might become useful yet."

"You said you were a merchant's kid. You sure you didn't mean *gambler*?"

"Gambling is done for pleasure. Now help me get Mr. Nadel up into the saddle, please."

Near noon it began to snow, obscuring the sun's descent. The Mare tolerated the weather with stoicism, and the concentration needed to pick her way mellowed the Nag. Horace clung close to Lilly's side, and admitted at last that he'd never seen *snowfall*— only ice and sand storms. He grew more nervous yet as they reached the town at last and walked the streets lined with shuttered and empty buildings; he whispered, "This is a dead place."

"It'll rise from the grave once news spreads that the bandits are gone." She paused under the sign of the tailor; there was light in the front parlor, to her surprise. "I suppose that was a grisly thought."

"Probably true, though! I smell a stable. I should bring these two around back. We *are* staying awhile?"

"I don't know. I'll knock, then—"

Mr. Nadel threw back his head and gave a shrieking cry. In answer there came the sound of pounding feet, Miss Reiniger's voice raised joyfully. Shutters banged closed in the distance; apparently this was too much even for the brave souls who dared leave them open at night. Tomorrow the neighbors might creep up to the tailor's house and peer in through the windows, expecting to see the aftermath of violence done in the night. The front door was flung open with a moan of its hinges, and lightly as any girl going to her best friend the woman skipped over the front steps and startled the horses by coming up on the wrong side of the Mare, her hands reaching for Mr. Nadel.

The sound of his laughter was more terrible than his greeting, and it took some effort for Lilly to soothe the Mare while Miss

Reiniger got the dead man down from the horse's back. It should have looked strange to see this woman with a corpse leaned on her arm, but their smiles matched, as did the way they tilted their foreheads close. He might not speak, but here was communication. Miss Reiniger said something, voice breaking. It was all very touching, but the night was cold. Lilly cleared her throat.

"Oh." Miss Reiniger turned unwillingly towards her. "I kept a watch. There was nothing else to do, even after I thought you were certainly dead."

Horace said, "This is all really disturbing. Can I take me and the horses around back? What have you got, a pony?"

"Yes—she's a pony. She drew a cart for us, when we needed her to." Those words were mechanical, automatic, as she peered into the dark at him. "You're weren't here before."

"I'm here now. How about that stable?"

"Yes, of course. There's room enough for you to take a bed." Mr. Nadel tugged at her arm, impatient, but she was shame-faced. "I should have said first that you're welcome in my home. I can set you up—feed you—oh, you're a stinking mess. I'm sorry, but you are. I'll get you clothes, too."

"Thank you, ma'am." Lilly surrendered the reins to Horace, who went around back with quick-footed avoidance of the Nag's cantankerous nips. It was an impressive show given his weariness. He wouldn't be taking up the tailor's offer of a room, Lilly knew; he would doubtless bed down in a nest of blankets and hay as soon as the horses were settled.

She envied him some; Lilly could feel the beginning of a bru-tal soreness in her limbs, and her eyes were gritted with the cold and a desperation for sleep. "May I—"

"Please come in." Miss Reiniger knew how to support her companion so that they moved quickly, him leaning hard on her and hopping along on his good foot. Up the stairs they went like an gymnastic act, and Lilly plodding behind feeling wistful. This reminded her of Octavius again, and she wondered: *Is he alive yet? Is Gero Alt, or will there be no trade?*

Lilly dragged her boots off at the door. Miss Reiniger grunted with a cutoff scream at the grubs that were still caught up in the socks beneath, but for herself Lilly could only summon up enough horror to knock them off. The tailor nigh dragged her into the building with her free hand; the front parlor had been dusted and was now well-lit by the lanterns Miss Reiniger had put up during her watch. Thus presented, its richness would not have been out of place in the chateau. Except for one detail: there were half-sewn garments spread across the floor; the mess of nervous work.

"Are you badly hurt? Oh, honey, you look awful. Quit nagging, you old man, Lyle saved you and he deserves all we can give him." There was too much fondness in the remonstration for it to be the least effective. "Did you shake your head to being hurt, Lyle? Sore? All right. There's a pump in the kitchen and a basin, too. Could you— I'm sure you'd like to do what you can to clean up. Tomorrow we can fill up the bath. I'll bring in some towels and sleeping clothes. You remember the way to the kitchen?"

Lilly nodded, having processed half those tumbling words at best. Grinning, Miss Reiniger turned away, dragging the corpse into the warren of their home, probably to go about the silly, teary portion of their reunion; and perhaps somewhere here they had a means for him to communicate, a tablet or suchlike.

Christ, she needed sleep more than a bath; she'd been filthy so long that she didn't give a damn about it. But the water might soothe her body some and keep her from waking in the middle of the night with the agony of cramping muscles. The halls were as tangled as she remembered, the kitchen as crowded. The heating of the kettle made her think of the witch's baths. Her leather coat she shed easily; the habit of shyness had at last broken enough that she peeled off her shirt without pause. She folded it carefully, then shook her head and dropped it in the bucket of peelings and other unacceptable foodstuffs that sat to the side of the counter. The garment had enough organic matter ground into it to make good fertilizer.

A tap on the shutters startled her; she swung them open, one hand on a knife that lay on the counter. Not a ghost leaned into the room but Horace, peering up at her with a contented expression. "The stable is nice. I want radishes—I fed all of mine to the Nag, though it hasn't made a bit of difference. Also, glad to see this tailor didn't make you into leather boots."

Lilly found him an onion—he accepted it alongside an apology—then asked, "Leather boots?"

"She smells like the Devil and her friend is undead. That seems a wicked sort to me. Do you want to sleep in the stable?" The latter part of his sentence had been obscured by cheerful, open-mouthed chewing.

"It's not really my habit. Here, have some bread, too. I don't think our host will mind." She shivered, skin prickling. Though grown tough against the cold courtesy of her girlhood, the winter on her bare chest was a tad uncomfortable. "Goodnight, Horace."

He flicked a salute her way—had he learned that gesture from soldiers the bandits killed?—and went ambling away to the heat of the horses. Closing the shutters was a relief, a return to the stove's warmth.

"Clothes and everything are on the counter here." By the time she turned around, the tailor had gone.

Did she stink so badly that being in an enclosed space with her would keep a woman from her own kitchen? Well— yes, she could imagine she did. The kettle whistled; she had become quite skilled in making the temperature of baths just so. It surprised her to laugh when she saw the holed, ancient rags the tailor had given her to wash with. She was a practical woman even when thrown by gratitude, it seemed. Judging herself to be safely alone, Lilly kicked aside her trousers and scrubbed what she could, for once not chary of her own body. One could have hid the blood-stones' glow in the bottom of the basin by the time she had finished, the water was so dark, and once dried and clothed again, she tossed it out the back door. After a moment of thought, she took out the slops bucket, too.

She rummaged in the kitchen and found willow bark, salve, bandages; while a new kettle of water boiled she tended to her hand, then made a cup of tea to drink. Slumped at the kitchen table, she nibbled on the heel of the loaf from which she'd taken a slice for Horace. It seemed to her that in the past she would have been fussier about commandeering another person's home, but that had been before she lived in any but a noble's, where the kitchen did not belong to a lady of the house. Or per- haps she'd gotten some bad habits from the bandits. She could cope.

Miss Reiniger stuck her nose in first, then an eye to glance around the door. "Oh, good, mostly washed and clothed. I have a bed set up for you—and you didn't stand on ceremony, good, good. Come along now."

She stood knee-deep in the ocean; Octavius turned his gold eye on her, an inscrutable look that could exist in dream alone. He went slowly into the ocean that was like a sun, leaving her. She held the blood-stones in her hand and knew them to be enough. Someone stood behind her, the waves retreated from that presence, and the rocks lay bare; on them lay three women with spears and scaled skin, and a shark rent in two. This was the strongest part of her, but she felt fear in turning—yet turned.

This was not Ermentrud who stood before her—not quite. Other shapes moved within her voluptuousness: temptations, predators. There was no need for her to come close, for Lilly could feel the heat of her tongue—and more, that which she had never touched.

Who brings a lantern into my loft? Not Horace. *But that was the light of the moon on her face, and herself change-sensitive enough to be woken by it. The room Miss Reiniger had given her was small but comfortable, with a featherbed and all amenities. It was clearly the main bedroom of the house, quietly given over to her as another sign of gratitude, and though she fully intended to protest the next morning, she'd been too tired for an argument and had simply fallen facedown onto the bed when Miss Reiniger had closed the door behind her.*

She wondered that the moon would be so cruel to wake her. Had she not been its creature once?

Silly, strange thought. If anything she belonged to the sea; there she would return, and it was the touch of the waves she longed for. Some part of her believed that those salt waters could wash away all the alterations done to her body and mind. The former had not troubled her much in the last—how many months?—not since fall. Other than a certain circumspection, an insistence on clothing when one of the others might see her, she had little time for crises about her reproductive status.

She had explored herself only that once, then laid the issue aside.

"What worries to have when the body is so weary," she muttered, and turned over on her side so that the moon would not bother her more. Yet it had done its work, and the question of herself circled in her mind. Of course she remembered the dream; it was not the sort of thing swiftly forgotten. The heat. What precisely did her mind expect of her body by introducing such sensations? That first investigation had made all matters clear, and squeamishness alone had not kept her from further learning of herself. What more was there to know? Perhaps some comfort could be found in the fact that her mind *did* bother to remember these things, but now was a time for rest.

She heard that hypnotism could clear a mind of a certain topic; if this continued to keep her awake, she would be detouring to find a person skilled in that art. In her memory, Ermentrud's teeth pressed sharp, wolflike.

This woman on her dark horse, free of all bonds but that of her wild hunger—she came by her prey honestly. The blood pumped and the mouth dried in anticipation of her; such things were called the base nature of humankind, a phrase that did not know its own meaning. At one time Lilly might have shied from these thoughts and labeled her feelings as envy of the creature's freedom and power. More honest to herself after months of lies to others, she would not falsely label lust, nor ascribe it to her male disguise.

Disguise—no. The self that answered to the name Lyle would not stir if called Lilly, but Lilly would let herself be Lyle.

So what of Lyle? Bald, ugly, callused, a half-trained menial servant with a useless knowledge of etiquette. Efficient, though; determined. She would give herself that much. Neither of which qualities she displayed at the moment, thinking in circles about a topic she tried to dismiss. With a huff of annoyance, she reached down her body and palmed the space between her legs; that smooth skin framed by the twitch of thigh muscles, interrupted only at those places that allowed for elimination. Bald as her head—she resented still that she had been denied hair enough to camouflage her nether regions.

Detached, she thought: *How would I describe the sensitivity of this? As like unto one's throat, or the crook of the elbow? No: it is less sensual than them.*

Yet the touch of Ermentrud, however illusionary, could not be denied because of this numbness. Lilly flopped onto her back, feeling very young and foolish and apt to make bad decisions. Surely a matron would not give these things a second thought, nor an aged man. She had no energy for deception, much less of herself: if it were not for her loyalty to Octavius, she might well submit to Ermentrud. She trusted there would be something worthwhile before the final consumption: a coy chase, the press of lips, the pleasures of courtship. The discovery. The prompt negative reaction and reduction to supper rather than mate.

In such a world in which that consumption occurred, Horace would be fine, sent off with the Mare and Nag. He would mourn, but not forever—not as Octavius would. With that thought she rejected the sensual self-destruction of the dream and, rolling over onto her face, fell back to sleep.

She woke at noon to snow thick on the ground and as much pain as she expected. The latter she brushed aside; the former looked more beautiful than she remembered, though practicality knocked at the edge of her mind with worries about travel speed and outfitting herself for such weather and the possibility of Horace's toes becoming frostbitten.

She had not been awake long enough for these worries. Changing into the clothes that had been placed on the dresser, she found herself the back door and went out to the stable. It was smaller than the bandits', draftier but adequate; she greeted the horses, checking them over though she trusted Horace to have tended them well. As to himself, she near stumbled over him, he had so well concealed himself in a number of horse blankets. He opened one eye at the sound of her footsteps, made a faint pleased noise, and promptly went back to sleep.

Not for her fellow beings alone did she come first to the stable. Rational thought could not accomplish what a single gesture could; she emptied the rags from her saddlebags— those which the troll had bid her discard, those months ago— and set them aside into a neat pile. They were taking up space that could hold useful supplies. The smell of cooking came through the open kitchen shutters; enough of this symbology. Lilly followed this desire of the body.

Tried to; soon as she edged into the kitchen, Miss Reiniger said in a bright and inarguable voice, "I set up a bath for you. And more clothes. Here, let me show you where."

"Let me bring along something to eat, please," Lilly said; to faint of hunger and drown in bathwater would make an unquiet ghost of her.

The woman apologized for the lavender soap; Lilly snickered over the thought of herself fussing at femininity and must have seemed quite mad to the woman, who edged out of the room. Lilly alternated between scrubbing at the filth caked into her skin and taking bites from sausage she had taken from the kitchen. Though it proved pleasant to be truly *clean*—and free of vermin—for the first time in months, she reflected ruefully that Horace would once more seem rancid as when she first met him.

A theory proved when she walked into the kitchen and muffled her reaction by coughing into her hand; Horace, seated at the table, looked like a sleepy clod of earth carried in from the stable yard. Miss Reiniger, cooking at the stove, looked mournfully into her pan. "Oh, Lyle. He *really* doesn't eat meat? Or eggs?"

"Or butter," Horace put in.

"He's not having a laugh at me, then? Well, Lyle, if he got the idea from you—I don't intend to make you into clothes." From the pleading note in her voice, she had made this assertion several times. "Your boy won't let the idea be."

"He doesn't mean to be alarming," Lilly said. "In fact—" Said *he*, risen from the table, sniffed at her shoulder. "Good morning, Horace."

He replied with a grunt and an oddly wistful, "Lavender?"

"It's soap. I'll get together another bath," Miss Reiniger said brightly. "Lyle, can you tend to breakfast?"

I hope you have a bandit's tastes, Lilly thought; then: *I hope I readjust to being among normal people who I do not feel resentment towards, soon.* "Yes, ma'am, gladly."

"Please. Frieda." She ushered Horace ahead of her out of the room.

"He's always polite," she heard him say. "Even with the bandits and the witch and me, and I tried to kill him once."

Lilly had the boiled eggs peeled and the toast buttered by the time Frieda returned. The woman's shirtfront was somewhat wetted and she appeared frazzled; if Horace took the same attitude towards bathwater as he did to the stream back home—back at the bandits' home—then it would have been an interesting experience. Lilly asked, "Do you start your work today, Frieda?"

"I started it last night. Sit down, I'll get the plates together. —I shouldn't have promised you anything." She turned away, her shoulders very straight. "I can't do anything without Hans' consent, and he doesn't always give that."

Lilly hesitated; sipped her tea. "Pass on my thanks to him, please. How long will it be?"

"I have seen what happens to soldiers when they come home from war. Even if the rations were sufficient, they are thin with energy expended in the agonies of doubt and death." The tailor glanced back over her shoulder. "Two months."

"It is not my place to say how long such things should take." She said it to those stiffened shoulders. "But I would wish it to be a shorter time."

"You're calling me a liar?" Her laugh was a long-night,

sob-rough sound. "I thought about this while I talked with Hans all last night, and I thought about it through the morning, and I wished you would wake up sooner because I kept changing my decision." She came over with the plates, a third for Horace: bread, apple, some sort of root vegetable mash, though he had not yet returned. "You'll make me change it again."

"I request only honesty." Lilly sat back, made eye contact. "I can tell you truly that more time will only waste me away, for even at this distance I can feel the sickening of my friend, and I cannot be well while his health fails."

"It's been months." The tailor sat down heavily.

"And hope can last years, can't it?" Lilly reached across, touched the back of the woman's hand. She could make this a demand, and she would if need be; but however unsettled Frieda Reiniger was now, Lilly had seen the metal beneath that.

"Yes. Damnit. A month. But come back once you have your friend." Frieda looked at her, fierce, brows drawn down. "You need to rest. I know how these things are, and dying of it—"

"Ma'am," Lilly said crisply, and speared a piece of sausage. "You set an excellent table."

Grumbling, the tailor subsided; by the end of the meal she was eyeing Horace's plate and tilting her head towards the back of the house.

"I don't hear splashing," Lilly put in, and rising moved to collect the plates. "I'll bring it out to him in the stable."

"Here, I'll wash up. He's skinnier than you." Frieda shooed her from the kitchen after making sure she had her coat on.

Lilly paused at the door. "Do you happen to have children, Frieda?"

"Never wanted them and never got one by accident." She grinned, fond, focused far over Lilly's shoulder into a different part of the building. "But keeping Hans taught me plenty. You had to keep a sharp eye on that man to save yourself the bother of curing him of greater ills. It was always, 'Frieda, I can't eat, I'm sketching,' or 'Frieda, I can't bathe, I'm staring at our stock.' Meanwhile he didn't do a jot of real work, either."

Lilly could not say she understood, but she forgave Frieda, a little, for her meddling. "Would you like your room back?"

"Not particularly." Frieda winked at her, a hopeful smile tugging at her lips. "I'd have to change the sheets again."

Lilly smiled back, letting the woman know that she had taken the teasing as meant. Besides, she was glad of Frieda's answer; nightmares aside, she'd slept well enough the night before that, in waking, it had taken her a full minute to crawl from under the sheets. It almost tempted her to return there to sleep off a warm bellyful of food and the assurance that her work would soon be done. But there were things to be done, yet.

She found Horace clumsily using a hoof pick to free a stone from the pony's hoof; it had its head hauled around to watch him with mellow, blue eyes, chewing a mouthful of oats meanwhile. Frieda had managed to do what Lilly had tried for months and gotten him into new clothes, the light brown cloth catching the light. Silk? Surely not. Whatever the case, that and his ruffled but essentially clean hair made him look quite civilized, bare feet aside.

He cast a look around at her and smiled hopefully; placing the plate to the side, she went to the pony, greeted him, and then took to the leg. *She* had to hold it between her knees, as he wasn't quite as accommodating to her as with Horace, but she was also better practiced at this particular skill and managed to clear out the rock. "It doesn't look damaged."

"No, I didn't think it was. He said it itched."

Finally free to do so, she asked, "*Can* you talk to them?"

"Can't you? Look how he stands." Horace straightened up and went to inspect the food on offer. "She fed me twice. I think I like her. Once she assured me she didn't mean to turn you into any sort of garment I felt better anyway. I had to explain to her about all the ways human skin can be made into magical things—and she claims power! I know that just from overhearing the witch."

Lilly held up the fine-toothed comb she had gotten from her saddlebag when she took out the rags. "Can I pick the nits and ticks from your hair while you eat?"

His expression brightened; she sat cross-legged on a crate behind him while he made swift work of his food. Once he had finished he leaned his head against her knee, and with a heavy sigh seemed to doze. It was disgusting work to clear out vermin— but, she admitted, satisfying too. Voice sleepy, he said, "I'm sorry you don't have hair. But there's a piece of straw on your shoulder. Leave it there, I'll get it."

Horace knocked at her bedroom shutters that night and crept in over the sill, glancing suspiciously around the room once before flinging himself down on the coverlet bunched at the bottom of her bed. She had been sleeping under that, but she contented herself with the blankets. It became his habit to sleep thus as long as they stayed at the tailor's, though he wandered by day. She did not imagine he stayed within the confines of that small town with the whole world open to him.

She asked, on the third night, as she might not have if she were not still tired with lingering nerves: "Do you mean to go somewhere?"

"Of course," he said, "wherever you and the Mare and the Nag are going. Think how cold you would be without me."

"You do keep my feet warm," she replied.

"No, I meant your *heart*. Godssake, Lyle." He sulked a while before saying, "You wouldn't have saved that hostage without me, would you have?"

She lay silent a long while, trusting not his wisdom so much as his bluntness; if he saw it, he would talk about it. "My ability to be compassionate would have grown rusty."

"Yes, see? I'm that wise talking animal that keeps heroes from screwing up in all the stories." He snuggled down into the comforters. "Which is good. Otherwise I'd be the maiden in distress—not even the princess!—that you saved from the evil wicked creatures, and that's . . . Ugh. Terrible to think."

"Are you sure I don't need to return you to your lord in some close-by kingdom, Horace?"

"Please, as if I need you for transport. Tell me when you want to get back on your quest to your true beloved—I hear he's a kraken?" He snickered to himself for a while; she figured that he had fallen to sleep when he quieted. There came his voice again, though: "It's not as easy as people tell in stories, you know. You're doing fine with all this. A lot of the time the storytellers are not so much lying as making their tales endurable. A lot of damsels don't want to be saved, and the animals always want something for their service, and the prince sometimes is running away from danger, not towards adventure. I've seen a lot. Traveling for Gottschalk—traveling for me, when I could take the time."

What he saw, he would speak. "O wise animal: What would I do without you?"

It came across as honest instead of dry; Horace patted her ankle and said, "You'd probably forget your own name or something. G'night, now. There's always more time for stories."

The next morning, in the window between breakfast and an embarrassingly long afternoon nap, Frieda came to her with the few garments which had survived the bandits, freshly laundered, though the woman said as she handed them over: "Promise me you won't wear them unless you're knee-deep in manure. Oh—here. I found it in a pocket."

Lilly took the key to Mr. Nadel's manacles and considered tossing it away. But why should that be her first impulse? By her work she had won it. Folding it against her palm, she smiled thinly and thanked the woman before retreating.

She slept most of the first week; by the second, convinced Frieda to let her take over the cooking and routine cleaning, so that the tailor could work longer hours. Each time Lilly saw Mr. Nadel, he had less flesh and smiled more broadly.

The respite cured her bodily ills but did not give her enough distractions to hold off nightmares; she spent days pacing the halls and imagining how best the woman's things could be organized—dwelling in the comfort of knowing she could no longer be ordered to take on such tasks—and time spent trying to befriend the Nag, though the bespelled horse maintained the same clingy aggression towards her.

There was something that she had to do, but she did not wish to know it. Pacing was far less destructive.

Then came a morning on which she woke to the sound of eaves dripping and knew that the warmth of the day bid her complete the task. First, she asked Horace, "Would the witch's land thaw also? What of the soil?"

"It plays along with the weather," he said, "and this early the soil's still loose. Sometimes Duerr would churn it up a little— he was such a bored and boring man, wasn't he?"

Leaving the conversation there, she went next to Frieda. "I don't have a cross of my own," she said. "Might I have one of yours?"

The tailor was eager to respond and showed her a full case of them; apparently she was a collector of most things, not just cloth and shears. Lilly chose one two feet tall and made of iron, a thing which once served to ornament a building. She thanked the woman, but could not escape before Frieda asked that she go down to the cellar; there bolts of cloth leaned against one another, red to the right, purple to the left, and between them all the colors a human mind might imagine, hints of pattern among them. Lilly's breath caught in her throat. "Most of your wealth is here."

"More than most. Almost all of it." Frieda smiled, pleased. "You appreciate good things."

Though she wished to have her business done as swiftly as possible, she did not regret having made the broad offer of help which obligated her to this. She would find pleasure in going through this room. "You wanted my help looking for something?"

"There's a brocade printed with fish. I either put it with the golds—" she gestured to the glitter of them, there between yellow and brown "—or the blue. You paw through the former, I'll sort through the latter, and we'll find it in half the time."

Better kept though she might be now that she had access to more privacy, time, and soap, the task made her feel grubby. There was nothing here less than gorgeous, and of a sudden it made sense that Mr. Nadel could lose himself in staring at this stock. Her search turned up dragons, flowers, a winding pattern that suggested in its twists and turns some biblical story told to those who could understand; then, at last, met the protruding and faintly puzzled eye of a carp.

She hesitated. It was worked with gold thread, yes. It mimicked real fish most masterfully. But this particular brocade also had something *too* honest about it, as if any moment one of those fish might defecate. Nonetheless, Lilly called Frieda over, who declared, "This isn't what I was looking for—it's better. Now come along, I'll have you look at what we've labored over."

There was little enough of the fabric that the tailor simply threw the lot over her shoulder and went back up the stairs, Lilly going ahead of her.

"Like a kid on Christmas," Frieda teased. "I thought you might have a soul under all that precision."

Mr. Nadel raised his hand in greeting; he no longer had his bottommost ribs, and the withered leg had been replaced with a wooden peg. For all that, he indicated their masterwork with a flourish, the smile that showed the fault lines in his face by all appearances genuine. Lilly felt awkward over the whole thing on account of finding the coat quite hideous, a ragtag assortment of fabrics for which one could only say that they were the same length. There was a patch of knit at the thigh, leather lapels, lace on one breast and chainlink on the other. It seemed to borrow its lines from vests, evening gowns, housecoats.

She made some awkward, socially polite little exclamation before she could help herself.

Frieda bent over with laughter. "No, no, don't say that. I don't think that you are blind. This is our most hideous effort yet—and that makes it powerful. We're going to incorporate some more metal, too, since you seem the type to need protection."

"It's meant to be hideous?" Lilly confirmed as she stepped up anxiously to it, touching a velvet pocket located beneath the armpit of the left side.

"Oh, very much so. Why else would I use these fish?" She shoved aside a tangle of other cloths on the central worktable and spread the brocade out. "A client brought it to me and insisted I do something with it. I refused to put my initials anywhere on the piece. Now, I don't want to be rude, but go do whatever it is that occupies you, because I want to finish this in the time frame you gave. The way you looked at me—as I remember it—promised all sorts of things you learned from the bandits if I didn't manage it."

"Of course not," Lilly said, too distracted to be entirely convincing. Her mind was on what waited for her. "I must ride out, come tomorrow morning. I expect I will be back before dark."

When she rose before dawn, Horace followed her to the stable; the space, warm and hay-smelling and filled with the stamping of hooves, had meant nothing but comfort for the past weeks. It did not seem so now. The manure shovel would do for the work she intended, and she knew where in the house she could replace the tarp that was laid over the hay. These supplies gathered, she removed the Mare's headstall, but Horace caught her wrist when she reached for the reins hung on the wall, asking, "Where are we going?"

"You don't have to," she began, then: "To the witch's territory."

He closed the Mare's stall door. "A mountain road all drifts and ice is no place for horses if you can help it." Then he put the shovel into her hand and the tarp over his own shoulder; he caught up her elbow in his and they were away, that rushing-billowing unnatural mode of transport that did not allow breath and gave the eyes only impressions of the landscape that passed. She thought: *I could almost, almost understand how he can do this daily*, and then they had stopped in the familiar clearing. Some of Ms. Gottschalk's magic must linger, for the ground was frozen yet, not snowed deep. He handed her the tarp, looking pleased with himself.

"You don't have to," she repeated, "but I'm going down to the witch's clearing."

He followed her, silent. When he fell back, nervous, and walked at a greater distance back, she knew he must smell it; and not long after she did herself, a putrid, sweetish stink that reminded her of the ocean, of the things washed up on shore. At the edge of the clearing she set the shovel next to her foot and made herself stare; for she was an agent in this.

The cold had not preserved the body as well as she'd hoped, primarily because the witch had gone about a thorough work after Lilly fled, and Ivo had been divested of his skin from scalp to foot. Some of it still hung in tatters from the trees, though she couldn't say whether Ms. Gottschalk had flung them there or the crows carried the scraps to the twigs. His entrails were in a long line from his belly to the trees, making him look not at all as the witch had, skinned but fearsome; he was more like a stray cat hit by a cart wheel.

Did it matter if a person was buried with all their organs? Lilly turned to ask Horace, but he was three yards back and giving her a sad look. "Dead bodies attract predators," he said.

"I'm rolling him in the tarp," she replied. "Do you think . . . Never mind." She came closer, forcing herself to go around the side where she could see the damage to his abdomen and assess her options. Relief: the animals had separated the bits entirely, leaving her clear to shovel the body into the tarp without having to worry about detaching a coil of intestines or else shoveling it in with the rest. Should she feel guilt for that?

Perhaps, but she would not.

Though the edges of him had frozen in bloody icicles to the ground and took some chipping with the shovel edge to free, some of his insides were still soft, bloated, rancid to retching. She felt glad not to have eaten before she came; though bile burned terribly on its own, it was at least not a waste. Using the shovel as a lever, she got first his foreparts—watching the bare bones of the spine twist, pulling slightly apart—and hinder parts onto the tarp, having to shovel one leg on separately. The rolling up of the tarp was not so easy as she had hoped and forced her to discard one glove—not the one on her still-healing hand, at least—when some unmentionable fluid wetted the palm.

Horace tapped her on the shoulder, or perhaps the better word was *petted*; then he went around to the other side and picked up the foot-end of the tarp. She would not have to drag it, at least. Yet she could have lived without the knowledge of how light a burden was a body missing many of its essential parts.

Gouges in the earth marked the place over which Ignatz had been buried. The witch had tried to dig him up, she thought; then chose to believe instead that a wild animal was responsible. Lilly erased these signs of attempted desecration by the expedient of digging a hole beside them, flinging the loose earth over the other burial spot one difficult shovelful at a time. It took effort to move the ice-heavy soil, but Ivo had been over-zealous and dug the original grave wide, so that the earth was recently disturbed; the task could have been more difficult.

After some time had passed, Horace made a small, hurt noise. Looking up in alarm, she saw that he held up a long strand of familiar black hair, long as he was tall. "She danced on it," he said. "Danced on his grave." He flapped his hand to get the piece of her away and chose another place to sit.

Breathing hard, Lilly leaned on the shovel haft and stared down into the foot of progress she had made. Six times this. Glancing up at the sun, she figured she had three more hours of useful work left in her and the day.

Well. One did as one had to. She dug. When her ungloved hand began to bleed, Horace casually shouldered her out of the way and took up the work, no faster than her but cheerful enough, singing a song in a dialect of Arabic, his voice all nose and tin. She held her shaking hands between her knees and did not look towards the shrouded body. Or was the term "tarped"?

She took over from Horace when he stopped singing.

Despite their efforts it became clear that the work would not be done before night fell. Horace trotted away to fetch camping gear from Frieda. She glanced towards the body wrapped on the other side of the clearing and said, "I'll meet you at the mouth of the path that leads out of here. And—could you get a rope, as well? Two lengths, I mean?"

It was a quiet spot, peaceful, the rise in the land where the cottage once sat hiding corpse and gravesite while being within hearing distance should she need to chase a predator from it. She did not think so; these woods were dangerous yet wary of humans, having learned from the witch what damage men could wreak. A fire should be enough to warn them away. It unnerved her that she could venture far into the trees and not lose her way; the geography of this place was familiar—as much as the coast had been.

On returning, Horace brought Lilly a new pair of gloves and a shredded roast stuffed into a bun; he handed the latter over with an exaggerated expression of disgust, and after she dusted off her hands they sat together on the bundled camping things. He had brought a bag of odds and ends for himself, dried fruit and nuts and oatmeal that he chewed raw. She asked, "What did Frieda have to say about this?"

"Oh." He spat a small rock that had been in with the oats. "I was supposed to tell her?"

With a sigh, she shrugged away the issue. Frieda was most

understanding of her guests' peculiarities, and this would be a small addition to what had come before.

It took them two more days to finish, and on the morning of the second Horace arrived an hour after having set off, somewhat frazzled but with a basket of viands and news that Frieda had been only somewhat panicked and that she had only wasted some time that would have been better spent on the coat looking for them. Lilly had laughed at that, asked, "Do you think Hans Nadel would allow her that? When a craftsman gets to that point in his work, he *works*."

Horace, never having been around such a fanatic, shrugged and made fond noises about the cinnamon roll Frieda had given him. Lilly chose not to point out that it probably had eggs and butter in it.

At noon, with the sun making the grave look brighter than any pit had the right to, they lowered Ivo into it by knotting the rope around the tarp at either end and easing it down. She had worried for some time that they had gotten the spot wrong in digging and would come upon Ignatz's corpse, but such a trauma never happened; now she wondered if they had not dug this one too far away.

The lowering done, she threw the rope in after him, flinching at the noise it made as it struck the body. Then she took up the shovel and began to move the earth back into its place. Often it was expressed that the dirt patting onto a coffin lid was a terrible noise; when it fell on a corpse, it had a soft, rain-like quality. She found it difficult to remember that there was a corpse at bottom of the grave, however, for the act seemed a burying of sins. What did it say that the bandits had left so many of their victims hung from a tree? Did they feel no guilt?

Well. She never held the illusion that they were *good* men.

It was quicker work to cover than to dig, and they had it over by evening; Lilly had tied up the camping things while Horace packed the dirt down. There they stood at the grave-sides, Lilly chafing her hands against the cold that her gloves did not quite chase out.

"You speak words over a grave, right?" Horace cleared his throat. "Well, I'm glad the bastard is dead, but that was an awful way to go. At least he ended up useful for the crows and now for the worms. What? Did I do it wrong?"

"Most people aren't honest. That was more right, I would say, but others would disagree with me." She smiled at him, wry. "What would you say at *my* funeral?"

"You'll have to learn when you're dead. I wouldn't want to break any traditions." He nodded at the mound of dirt. "Aren't you going to say something? Throw a flower on it, maybe? I could go get a flower."

"No. Thank you, Horace." She thought of learning from these men how to sew, butcher, cook, turn a blind eye. Taking the cross from their pack, she knelt and laid it not on Ivo's grave but Ignatz's. "Useful. I would put that on his gravestone."

"Psst." Horace nudged her. "You're supposed to say it *to* him."

"Thank you," she said, dry, "for the useful things."

A raven landed on the oak that spread its tangled boughs above the bandits' heads and, ruffling its dark feathers, cawed, feathers flared. Did it ask, *Why would you bury a feast*? As it flung itself back into the air, the motion of its wings recalled to her the dancing witch, the feeling of her hair.

It was too much. She did not want to know that such delight could come at the death of a man.

"Lyle," Horace said as she fell to her knees, hands over her eyes. "Lyle, hey, I don't know about this, what's this? Are you all right?" The pack hit the ground with a thump and he knelt beside her, leaned hard enough almost to knock her over. He muttered, "Are you crying?"

"No." She cleared her throat. "I think not." The world was nothing but red and the pressure of her hands. "I've never known someone to die before. Isn't that odd? And now I've seen two in the process—two people dying, one killed."

He laid his head against her shoulder. "I've seen lots of people die. You should have been there when the Buck did."

"I'm sorry." *Now* tears prickled at her lids, and she let her hands drop, ashamed at her own hiding.

"No, that's not what I meant. I mean, if you had, then you would understand that this isn't unique. That doesn't make it hurt less, but it makes it so that you can hold onto it. I mean . . . Once I saw an elephant die. Before that, she explained to me that, hares to horses, every creature preyed upon is allowed to go in peace. I was a foal then." He was silent a long while, warm at her side. "She was talking bullshit, though. She screamed just the same as anybody when they killed her."

"Are elephants prey?" Lilly had seen pictures; they seemed too fierce for that.

"Yeah. Little ones get taken sometimes, and there are big birds and serpents and humankind that hunt the adults." He heaved out a breath. "I like you, Lyle, but I don't like humans. I never liked them on my back, or the bit in the mouth, and the last few years have not really impressed me." He stood, and she followed. "So, this friend of yours. He's as important as all this?"

She raised an eyebrow at him. "Yes. I don't think I would have done all this for someone I felt so-so about."

"You would." Horace grinned. "You would do it for Frieda or for Nadel or even for Ignatz and Ivo, once, because you're a little bit mad. Now, if you're crying about these bastards, should I stand clear when you rescue this friend of yours? I can imagine the tears, the blubbering, the—"

"My parents would have gotten along with Ms. Gottschalk." She thought, first: *A little bit mad is right.* Then: *Though she killed them, they bound her for many years.* She sighed, knowing that she did not deserve the peace of a sham justification. "For Octavius I'll smile."

Snowfall began again—no; for the first time in decades. Horace muttered filthy curses and put the pack over his head. Then: "I'll say thanks to Octavius. I bet he wouldn't like Gottschalk and didn't like your parents and anybody who doesn't like a friend of Gottschalk is a hero to me. None of which is real, but I'll take your word for all of it. Come on, we should really leave before our feet get frozen to the ground and we have to read a whole service over them."

"You've been hoping this whole time that I didn't have the Bible with me, haven't you?" She pulled it from the inside pocket of her coat and waved it at him; with a yelp, he caught up her arm and dragged them back up the mountainside. That left the shovel behind, but then, the horses did not deserve to smell it.

She left Horace in the stable; his reunion with the horses had involved much noise, and he declared that he would stay with them the night in compensation for having abandoned them. Darkness lay heavy over the tailor's house, and the fire in the kitchen stove burned low. It was an empty *house—or an invaded one?*

After considering a moment whether she should get Horace, Lilly opted instead for a large pair of shears and crept through the house, listening. At the workroom in which she had seen the coat of illusions she paused; underneath the door came light, and inside was a furtive noise, too low to interpret clearly. She pushed it open, imagining the coat destroyed, stolen, the tailor dead and Hans Nadel more dead than previously.

No, they were still alive and mostly dead respectively. Frieda threw herself in front of a half-glimpsed mess of fabric, waving her arms. "You *cannot* see it this close to done! Get out. We can give it to you tomorrow. And welcome back. I don't want to know what you were doing. What are those shears for?"

"I found them on the ground," Lilly said, which was not actually a lie. She laid them aside. *Tomorrow.* "Is the bedroom still mine to sleep in?"

"I bet your friend is already curled up on the comforter. Lyle, you *do* want this tomorrow, right?"

Lilly closed the door behind her.

Horace had flopped across the foot of her bed sometime in the night; perhaps he'd grown used to the luxury of feathers and found hay too rough. Being muzzy-headed, she stared too long at him, though she knew such things woke him—as this did. His eyes were alert, black in his dark face and the shadows of the predawn. "You have a question."

It should have been easy to ask this of him. "Can you carry the two of us there?"

"'Course." He laughed at her, a happy snorting noise. "This is way better than the time you made me help kill someone."

"Technically, you asked for help killing him, first." She flung her blanket off, over him, and was not surprised that he snuggled down with it. Horace would sleep as late as she allowed. "Is cheese acceptable today?" Frieda had thoughtlessly given him a grain mash with cheese, upon the taste of which he declared the food acceptable. It was not *flesh*, after all.

"Yes. Make me potatoes with it." His voice had already gone faint by the last word.

She rekindled the stove and made coffee; besides the usual root vegetables and wheel of cheese the tailor kept by, there was no bread in the house and a single link of sausage, so she fell back on her standby of porridge with dried fruit for herself and Frieda while the potatoes fried on the stove. The snowfall was heavy today; soon Horace would be drawn out of bed by the cooking smells, and somewhere in the building the coat was finished, and probably the tailor was collapsed across her workbench snoring after the long night's work. Lilly savored a lungful of peace.

She was on her second cup of coffee—she didn't even like the stuff—when Frieda stumbled in, eyes darkly bruised, one cheek still red from whatever hard surface she had slept propped against. She glanced at the set table, the bubbling pot. "Want to take that off the heat and come see the coat now?"

"God, yes." Lilly followed her out, near tripping over the clutter in her haste, catching herself badly; she had been occupied rubbing her palms against her thighs, as if drying them of sweat. There could not be any of the grave left on her, not after she scrubbed herself raw, but approaching the coat reminded her of the payment tendered for it. From the workroom came the creaking of the spinning wheel, and she could almost believe opening the door would lead her out to that yard where she had chopped wood, six months ago, waiting to see if the bandits would kill her.

The coat hung on a dress form, whole: the fish on one shoulder, staring out at her with its too-real expression, a full skirt on the left and a narrow tail on the right, and the iron of chainmail visible on the left breast over the heart, leather beneath it, lavender fringing it. There were tassels, gold and purple, on the right breast, as if to balance the left. They did not. Lilly circled around the back, fascinated; it narrowed to the waist, its panels in fabric like a rainbow calico cat punctuated with fabric that might have been an Eastern tapestry once.

She said, "It's—" She looked to Mr. Nadel spinning contentedly on the opposite side of the workroom. "It looks very effective, I think?"

"That's the most emotion I have ever seen on your face. Pure startlement and a tinge of hilarity." Frieda sounded as proud of this accomplishment as of the coat. "Go on, try it."

"It's not—"

"I know. You told me already. The future owner won't ever know you did. Go on, I can't watch a masterpiece walk out of here without knowing how beautifully it serves its function." She grinned widely. "Not that I'm worried it won't." When Lilly still hesitated, the tailor rolled her eyes and strode forward; taking the coat from the form with a swirling, practiced motion, she turned it over Lilly's shoulders, sayings as she did: "Arms through the sleeves, now, and imagine it whatever suits you."

Lilly pulled straight the bottom of a plainly cut, dark grey jacket.

"Creative," Frieda said, dry, and chuckled when Lilly spread her hands: *What can you do*? "It does other things. Armor, robes, whatever goes over other garments. I've made pretty ones, you know—subtle, with the threads of Hans showing like distilled magic at the seams. But I wanted this one to suit any task, and that requires a workhorse ugliness."

Lilly shrugged it off her shoulders and held the coat in its true form; Frieda took it from her and gently folded it.

"I'll parcel it for you."

"Does it have a name?" That caught her a look of startlement. "It seems the normal way of unique magical things."

"The Raggedy Coat." She patted it. "I do like a little humble to even out my bragging, and you don't ever want to let someone know just how good a thing you've got. I hope this man who's buying it from you is worth all this."

"What he's giving me back certainly is." Lilly nodded to Mr. Nadel. "Thank you, sir. And thank you, Frieda. Once you have it packaged, myself and Horace will be on our way."

Frieda turned away to muffle the Raggedy Coat in paper. "Now, how do I convince you otherwise? Where will you get supplies?"

"Along the way."

"And is it not too late to start traveling?" Frieda enfolded the wrapped Coat in innocuous brown paper, rough twine—making it a less likely target for bandits.

"There is not a 'too late' for us."

"Then I'll have to throw my pride away yet again—do you realize how often you make me do that? How much guilt you've caused me? You made me spend almost all of a month slinking through my own home, apologetic, heartsick. The only thing that has cured me is making this coat, handing it over, carrying this deal through. When I said two months, I wasn't really lying, like you thought—though I don't blame you. You don't know me, and I've always worn nervous like deceit. But I'm not ashamed anymore, Lyle, and I'm okay with being selfish." She took a deep, heaving breath. "So. Wait here just one more night. Please."

"If I cared more for my self-respect than the life of my friend, I would stay another night and see you repaid in this way. But I cannot." Lilly held out her hand for the package.

Frieda shook her head, smiling wryly. "Ever the compassionate soul."

"Pragmatism is my monarch, I'm afraid." Handed the package, she pressed it against her chest. "But might we meet in the middle? If you would not mind stabling the horses, then you would guarantee I will spend the night at some future date, and whatever crime you feel you have done against me would be done with."

"Your father was a merchant, you told me once." Frieda stuck out her hand, work callused, slender of wrist. "Shake on it."

Lilly did; it was an honest deal, for though Ermentrud might be the end of her, death absolved all debts without heirs to take them on.

———

When they emerged into the shadowed wood which bordered Er-mentrud's estate, a somnolence descended heavy as the moon on the horizon, and Horace dropped to his knees beside her, eyes roll-ing once in distress before he slumped forward. Lilly dropped down beside him of her own will, checking that he still breathed, bent over him as if her body would protect his. There came a call: Don't you desire me?

"No," she replied, and touched her pack as if to draw the small knife she kept for everyday tasks. Useless, that—if it were not iron. Afraid of being foiled at so late an hour, she palmed its handle. Standing, she turned on her heel. "Ermentrud—"

"You lied. You *do* want me, to come into my grove and lay your head on the downy slope." A shadow of her curves moved between the trunks of two leaning oaks. "Why don't you? I see your scars. The journey has been long."

"What use rest eternal when a task is to be done?" Lilly shifted to stand between Horace and the dark-wife, though she suspected her companion would be of little interest to her.

"A momentary rest." Her smile flashed, and in it was the falcon. "We have games yet to play."

"I hope you will pardon me, ma'am, for saying that I believe the games would be fixed."

Ermentrud made a pleased noise. "If you are still incapable of pleasure, then let me propose business: for a moment to talk I will give you a kiss and safe passage."

"And if I would accept the latter payment but not the for-mer?"

"You do. To say otherwise makes a liar of you, and that is a terrible trait for a trader to bear." Ermentrud held out hands with the beauty of cathedral windows. "Walk with me, Lyle."

Lilly set their pack underneath Horace's head. "Will he be safe?"

"This wood is me. He is protected." Her hands closed over Lilly's soon as she came close enough, and she drew her close, breath hot on her lips; but she brushed her lips against Lilly's cheek, a greeting. "You've been away so long."

"You said that you have something to speak of." Lilly drew back, shaking her hands free.

"Walk with me. There is a stream this way with a song that you will appreciate. I have heard Octavius produce similar. It's a longing for the ocean, you see." She strolled alongside with all decorum. "Are you a virgin?"

"What is the meaning of virginity?" She laughed, bitter. If it were innocence of sensuality, she lost it at her own hand. If it were penetration— "I am not inviolate."

"Then I admit myself baffled at your resistance of carnal pleasure." Ermentrud lowered herself to the bank with a grace befitting a matron long learned of her body. She rested on one hip, legs tucked modestly one over the other to the side, and leaned on a bent elbow. A painting dwelt here, for art alone could be so intense.

"I understand that the imaginations of virgins generate more temptation than the knowledge of whores." She lowered herself to her knees, feeling the give of the soil, hearing the song. "Are you also these waters? Yes, I know it. This is his song that you reproduce, but it is not his breath behind it."

"What is he to you? A—"

"No." Lilly cut the words off with a gesture. "He is my friend; but more than that, he is the ocean's, wild, untameable. Octavius is as much to me as he can be, as I am to him, but touch is not a part of it."

"Intimacy grows where love does."

"Intimacy is not sensuality." Lilly shook her head. "You have a great advantage in this debate. Debased but unlearned am I, and this is all observance. From my own parents I can say that a couple might have love and no sensuality, and that sensuality exists between the horses mating in the field. Though the passions nod to each other and might braid together, they are not siblings. So I say: when I look upon you—" and she did, seeing the dark-wife's body move against the thin cloth of her dress "—I see great sensuality, and if I were not devoted elsewhere I would fall beneath that. There are many worse things to die for. But I am devoted, and at this moment intimacy is valued more in my heart than sensuality."

"I admire your honesty," Ermentrud said, "and that when I demand talk, you overcome your muteness. But I still doubt your truthfulness. Do you really know yourself so well?" She ran her tongue across her lips.

Lilly watched the obscene gesture. "Do you mean: You will kiss me, and we shall see how much I know?"

"No. You will kiss me and you will see how little you know." Ermentrud stretched forward with lioness grace and brought their lips together. Again the heat of her mouth, the press of her smooth lips catching against Lilly's chapped ones, her other hand settling on Lilly's hip. Anticipating this time, she held close to it, shivered in the sensation of Ermentrud's fingernails running lightly against her scalp, the dark-wife's breasts pressed against her arm. When the other would have drawn away, Lilly followed, and savored a moment longer before turning her face aside.

The dark-wife waited, lips reddened. Lilly said: "You are a worthy end for a soul, but I cannot allow you to have mine."

Ermentrud traced Lilly's bottom lip with the pad of her thumb; smiled. "You will remember this for the rest of your life, even if you escape me and we never meet again. I possess you."

"Possession and consumption—I was warned of that." Lilly stood, dusting off her knees. "Is half a meal as satisfying?"

"It is like the scent of wine swirled before one tastes it. A different pleasure." The stream trickled to a stop. "Your friend awaits you."

It was not that the woman left; she merely turned her attention away, and in doing so became another stretch of grassy bank.

Lilly found Horace standing with head down, nostrils flared, feet planted. Ready to fight. "We are standing in a body."

"It is the dark-wife's. Her magic touched you briefly." Lilly licked her lips, turned away to hide the blush that abruptly came over her. "But it will be over soon. Come, it's just over this ridge."

One tent with pennant torn and a cage toppled onto its side remained in the fields of the dark-wife; the snow covered the earth smoothly as an ermine's winter fur clothed its body. Horace stood close to her shoulder, shivering from the cut of the wind. "Your friend . . . We would be able to see him from here. Are you going to kill someone?"

"No." Her heart said, *I will give everything I have left, and I have more than death.* The Raggedy Coat weighed heavy in her pack—worthless? No. If she could deny his death for months, she could hold that belief for some minutes more and determine whether her mourning was yet justified. "I believe this will be complicated. Would you like to go back to Frieda's?"

"Yes," he replied, and followed her towards the cage.

It smelled of fish, and in one corner lay a piece of tentacle frozen by its own fluids to the metal. It would be difficult, she reflected, to dig a large enough grave for Octavius in this frozen soil. Impossible. She would have to wait until the spring thaw.

A pair of oxen in a makeshift corral to the side lowed pitifully on seeing them, nuzzling the chewed-over wood of their fence; Horace left her side to paw among the mess of toppled crates and torn tarp which rambled beside their pen. There he found feed enough to give the beasts; she left him to it.

The tent drew her forwards; pulling aside the flap, she saw a great deal of personal effects strewn about—not as an animal would damage them, but as a man would shove them aside to gather what was most important.

Horace—smelling of hay and cattle spit—caught her elbow, turned her around. Pointing towards the manse, he said, "That. It's alive. Look at its eyes."

In the cornices flared the wings of the falcon, its flanks the stallion, its pillars the woman. "Yes. You could—"

"No, no, say it again and I'll take you up on the offer." He forged some distance towards it as if to get away from her temptations to abandonment, then said: "But you'll have to break through the snow. It's hip-high on me."

The front doors were heavily carved, nymphs and fainting youths twined by reeds on riverbanks, each holding a pomegranate—to their lips or tumbling from their palms. The knocker was an exquisitely worked replication of a pomegranate half-opened, each seed defined. Lilly did not bother with this nicety; setting her hands on the handles, she sought to heave them open. The wood burned against the palm which the witch-poisoned oak had torn, and she stepped back, shaking it. There was the heat of blood under her glove.

If not the front door, what? The windows were all above head height, the gutters ice-slick, and no trees reared close enough to climb. Even if she felt like indulging in acrobatics to seek entrance, she'd get herself no further than a broken back. "We should have brought an ax."

"You're not going to try knocking?" At her look, he said, "You're the type that leaves their card at the door."

"It's a special case." She shifted the pack on her shoulder, thinking of its contents: provisions, flint, the Raggedy Coat, a small knife, the bag of the automata. Taking the latter two from their places, she set the edge to the sinews, arched an eyebrow at Horace.

He backed away, but he did not leave.

The sinew cut easily, as if old and strained by much use; the pieces lay on the stoop withered as worms in the sun. Her knife-work was more ostentatious than the bag's action: it slumped, empty, from her grip. After the anticipation had faded into an awkward pause, she cleared her throat and asked of it, "Could three of you please come out a moment?"

"Please," Horace said, laughing. "See? Calling card manners."

Lilly flung the bag to the ground as fingers wriggled from it. There followed the arms, the heads with the features pulled back taut, lips white over yellow teeth, eyeballs rolling round in their sockets, until at last their necks and shoulders and bodies emerged all in a liquid, undifferentiated lump, from which the automata dragged themselves apart; knelt, then stood.

"Hi," Horace said, like he wanted them to know he didn't have any hard feelings about their punching him.

Their eyes were on her as they had only looked at the bandits before—and was she not become their master, in the absence of the others? Their muskets were at her command; this numberless host would do as she wished. The realization made her feel sick. So many lives to be lost and taken stored within this sack, and that so easily held in her hand. For Octavius' sake she would use that loathly power. "I need to get through this door."

They set their shoulders to it all at once, and though their flesh smoked and melted upon touching the wood, they put their strength behind it. One of them fell; three more emerged from the bag to take his place. Their numbers increased until they were a writhing mass in which their destruction became impersonal, quickly hidden. For her coldness she earned the breaking of the lock, wood and globules of automata spraying into the manse's front hall. Catching up the bag, she gestured the men back into it, then hanging it from her belt, stepped carefully around the remains of their brethren.

"*Buildings,*" Horace moaned, and followed her over the mess into a space all marble, subtly malformed classical statuary, threadbare rugs. The halls were bare of dust, empty of servants.

The sound of a woman's sultry voice throbbed in the walls, stronger down one corridor than another. Lilly followed the noise and knew they were close when Horace wheezed fearfully and edged close to her.

The doors at the end of this hall opened under her hands.

Ermentrud must have resigned herself to the interruption—
yes; the dark-wife lounged on the carpeted steps of a dais, the
smoothness of her curves hugged by a gunmetal grey robe
fringed with jet beads. Behind her—Lilly clutched the bag of
automata and wondered if they could kill Ermentrud for her.
Octavius curled on the dais, surrounded by a fence of broken
glass in which the faces of saints and crying angels were
wrought in gold leaf and colored panes: he was not well. The
skin which should have caught the firelight and intensified it a
thousandfold was flat and flaking, his golden eyes were sunken;
his tentacles trailed and curled at the ends like limbs caught in
the cramps of disease.

He raised himself up as he did when narrating a boastful
story and cried to her, "I waited for you." That voice had not
changed, and with the hissing noise of rough fabric being
rubbed against itself, he lifted a limb to show her the jacket he
had saved from the sea.

"How sweet," Ermentrud interjected. "Here is your rival
come to court me, Gero."

"No." This from Gero Alt; he knelt at Ermentrud's feet. "No,
he went to fetch me the coat. Boy—please. Give it to me."

Low, Lilly said, "You sold him to her, didn't you? Yes. I see it
in the way you hunch forward, Gero. I will not make a gift of
what I promised as payment."

"I did not think you would succeed! How am I to value a
deal made with some mad-eyed boy over a chance to have my
love?" He struggled to his feet and turned to her. Like a beggar
in the street, he had gone to a ragged beard and jutting bones,
the hollows of his eyes greenish, skin yellowed, veins purpled.

The proud sky-blue of the coat had been reduced to mud-spattered tatters. "Would you kill a man?"

Yes. And: *You are already dead, sir.* "Ermentrud, ma'am. What can I give to you that will return to me my friend?"

Gero Alt said, "Give it to me. One show is all I need, and then *I* will make a gift of the kraken."

The dark-wife gave him the fond look of a gentlewoman indulging her lapdog as it yapped at a visitor. To Lilly, she said, "I would have your body." When Gero turned on her with jealous anger snarling his features, the carpet slid out from under him like a snake's tongue withdrawing into its mouth. He went to his knees with a terrible noise of bone and flesh impacting the wood.

Lilly put the man out of her mind; words were on her tongue, but they were insufficient. She had become proficient at opening trousers since that first awkward fumbling on the slope of the Three Crones Mountains. She bared herself, asked, "Are you still interested?"

Horace murmured in her ear: "Like a mule, of sorts."

She would thank him for that, later, and the way it offered her a place in the natural order. For now the dark-wife was pouting; said, "Put that lack away. I'm a consumer of whole things only." She tapped a finger against her lips. "It need not make you useless. Circus master?" Gero Alt held out his hands to her, mouth opening between sagging cheeks. The dark-wife, petting Octavius on the eye ridge, said, "Give the coat to him, not-boy. That is my first requirement."

"At her request—and no other reason," Lilly told Gero Alt, and tore open the parcel; she held forth the tailor's work, in all its patchwork, gaudy confusion. When the circus master swirled it around his shoulders like a king's robe—it became thus, and more.

He became everything: a strongman with another balanced on his hands, bodies straight as planks; an acrobat who twisted through the air as if he could fly and tumbled when he hit the floor only to spin back to his feet and spring off to another trick; a fire eater, mouth stretched wide as a column of independent flames filled his gullet, wider as he heaved it out again, blacking the ceiling; a tattooed man, kneeling to show his back, raising up to spread his arms. It was Ermentrud's naked body written onto his skin. He bent forward and was a lion—a sphinx, stretching massive forelimbs, opening his muzzle to roar, but his hind legs still a human's, skinny, shaking. His forearms were swords that he swallowed, and finally he was just a man: one in all the splendor of the circus master, the rich red coat, gold braid, the boots of shiny leather.

His face was a dead man's. Broken, he fell forward, the coat returning to its natural form around him. Legs at odd angles, fingers tweaked, face burned; his abdomen was bloated as if something had gone wrong with his innards, as well. He began to cry, heaving sobs, and asked: "What am I?"

"Do you see?" Ermentrud looked to Lilly, head on the side. Over Gero Alt's constant mutter of *what am I what am I,* she said, "Flesh is useful for pleasure, but it is memory that gives me sustenance. Hence *dark*-wife: where once was past, there is now nothing but a pit, and however you peer into it, it is something more unseeable than the night sky between the stars, or a cavern that is deep in the belly of the earth."

Lilly thought, *I have killed a man.* She said, "I will make a deal with you, ma'am," but her mind was elsewhere. She knelt beside Gero Alt; his eyes rolled but did not fix on her—blind, whether from injury or pain. She laid her hand on his cheek and said, "I'm sorry. I'm so sorry."

"I want this off of me." His voice crackled like fire and ash. "It's heavy. It hurts." His broken limbs moved in uncoordinated jerks, flexing into unnatural shapes whenever they were pressured.

Despite her attempts to soothe him, he continued to thrash and—after checking that Ermentrud still enjoyed the scene from her dais—Lilly helped the man divest himself of the Raggedy Coat. She tried not to hear the noises his bones made in the process.

"Tell my wife that she comforted me most, more than all the whores in the world—" his tongue, swollen and blistered and bloody, ran across the cracked remains of his lips "—and I want our children to know they are the best of all my acts."

She kept her hand on him as he sobbed through the last of his breaths. Another time she might dwell on the deaths she had seen; for now, she came to her feet. "A portion of my memories for Octavius, ma'am. I will make that trade."

"Then I will have the memories of your kraken for my own." Ermentrud stood, stroked the ridge over Octavius' eye. "If I cannot have it as a pet, I would remember him as a friend."

The kraken keened, low and reedy. "Lilly, I have never done you a favor so great as this."

"All these years of our friendship have been my life." She smiled for him. "But what is the past to the future? Your living is worth more than my having lived, Octavius, and though you may become a stranger to me, at our reacquaintance I will know that you are worth any loss of mine."

Ermentrud stepped down from the dais, a curl of smoke uprising, her lips parting; and through them Lilly saw a nightmare vision, a crypt of human beings caught in emotion, love and desperation and ambition, all the strongest they could have—and that meant somewhere a soul wondered where their passion had gone. "Now," the dark-wife said, "give me all of it. Tell me. Your performance is your mouth." She smiled at the obscenity which twined in that phrase.

"Octavius goes first." Lilly stood, the Raggedy Coat over her arm. "No—do not look thus; that is a condition of this trade. I know that *I* will not default." Her voice was her father's at its most low and cold. "Do you think I would bother to make so many deals honestly, only to break at the last? I will see him freed while he is yet my dearest friend."

"I don't see that you're in a position to make conditions." Ermentrud came forward another step, sensuous, predatory. "I want you to whisper your most intimate secrets into my ear, and when you cannot see him for anything but a monster, I will let you choose if you still want him."

"I won't leave," Octavius said, tone reasonable. "I won't leave you."

Horace's hand locked around her wrist, and in his nasal, loud voice, he yet managed some dignity. "Lyle won't leave if the kraken refuses to go or you refuse to release it, but I will—and I'll take him with me." He was stronger than her, and she could not yank free. He lifted his chin, staring down the dark-wife. "It would be a stupid deal if he doesn't make it certain, and though my friend here has a tendency to make that mistake, I'll stop him this time."

Lilly could have struck him; it terrified her. "I wouldn't forgive you." He shrugged by ways of an answer.

Ermentrud looked at him with interest. "What a strange little magic thing you are. You would do this for—"

"Yes," Horace said.

Ermentrud spread her hands; the glass shards shrank down into the dais. "Remove him if you can."

The kraken dragged himself down to level ground, passing close by the dark-wife, though he did not quite touch her; she flinched back from the look he cast at her, a shaming stare. He settled himself next to Lilly, whispered in a voice like the song through the smallest of pan pipes, "Will you remember the songs?"

"I won't talk of them."

One of his reduced tentacles curled around her ankle, as it had often before. "She let me free, once, so that I could tire myself fighting for an exit from this place. It is her right as a predator to mislead her prey—but to *me*, she has lied."

She pulled Horace close by the hand he still clutched. "How much can you carry?"

He looked at the kraken; said, "Hello, Lyle's friend. Not so much as him."

"Well met," Octavius replied, solemn. "I am much withered. There is little water in me. Do you know, Lilly, I remind myself of a sponge? All those holes."

"All right." Horace leaned against her shoulder. "I can try. It'll be interesting." He let her go, crossed to stand in front of the kraken, and asked, "Can you hold hands?"

It looked more like *hold arms*, those massive tentacles looped around Horace's wrists, and Horace looking most wary of the situation. Casting Lilly a last, pained look, he was away; and if the noise was more like thunder than its usual, at least he had managed that much.

She burned with a bizarre jealousy that the incalculable sensation of loss which burned her eyes and clenched her stomach would shortly be given to the dark-wife; Lilly nonetheless asked, "What would you have me do?"

"Come sit beside me on the dais. Yes, where the glass was." The dark-wife caught her elbow and led her to the place, sitting with a grace that would make the most elegant of women seem a crippled dog. "Be less frightened. Why would I hurt you now? Soon you will be killing yourself."

The dais was carpeted, plush, as if to invite slouching; Lilly held herself straight. "I would proceed."

The dark-wife bent her head close, her hair tickling at Lilly's neck. "Speak."

"What would you have me start with? With the urge to murder I felt upon seeing what condition you had brought him to? Or shall it be the first time we met? There is so much of the ocean in it that I don't know how you will take him and not that."

"I am a precise predator. I take the liver and no baser organs." She pressed herself against Lilly's side; it was no more sexual a touch than being bound by a snake. "You meant to kill me. Yes, you touch that bag of magic at your hip. But Octavius would have thought less of you—you have taught him to abhor murder. Oh, already I taste you." She parted her lips as if in anticipation of placing a morsel on her tongue. "It is not natural for the innocent to think first: I will kill. Fresh soldiers shoot above the heads of enemies, and a slaughterer new to butchery will not look their first veal calf in the eye."

"Is that a question? No. I won't be so intractable." Lilly shook her head. "I have played a Judas goat and let a man be led to his death. A child who has watched the slaughter of chickens and hogs all his life does not hesitate at the knife. Thus with me."

"All that over one death?"

"We don't speak of Octavius anymore." Lilly slanted a look at the woman. "Are you taking more memories than you are due or savoring the scent before turning to your meal?"

Ermentrud laughed. "Perhaps I find you interesting. Humans are frequently thus—do you not watch the gamboling of meat while it still lives? Fine, though. Tell me the first murder you committed for Octavius' sake."

"Myself. My female self. That is the middle, though, and I have already muddled this enough. I wouldn't want to short you a morsel." Lilly closed her eyes. "Such a friendship as that starts on a beach where the gulls strike at something small and red and shrieking among the rocks, and a girl drives them away for curiosity. When I picked him up his beak was sharp but he did not bite me."

Ermentrud was a suffocating weight. "You—"

"If you would be a compassionate killer, do not interrupt; I might forget a detail. It is not for you that I don't wish scraps left behind, for such things would be torturous: campfires too far off to reach on a cold night." The blood-stones were warm in her breast pocket, a gift to her current self. They would mean nothing after this excision, but before it, she could think: *I will* always have them and what they mean, even if I do not know it. "Without him, I would not be I."

She stumbled from the manse with an ache buried in her brain and an impression that she had come a long ways for a precious reason, though she could remember only the journey and not the grail. Such troubles fell away when she saw Horace leaned against the side of a coiling, powerful, undoubtedly ill creature, the limbs of which encircled her friend like the ramparts of a keep. Horace shoved himself upright, though his legs shook and sweat glossed his brow. He had carried a great weight.

She presumed this weight was the sea monster. But why? "What has happened? Are you all right?"

"Fine." Horace pushed himself away from the kraken and came to her side. After a close inspection of her face, he grinned. "You lived. Good. You don't remember him, do you? We talked about that while I was fighting not to pass out—it was a short, brutal, messy trip, and I'm glad you didn't ask me to take him halfway around the world. Anyway, his name is Octavius."

"Oh." She did not know that, but she went around to stand beside him, anyway. "I know that I traded something of myself for your life and that we are going to the coast. But why?"

"I am your friend," he said, then: "Please, do not flinch from me." He uncoiled a tentacle and touched her cheek—the one with normal skin.

"You aren't alarming. I just don't remember you." She failed to read any expression on that alien face. "I remember walking on the beach with anticipation. The sound of the gulls, the surf, and how I knew they meant I was home. But not you."

Horace touched her shoulder. "We should start out. It's getting colder and the manse frightens me."

She glanced at the kraken—her old friend?—but did not know what to say. Thus she left in silence to prepare them for the road. She took the blankets from Gero Alt's tent, first, and what supplies the man had not let molder. Seeing her companion shiver, she offered him the Raggedy Coat; he claimed it smelled of death, so she offered it instead to the kraken, who said only: "No, thank you. My home is the deepest ocean."

From there they yoked the oxen—the animals were glad to be free of the dropping-fouled pen and complied willingly— and loaded Octavius onto the cart. Lilly was engrossed in the task of sorting out how to hold whip and rein when the kraken asked, "May I speak while you work?"

"Yes. So polite." She struggled a while to get the oxen to move, Horace making suggestions beside her; he had, after all, seen many such animals being driven. Though difficult it became doable, perhaps because the oxen knew their profession.

"You taught me that." The sea monster made a rumbling heartbeat sound—laughter? "Being polite, not how to drive a cart. May I tell you a story? May I tell you *many*?"

"Yes, of course." She owed him something, didn't she? Otherwise her neutering would have been too much to bear, and she would have abandoned this quest at its outset.

"It begins with your first and only injunction: do not kill the species of man. Then you gave me the power of stories." He fell to a light, tuneless humming, and Lilly had no words to break the awkwardness. Then the monster spoke again: "I learned circumspection while I sought stories for you. I could not let humans see me, for to them I am a killer best killed. I learned how to *listen*. I suspect I will be wise someday."

"Speak on," she urged in his next silence, and allowed Horace to settle against her side.

"Do you care?"

"I— I see that it does you well." Those words must be brutal to him, but she could not interpret his expression. "I cannot lie—will not. I like to hear you, but it is not because your words ring in my heart: it is because you are new to me, interesting and kind and loving. It is beyond me to return the last."

"It is beautiful from here," he said, for they had reached the top of the ridge and the manse threw a long shadow, gold-limned, onto the snow. Then: "At the end of the best books you used to read to me, the last sentence was an echo of all that came before, a summation, and it only took remembering that one line to know the whole thing. If I tell you our lives, will the final words be thus for you?"

"Try." She laughed, hollow and afraid. "There is a ragged edge where I can feel an immense loss—something bigger than the space you now fill in the back of this cart, larger than you might ever grow, though you fill all the unknown territory of a map. Did you weigh more heavily on me than all the physical burdens in the world? Yes, I think so. I feel saddled but without a rider—and I am not meant to be thus." She reached back and rested her fingers on the tentacle within her reach, fascinated by the texture, the color. His eyes were the magnificent part of him, but now that she had learned to look past the lesions, she could see why her past self had valued this creature. "Do you think you could give yourself back to me in our little time?"

"I would speak forever, if that is what it took."

"And then we would both go on into infinity unfulfilled, for we would someday hit the beginning of the recitation and be forced to narrate *that*." She took her hand away. "If it pleases you to please me, then speak. You remind me of the ocean."

"I remind you? Those words are terrible to me; I do not understand your meaning."

Silence, snowfall.

The kraken asked, "Where do we go?"

"I know but one swift route to the ocean."

During their travel, the kraken elicited the story of how she came to rescue him. It became awkward when she sought to explain why she would go to such lengths and found her own actions inexplicable. At those times she would fall silent and let Horace tell his part. She liked how he shaped the thing despite herself—it almost made her out to be a hero, and she laughed at him for it.

When her throat grew dry with telling, Octavius took up the thread of stories. They were incredible, told piecemeal so that each was like an individual gem—and often Lilly would catch herself thinking that she would have liked such a friendship when young. More distressing was the story of how he came to be within the circus master's grasp.

The old trick to catch any monster, to put a virgin girl on the deck, couldn't fail to draw Octavius' attention, although for different reasons than the sailors would imagine. The violent capture and subsequent slavery that followed made her cringe, even as the kraken cackled and wriggled his limbs as he detailed how much he'd been sold for, to whom, and where. He painted them an awful picture of humanity with perfect delight, and that of all things won Horace over at last.

"The first merchant captain—the one who captured me, the clever one—knew how to take care of a sea monster. A foreign man, in bright robes, with a kind voice." His voice, resonant with the sea though he grew more withered each day, sent birds squawking into the air.

Horace huffed, said, "Wait, kraken, I thought you'd mentioned this man's leaving—did he come back, or are we revisiting the past?"

"I mean him as a contrast," Octavius explained, patient. "For Mr. Alt, you see, did not have the least concept of skin care and kept me quite neglected in that iron cage. I languished. So I felt quite glad when Lilly strutted through the camp like she owned it—" He laughed at the sour look this prompted on Lilly's face, and allowed, "Well, she meant to look intense rather than masterful, I am sure. The performers got out of her path, anyway."

"*His,* not *hers,*" Horace said, patting the kraken's bulk; he'd taken to using the creature's tentacles as a headrest and a place to prop his feet. "Otherwise it's just confusing."

"You are rather missing something, Lilly." He hummed to himself. "Your shyness and demureness. Something like the ruffles of a petticoat." Over the noise of Horace's sniggers, he added, "Do you see the change in yourself?"

"I do not know that I am changed," she replied, her focus on the oxen, who were growing truculent with the lowering sun.

Horace mumbled something to the kraken; this was not unusual. The silence that followed was, however, worrisome; she turned to look at them. How such different eyes managed to stare the same she did not know; she asked, "What troubles you?"

Horace answered her. "Sometimes you hold words back as if afraid of how we will use them."

She hesitated. "I've never been one to speak overmuch."

"And you thought things over," Horace agreed, "but you've given me answers like 'yes—no—maybe'—uncertain answers. You don't do that anymore."

Octavius murmured, "I do not expect you to be open with a stranger."

Lilly turned back to the oxen; could not but mock herself for proving their point when she kept to herself the words, *I do not remember ever being another way.*

Ragamuffin village children pelted after them, fascinated to see the kraken on the cart; they must have thought him tame, for they would reach out to touch his tentacles. When the bolder among them asked where she took this creature, she answered always, To the sea. *They would groan at the loss to human curiosity and turn aside from her, most disappointed.*

It was an old road that brought them near the shore. When the waves could be heard over the forest sounds, Lilly tugged the oxen to a stop and handed the rein to Horace. "Take them into town and see what you can get for them, please," she bid, and startled at the way her companion's face lit up. "Why so pleased? I thought you liked them."

"You're trusting me in a money matter." He bumped against her shoulder. "I've watched you buy provisions—I think I know the trick of coming out with more than the other person."

Lilly winced; she disliked the thought that the transactions she haggled over were unfair, but she could not decently contradict Horace's assessments of them. Troubled with this thought, she dropped down from the driver's bench; Octavius was making his painful way off the back of the cart, making the oxen nervous. They had grown used to him as a motionless lump—as had she. She wished for a way to help, only to feel presumptuous when she saw how he rose with a great flexing of muscles upon gaining the ground; he towered over her, as she'd forgotten somewhat while he lay deflated behind her. "Shall I come with you?" she asked.

He sat still as sea-wrack for a long while; Lilly shifted on her feet and gestured for Horace to start for town. Octavius said in a voice too small for his monstrosity, "Yes, please," and together they walked from the woods down onto the rocky decline that gave out on the ocean.

The sight of water stirred her heart; it must pain him to be so close. "Will you not proceed me?"

"I will not," he replied. "I have been drying for months, and a few more minutes will not wound me more."

The rocks were steep, but this presented a familiar obstacle. Her new strength made it easier than it had once been, for where she had been agile and clever in finding easy routes, she could now take those that were direct and difficult. Though the mood of the monster was somber and she wished to echo him—out of respect if naught else—she could not help but take pleasure in the exercise.

Soon they dropped down onto the pebble beach at which the waves lapped. "Wade out with me," Octavius asked of her, and she had come to know him well enough to sense the sorrow in his voice. "For just a moment more."

He valued touch, so she rested her hand on his side when she said, "Yes," and walked beside him until she stood hip deep. Beside her Octavius rolled in the water, whistling, perhaps hurting where the salt touched sores. If he had eyelids, would they have slid shut in pleasure-pain? She waited, fingers spread in the waves when they washed high enough.

At last satisfied with his ablution, Octavius said: "You could stay. Though you cannot remember, you are still my Lilly, and I your Octavius."

"I'm sorry. I can't torture you by failing to love you, and I don't think I can love. Not now. Somewhere there is life for me, a place to close that gap. And whether I do or not, we *will* meet again. I see that I owe you that. There will be a time in my old age when my mind is nothing but shadows and it will seem your stories and the traces of anticipations are a lifetime of friendship. Then I will return to you, and though I will never quite be your Lilly, you can pretend that it is the years that have changed me and not this lack—the lack of you."

"Oh, Lilly," said the kraken. "Never will you change so much that I do not know you."

"Lyle," she replied. "I prefer to be called Lyle."

He lay silent a long time in the surf, and she thought, *The sun must burn his skin, still, on the top of his bulk.*

"Might I sing you a song?" he asked at last. "It never meant anything before. Just a tune that I would hum while I thought, because you hated to interrupt me then but could not quite tell whether I was waiting for a reply or ruminating on my own. If you are to remember only one thing of me, it would be that—a simple, everyday thing."

She laid her hand on the ridge over his eye, thinking: *Did I do this once?* And the kraken sang, not as he had sung for her before—not of the deep or the whale or the surf or the storm— but merely a tuneless humming, a trace of melody, pleasant to listen to but not stirring. He reached up to touch her face, the unmarked side and then the marked. His was a cold, unpleasant skin.

"Until we meet again." The bulk of him whispered into deeper water. Twice more he looked back at her before the curve of his body could not be distinguished from the waves, and she turned aside. She felt she should weep at this parting, but walked away dry-eyed, her mind already turned to a place on this shore which might offer her closure. Unwise though it be, she would look on the chateau before she traveled from this place.

Her regret at the dimming of gull screams and wave breaks paled against the need which drove her up the path of shells. Ahead lay home, her father, the halls of her childhood glimpsed through memories of her sandy feet messing the carpets and the tension of being played out as a gamepiece in Father's manipulation of his business partners. She hesitated a moment, knowing that her child-self would not have been so anxious to return to the chateau; it baffled her until she realized that Octavius must be the author of her original loyalties. His memory being no more, she recalled her father strongly. Though he betrayed her, he loved her, also. Perhaps he would like her better for the changes wrought in journeying.

She came to the crest of the path and halted.

The grounds were come to ruin by their old standards, the hedges leggy with the first new branches of spring, the flower-beds a mess of the previous year's dead annuals and a sprouting of weedy green. The paths were muddy where not icy, and the building itself shuttered, though the sun would have cast warmth through the windows on the near side of the building. Lilly stared, sickening, then with such haste that she slipped twice, she came to the front door. Knuckles, knocker, fist: none drew the attention of the servants. Frustrated, she tried to open it, found it locked; she went around the back. As expected, the servants' door came open with a touch of force; she had known for years that the latch was weak.

She wandered down the corridor, looking into the kitchen and the laundering room, running her finger through the dust accumulated on Miss Hannah's dresser. She had left behind all but one of the books of Arabic and French with which she taught Lilly; it was a pocket-sized one, a detailing of an ancient myth whose hero was wily rather than strong. Likewise did she find the rooms of the other maids emptied of personal effects—except for one.

She touched the rumpled covers of the narrow bed and noted the cradle pushed against the far wall; she could remember, faintly, that one of the servants had been expecting, much to the mean delight of the household at large. She opened the bedside table's drawer; therein lay a very small pistol and rosary, as if the power of the two might cancel out the guilt which attended both. She checked the chamber of the firearm and found that it was not loaded, nor were there bullets in sight. She lay it back down and went out of the room. If she encountered the inhabitant, then she would question the individual;

she suspected that the individual had snuck in, however, and did not expect them to know the intimate details behind this corpse of a home. Going out into the hallways of her childhood, she looked into parlors stripped of all their trappings and living spaces with furniture shrouded.

In what had once been her room, the only mark of her inhabitance was the statuette of her mother, which remained alone in its little casket at the back of the wardrobe.

She put it back and meant to leave, knowing what she would find elsewhere and unable to face the changes wrought upon her home. The route she took brought her to the stairs up to Father's study, though, and without so much as a pause she took to the treads. Perhaps she had meant to do this all along. Tired, heart-sore, she ached for closure.

The statue and the screen were still here, along with the smell of cigar smoke and the harsh salt scent of sea captains. Over it all—blood. More than blood; the putrescence of rotting flesh soured the air. She shouldered aside the door as if haste might save a rotting corpse; it was not such a sight that she found, but merely what parts of a mutilated human body could not easily be carried away—as she knew from experience. Bone shards and brain matter speckled her father's chair; a tooth sat on the blotter, gold-capped. There was an enormous amount of blood on the carpet and walls.

She went around the desk, flinching as the toe of her shoe came down on the soaked carpet; careful to avoid contact with any bodily matter, she slid open the righthand drawer and found the pistol missing from its customary place—though a small bag of coins was still there. Her breath shuddered from her lungs as she looked at the ledger laid out neatly on the table; if a stranger had been here with a mind for theft, the gold would have been gone or the papers mussed. Instead—this. Whatever he said of them in private, Nikolaus Rosa assumed a solemn but inoffensive temperament in his dealings, and thus did not make such enemies as would murder him.

Strange for him to kill himself; though not vocal on the subject and content to leave his wife and daughter to their own beliefs, he had been a faithful man. Then she thought of how he baited Anna Rosa, the story of the King's despairing of his favored servant's will to live, the drunkenness which pervaded her memories of the man. On the sideboard sat two empty bottles of what had been a very fine and quite expensive liquor, one of the sort that Father would not drink without occasion to warrant doing so.

She closed her eyes against the heat of frustration, anger—the inescapable awareness that this did not surprise her. Desperate for distraction, she took the ledger in hand; it had largely escaped the gore, the majority of which decorated the wall behind the desk. Something must be significant in it for Father to choose it as his last sight before death. The neat numbers of the expenses column were interrupted in one spot by two words: the *Dispatch*. Lilly gaped at it; she remembered the weeks after the ship had left its yard and proved itself seaworthy, for her father's genuine cheer had been alike to a visitation by an angel.

The *Dispatch* was a beautiful ship, he said; she could hold as much in the way of goods as two of his others and could hold up in waters rough enough to drown a whale. She knew what it meant—knew, even, that she would walk away, for the room had filled with sharp-edged claws from the past. All the same, she found the box in which the man kept signed contracts and ruffled through for sign of an item bought on the back of the greatest ship plying the trade routes between the land of spices and the coastal kingdoms.

She went directly to the records of Nikolaus Rosa's dealing with Saleem, and touching the contract signing over the *Dispatch* for the capture of one sea monster, she asked herself: Was that monster worth a ship to *her*, as it had been to her father? And what motivation could he have, taking away the friend of the child he drove from his home? It must have been at some cue from her. She could see her actions in the past, the emotional distance she put between herself and the household, but she could no longer understand her own behavior—her rationale had died with her memories of the kraken.

She thought of the ocean's spray flashing over dark stone, touching her cheek. It often called to her thus; why, then, did her child-self not answer it? With a flicker of resentment, she came to the same answer: *Octavius.*

An inarticulate, crying sound turned her around, the papers in her hands scattering as she dropped them; Mary stood in the doorway, a hand held over her heart, expression working through shock. Time and pregnancy had changed her, putting fat onto her hips and breasts; Lilly felt abruptly self-conscious of her own flat-fey body. She held up her empty palms, said, "I am leaving, ma'am."

"Oh," said the other woman, and in the next moment she had swept across the room and wrapped her arms around Lilly's chest, cheek pressed against her neck. "Oh, Lilly, you are alive."

Lilly stood limp in the embrace, unsure what to do with this gesture; at last her stepmother backed away, cheeks wetted with weeping but smile wide. Lost, she asked the woman, "Where—?"

"I was hiding," she said, frank. "There has been a misunderstanding and I am waiting . . . When I heard how long you paused in this room, I could not suffer to be ignorant of who disturbed the place of my husband's death." She spoke the last in a frank, somber manner; not mourning, though she wore black, yet regretful. "They believe I murdered him."

Lilly closed her eyes, gathered up what wits remained to her. "I knew him too well to believe he would die by any hand but his own," she said, and set it from her mind that she would not weep. "The babe . . . My half-sibling . . . ?"

"He is healthy," Mary said, then: "Are you?"

Lilly looked over her shoulder at the bloodied chair. "Might we go out? Wait." She knew where her father hid his wealth; one such stash was an innocuous, battered pouch jammed between two ledgers from his first decade as a merchant; it was a small portion of her inheritance and enough to keep her in ascetic comfort for a year.

The skin around Mary's eyes pinched, and grasping Lilly's hand she said, "I am comforted: I found what I could of his and took it, but did not know what to feel about my actions. Now that you do the same . . ." She laced their fingers together, and somehow smiled—genuine, pretty. "Come along. I am so glad that your brother will meet you—I did not think it possible."

Lilly followed silently behind the woman as they went towards the servant's quarters; if she had borne Nikolaus a son, why the suicide? She formulated a dozen ways to ask the question and rejected each as inadequate. Outside her own old

room, she balked at last, the questions too heavy; the first that
found her tongue was, "How do you know me?"

"You are yourself. I have seen your eyes many times, Lilly,
and your bearing is your father's. Whatever else is changed—
those things and more remain." She touched Lilly's shoulder,
smiling faintly at the embroidery carp—she must be wondering
about the Raggedy Coat, but certainly a woman who did not
inquire as to one's bald and breastless body would not question
one's attire. "I see it has been a hard road. But your friend . . ."

Lilly had shaken her head on reflex, but now said, "He is
returned to the ocean."

Mary's eyebrows drew together, but in either compassion or
the desire to hold her babe, she did not pursue the question.
They stayed silent as if in respect of the dead house; for without the rustle of attentive servants and the boot-clacking of
merchants, its right name was *grave*. Lilly felt distracted and
anxious at the delicate hand which still held her own—scarred,
callused—fingers in a sure grip. Could she believe murder of
this woman? No; she had run a successful household before
Lilly's departure, and though her marriage wore at her, she
never showed the restless-fox nature of Anna.

A happy, bubbly noise of greeting emanated from the cradle
when Mary pushed the door open; Lilly would have hesitated
on the threshold if not pulled forward by her stepmother's sure
grip. They stood looking down on the babe, then. Lilly checked
Mary's expression for some sign of meanness, but her expression was one of enraptured love and tired patience as she
reached down and brought her son up against her breast. She
turned a steady look on Lilly and said, "His name is Friedrich.
Do you wish to hold him?"

Most definitely not; she shook her head, but reached out to brush a lock of wispy blond hair from the child's face. His eyes were the same brown as her own, as Nikolaus', and across half of his face was a birthmark the color of red rose petals—the left side, like hers. *Well*, she fought not to say, *at least my father died knowing that he was not a cuckold*. A strained chuckle made it past her lips, and in a bitter tone utterly at odds with it, she said, "He did not get the heir he wanted, then."

"No," Mary agreed. "For however much he searched for you, he could not find his daughter."

Lilly looked up, startled, and further surprised when Mary laughed at her, a gentle, sad sound.

"Oh, sweetheart." Shifting the burden of her babe, she drew Lilly close with her arm. "He went on for days about the curse of the serpent he killed to win his wife, and he would hold his new child and ask me, *How will you raise him*? I never could give him the correct answers because he wanted the ones Anna would give—I had heard enough of her to know that she would 'give the babe all the knowledge of the rough world when he was still young enough for it to imprint on his mind.' That and more." Mary shivered with the memory, hugged Lilly tighter. "When he realized that he would never again have the daughter of his soul, his wife's child . . ." Mary shrugged, lowering her eyes. "I am sorry."

"You have no cause to be. See how he laughs?" Lilly stared down into that pudgy face with its active, bright eyes, and felt for a moment nothing but fierce protectiveness. How could Nikolaus abandon a babe? But then he *did* have a poor history with regards to his children. "Do you know, Mary, why my father took Octavius from me?"

The woman chewed her lip, began to rock as the babe fussed at her change in mood. "I could guess—*you* could guess. He wanted you to be severed from the sea, I always thought. Sometimes when you looked out towards the horizon I feared for you, too."

"I get the impression that Octavius would not have allowed me to drown, whether by nature's hand or my own." She did not know, though; and something must have been off in her comment, for it won her a strange look from Mary. "My father succeeded, I suppose. I am not dead."

Mary squeezed her shoulder and then backed away. "I am waiting for my brother—I sent a letter to him by pigeon, and if God wills it he will reach this place before the food in the stores run out, or the von Graf family arrives to sell the land. I do not think the townsfolk will disturb it now that the maids have straightened things and gone. It cannot but have a reputation for being haunted. So—I will be well."

"You expect me to leave?" Lilly ran a hand back across her scalp, wondering what about her appearance was so cold. "Mary, you *are* my—"

"Friend, I hope," she cut in. "You are too old and I too young for the word 'mother' to be between us."

Lilly accepted this with a nod. "Then I will say: you are the mother of my brother." She offered up a slantwise smile. "I have a companion who will make flight a simple matter." The introduction between this refined woman and Horace would be—well. Mary *was* a good-natured woman and might be of such stuff as could appreciate him.

"I will trust you with him, of course," said Mary, and pulling a lock of her hair from the babe's grasp with a muffled *no* continued, "but I would be comforted to see you hold him a while before you go."

"*I*? I would no sooner travel alone with a babe than swim from here to the Orient. Mary, there is room enough for you. Besides—" she made a gesture that encompassed the servant's lightless room, the shrouded house behind them "—how could I leave you here to be discovered? To be hung as a marricide?"

"If I am followed—and I will be, for there is no method by which I can remove all traces of myself from this place to thus baffle some magician of the King—*when* I am followed, then whoever harbors me will be punished, as well. Then where goes my babe?" Said babe began to make noises, at which Lilly looked askance but Mary merely raised her voice to be better heard. "So go with him and go with my blessing: it is little cost if I am given over to spare him. Or do you go on some errand now which cannot bear the burden of a child to watch over?"

"No," Lilly said, and could not suppress the bleakness of her tone. "No, I haven't any obligations at the moment. Mary— give me your trust in this. There is a safe haven for all things."

Mary stepped away, her attention for her boy, her expression distant. "I have had this plan so long—and I had resigned myself to death. It seems dangerous to abandon that, for I would like to go merrily into the grave. Promise me something, Lilly." She looked towards her. "Value his life over mine."

That took Lilly aback a moment, but at last she said, "May I never need to abide by it, but I will swear to do so. And—one more thing. Please. Do not seek to repay me."

———

To make their way more quickly to the other side of town, Lilly checked the stable; Mary reported hearing an animal out in the field, though she was uncertain if it was one of the carriage horses. He was not; she knew the gelding as her father's show horse, a skittish, useless, and breathtaking animal. Seeing her, he arched his neck, tail flicking against the wind, nostrils blown wide. Mary could not tell what had happened to the other stock—pigs and cows as well as horses; Lilly suspected thievery. It would not have been worth it to the nervous men and women to waste time chasing a poorly tempered animal.

What was the horse's name? Marshal? Calling to him, she held out a handful of oats; recognizing her, he came forward and nosed into her hand. He was not thin nor weak, having had access to what feed the thieves left behind. A startling possessiveness came over her: she knew this animal well and disliked the thought of another's hands on him. She would have to sell him, for Horace could not travel with him, but for the moment she set aside the thought and indulged her mood. Besides, he was trained for a light carriage. It took bribery to convince the animal to wear the harness, but it made possible the transport of two individuals and a babe.

Mary came from the house with a small case in one hand and the sleeping child held against her shoulder. She stared at the carriage, lost a moment. "My brother will think some evil fate has befallen me."

"He will return home and know differently," Lilly said. "We cannot—"

Mary smiled at her. "Leave a note or wait. I know." She slid the case into the foot of the carriage and then turned. "Will you hold him for me?"

Without much choice in the matter, Lilly accepted Friedrich; he was heavy, warm, utterly limp in sleep. She found it disquieting; she brushed her thumb against the edge of his birthmark and wished she could ensure a good life for him. If he lived up to the family tradition, as a young man he would take up a violent profession and embroil himself in a plurality of plights. She said, "I hope he takes after you."

Mary laughed. "Give him here, now. Here's my hand."

Lilly accepted the woman's help up into the carriage and urged the horse into motion. They would have to make a loop around the town, going by winding back ways; both of them had reason to avoid recognition, after all. It was in the honeyish light of the afternoon that the carriage rattled to a stop in the center of the crossroads where Horace had agreed to meet her. Something had kept him, or else stolen his attention, for he was not there; Lilly came down from the carriage to soothe the horse, who stamped his hooves in irritation.

"Lyle!" Horace skipped in a dust-devil here-and-gone over the roadside ditch, flung an arm around her shoulders. He paused a moment to touch noses with the horse, laughing at the animal when it neighed and shook its mane—surprised to see a fellow equine in such a shape, perhaps. Then he went forwards, hand braced against the horse's shoulder, to squint at Mary with a doubting look.

Friedrich held to her breast, she stepped down onto the road; there she dipped a shallow curtsey, and said, "I am most pleased to make your acquaintance, for I'm not often in the company of magic. I am Mary, and if I am not mistaken, L— Lyle spoke of you as a friend." Her smile made her formality a gentle joke.

"What a lady!" Horace looked pleased at that, and playfully

bowed back to her. "I'm Horace. Now we're friends and can dispense with the etiquette, right? I don't like to sit at a table to eat."

Mary patted the babe's back; the creature did make a great deal of fuss when not paid direct attention. "Thank goodness. I didn't think to pack my good silverware."

"You found someone who smiles," Horace said, bumping his shoulder against Lilly's. "It'll be a nice little change. She *is* going to come with us?" He went to Mary's side and peered curiously at the babe, touching his face, with the same calm curiosity of a herd inspecting its newest member. Mary murmured the child's name and showed no concern that such a rough stranger came near.

That is trust, Lilly realized, *in me*. She cleared her throat. "Horace, I thought we would sell this gelding—" she patted the horse's neck "—and go quickly to the home of Mary's childhood."

"Can't." Horace made a face at the babe. "Little ones don't take it well. I think they see it all—it makes their eyes go funny."

Lilly breathed in, out. "Is it agreeable, then, that we travel by carriage?" Mary looked uncertain. "If it comes to it, I will not stop your self-sacrifice, and in its aftermath will care for the child as if he were my soul—but I will do all I can to prevent those things."

"I'm glad you didn't kill him," Horace said over Mary's agreement; he looked between the two baffled stares turned to him. "Lyle didn't kill this little fellow, I mean. In town they spoke of your coming from the mountains riding a hellcat. Once you got here, says they, you punched a hole in your father's head and then cooked up the babe with Mary and ate him up, then helped her hide from the attempts to catch her to hang."

"What else do they say?" Mary asked, voice soft.

"'Be sensible,' I heard the baker say. 'Lilly wouldn't ever. It was the lady who shot the marquis with his own hunting rifle and whisked the babe away to some ungodly end.'"

"He shot himself," said the woman, "with a pistol."

"I wouldn't have minded if you had beat him over the head with an iron saucepan," Horace replied, with a nod to Lilly. "Do you see him?"

"We should go on," Lilly cut in, "for a townsman might be traveling and come upon us, here." In helping Mary into the carriage again, she could not resist asking of her, "But how did you hide?"

Settling in, she took a moment to answer. "I went to your old place," she said, "the slope down to the sea where you met with Octavius. Your father told me about it. How he cried—oh, such weeping." She shook herself. "They did not think to look for me there, and once they had turned the house sideways, did not suspect me to go back to it. I did not suffer. It was merely . . . Cold." Friedrich squirmed in her arms; she opened her blouse that he might suckle.

Marshal would not be convinced to move until Horace took to his back and communicated that ahead would be better pastures and a night's rest. Her friend kept to his perch, though he had said before that riding made him nervous. The gelding preferred the company of his own kind, Lilly remembered. It seemed he went with a smoother gait now that he shared his harness.

Having been fed, Friedrich still showed signs of discontent, which patting and bouncing did not soothe and a check for bodily functions did not explain. Mary smiled, shrugging. "Babes have their worries."

"May I . . . ?" His mother gave the babe for her to hold, and Lilly hummed the kraken's melody to him.

At the hilltop where they stopped for the night, the sun's last light could be seen gilding distant waves. She regretted the sea; not the loss of it, but the having.

Enough; time would bring her to her heart's home, for the world did not have iron enough to chain her from it. So long as she provided the means for Mary to protect her child, pragmatism need win out over sentiment. Thus she told herself that thoughts of oceans and forgotten life must be left slumbering in an uninhabited harbor. Yet in reaching for the paring knife in her coat pocket, she found also the blood-stones; against her palm they beat with thalassic hearts. When she had fetched them, she remembered, the cold salt water cradled her. *How*, she asked herself, *did I reach the shore?*